DESPERATE ACTS

Other Five Star Titles
by Jane Candia Coleman:

Doc Halliday's Gone
I, Pearl Hart
Moving On: Stories of the West
The O'Keefe Empire

DESPERATE ACTS

Jane Candia Coleman

Five Star
Unity, Maine

Five Star First Edition Romance Series.

First Edition, Second Printing

Published in 2001 in conjunction with the Golden West Literary Agency.

Cover photograph by Jane Candia Coleman

Set in 11 pt. Plantin by Rick Gundberg.

Printed in the United States on permanent paper.

Library of Congress Cataloging-in-Publication Data

Coleman, Jane Candia.
    Desperate acts / Jane Candia Coleman.
        p.   cm. — (Five Star first edition romance series)
    ISBN 0-7862-3210-2 (hc : alk. paper)
        1. Abused wives — Fiction. 2. Suicidal behavior — Fiction. 3. Mothers and sons — Fiction. 4. Teenage boys — Fiction. 5. West (U.S.) — Fiction. 6. Ranch life — Fiction. I. Title. II. Series.
    PS3553.O47427 D47 2001
    813'.54—dc21   00-067706

For Glenn with all my love

PROLOGUE

In the garden at night spiders make webs across the paths. When I go out—to the garbage cans or simply to look—they stick to my face, my arms, invisible barriers. Think of it. A thousand bodies spinning fragile links from bush to tree while I, going about my business, rupture the fine highways, the lanes of silk. I, female, groping through the dark, violate order, disrupt lives. I, wife, stealing my few private moments in the dark, gathering my thoughts, break apart what took centuries to build.

Jake, who came home with the news he's been invited to Russia, is inside trying to make order out of the chaos of papers on his desk. I give myself these few seconds of solitude to watch moths rise from the grass, nighthawks diving from the sky.

So many lives, all mysterious. Even my own. I have bled a child. I have accepted Jake into my body so that it is not mine anymore. It belongs to him and he, knowing that, makes demands. Food! Comfort! The stylized writhings of sex. The body is always on call, giving willingly or not so willingly. It walks through life, dutiful daughter, shaped for bearing, for giving out what is put into it.

My brain races through the night. Feelings, those necessities set aside in the numbness of duty, whirl inside, gather momentum, shriek like sirens inside the vessel that is me. "What about us?" they clamor. "Without us you don't exist."

I know I don't exist. Maybe I'm afraid to exist. Or maybe there

7

is no one who would value my reality.

I have always loved my world—these webs, these hunting hawks, these poor moths doomed like flowers—and the loving rises in my throat that aches with silence. Who in this family talks? No one. My child hides, like me, behind his eyes. Jake has his work, his lists of duties for me. If I call out in the night for company, no one hears. I wonder how many more there are like me. Women wearing a path between bed, sink, stove, trampling their hungers underfoot.

Jake comes to the door. "Nan?" he calls. "Nan?"

"Here."

"What're you doing?" He always needs to know where I am, what I am doing. It gives him a sense of control. That's what my life is all about. Power. Control. I am never allowed to run free but am always on a leash.

What if I said, "I'm touching myself in the dark. I'm listening to the fragility of life?" Would he understand?

Of course not. He'd think I was mad. Besides, things like that can't be said. They don't belong to our life together. Our life has one pattern, aloneness has another, and it is mine to stitch at in spare moments, to spin like the spiders, to be broken by the violence of bodies pushing across the tiny pathways.

"I'm taking out the garbage." There's an answer that suits the situation. I am working. The piled-up detritus of three people's day is real. It stinks. It oozes over my fingers. Though the bag is filled with broken glass, it is still more graspable than spider webs, the gilded dust of moth wings like a veil in the yard light.

"Make sure you put the lid on tight," he says. "That cat left a mess this morning."

Chicken bones, corn husks, tin cans, a sanitary napkin in a trail across the grass. I know. I picked it up. Jake would never touch such things.

The cat was doing what cats do. If I do what I do, how does it affect others? How would they feel, picking up the shards of Nan? How would it feel to be free—of a past that taught me all the wrong things and that haunts me still, of Jake whose voice follows me across the yard? Or does freedom bring with it another set of responsibilities?

The fact is, I don't know what I want. Or who I am. Or what.

CHAPTER ONE

The day had begun more horribly than usual.

Nan's alarm went off at 5:45, disturbing Jake, who thrashed on his side of the bed. "What was that?" he demanded, and before she could speak, he repeated the question.

"The alarm," she said, thinking in the brief moment after she answered, that surely, after all these years, her husband should have learned to recognize the sound.

Instead his voice rose hysterically. "I asked you what that was!"

The room was dark. She couldn't see his face; didn't want to. "The alarm!" she shouted, not caring if Jamie got awakened early or not.

Jake sat straight up. She could see the outline of his body against the wall. "Jesus! You don't have to shout! I only asked a question. I was startled. Now I'll never be able to get back to sleep. You could have answered me nicely, you know. You really could have. I don't yell at you when you're sleeping. Now my stomach is sick. Make me some tea and make sure the milk is warm this time. You know cold tea upsets me."

"Everything upsets you," she said under her breath, feeling for her slippers.

At her muttered words, Jake threw off the tangle of blankets. "You upset me," he yelled. "You never think. You just

10

don't seem to care about me at all. You don't, do you?"

"I'll get your tea." She avoided the question.

"Answer me!"

"Of course I do." She forced herself to sound like she meant it. "I'll be right back."

"Hurry up. And I'll have a piece of toast, too."

She went out and closed the door. Usually she tried to get out of the room without Jake hearing, gathering the clothes that she always put out the night before and creeping down the stairs because Jake, once awakened, issued a stream of orders and commands that flayed that place inside that was hers, that she had been protecting for what seemed her lifetime.

The kitchen was cool in the first light. Outside the big bay window the elm trees stirred, and the small leaves caught the sun and flickered like fish in a great and moving sea.

This was her time to open the back door and go out into her garden, alive to solitude, to her fragmented self that needed a half hour alone. This was the time when she listened to her inner voice and dreamed, and, if she were lucky, wrote a poem or at least the beginning of one before Jamie got up. These thirty minutes were what kept her going, reaffirmed her person, her relationship to a world that, more and more, had nothing at all to do with Jake.

She had started writing again ten years into marriage. The first ten years seemed, looking back, to have been chaos, a scramble for adaptation, protective coloration.

"The survival of the fittest," she said to herself, smiling grimly, for why she wanted to survive only to be slapped down again was a question she couldn't answer, hadn't even asked.

Jake's hysteria had left her trembling. She felt violated; raped, not physically but inside where her feelings were.

11

The problem was that no one would believe her. What had happened this morning was a mere echo of a thousand other mornings and nights. Jake's rages over nothing at all were a constant. Thinking about them, what she heard was his voice going on and on, accusing, damning her and, too often, Jamie.

Poor kid. Since he'd been two years old she'd tried to shield him as much as possible from his father. Lately he had devised his own methods of protection, slipping away after dinner to his own room or to the houses of friends, not returning until bed time.

She stood on the stone patio inhaling the scents of spring—freshly-turned earth, the fragrance of new grass, the ethereal perfume of yellow daffodils in the perennial border, violets in the shade along the fence.

Everything was stirring, reaching for the sun, boisterous with the thrusting of instinct. *Everything but me,* she thought sadly. *I just stay the same.*

She put out a hand and gently cupped a daffodil, peering into its heart as if she could read the future in its waxen core, its red-tipped stamens, as if somewhere was hidden a secret she could not fathom and hadn't the words to elucidate.

Abruptly then, remembering Jake, she turned and went back to the house. Dutifully, she steeped the tea and heated milk in a small pan, feeling that she stood apart from herself at a great distance, her hands, shaking but competent, moving by themselves, doing what they had done every morning of her married life.

They arranged the old tole tray with cup and saucer, a plate of buttered toast, a folded napkin, then carried all down the hall and up the wide front stairs, the dishes rattling in time with the racing of her heart.

Maybe this was how all the powerless felt going in to audience with a wicked ruler who, quite conceivably could shout, "Off with her head!"

But no. With her head in a basket she would no longer be able to serve. The bitter smile shaded her lips once again as she balanced the tray and felt for the door knob in the dim light.

"I told you not to close that door!" Jake was sitting almost the way she'd left him, clutching the bed clothes to his chest. "I've told you and told you. I can't sleep in a closed room. It gives me a headache. But you persist in doing it. Haven't I told you?"

"Yes," she said, putting down the tray on the Queen Anne mahogany bedside table. "I'm sorry."

"No you're not," he retorted, turning toward the tea. "You're just trying to shut me up. You want to lock me away so you can't hear if I call you."

True, she thought. Very true. She hated to hear him calling her from the bed. "Nan! Nan!" She could recreate the sound in her head; that of a spoiled child calling for its mother; a wild-eyed Caligula demanding his slave.

She backed away trying not to call attention to her movements. "Drink your tea," she said soothingly. Oh, she knew how to calm him, knew all the words and phrases, the humble posturings, and her knowledge tasted bitter on her tongue. "I have to go get Jamie up. I'll come back later and see how you are."

"Come quietly. I'm going to try to sleep," he said. He set down his cup and glared at her. "Don't go anywhere. You aren't, are you?"

"No."

He hated it when she sneaked off to shop in the morning, leaving him responsible for the telephone or the doorbell. And more often than not the telephone would ring and

13

awaken him, so that he had to function without her. Cerberus at the gate of hell, she thought. A guard dog. That's me.

Oh, he was lucky. As a super professor he could set his own schedule, teach his classes late in the day, come home to dinner when he chose, and then spread his papers over the table and work until dawn.

"I'll be around," she said and left to wake Jamie who usually slept like the dead, probably in self-defense.

This morning, however, he was awake, his blue eyes watching her. "What was all that about?"

"Nothing. Just get dressed and come down quietly," she said.

"Mom!" He sat up and stared at her, a handsome kid and intelligent. "Come on, Mom. I heard it. Probably everybody on the street heard it."

"Not now," she said, anxious to be in her sanctuary out of ear shot of all but the loudest cry. She left him, moved on tiptoe down the stairs, avoiding the board that always squeaked.

Trying to write was useless when you were shaken to the core, when everything inside seemed to be loose and jangling like a piece of broken machinery.

Writing demanded peace; concentration; the ability to focus on the words, the thoughts that hovered in the mind's darkness. And today she had no mind. She was a million pulsing synapses, all out of sync.

Write something! commanded the little voice that was her constant companion. *What kind of a writer are you to let him win?*

"No kind," she answered. "I'm not sure anything I do is worth the effort."

Bull! said the voice. *He'd like you to think that. To be a nobody. Write what just happened. Get it out. Get rid of it.*

"Maybe I will. Maybe I'll just start keeping a journal."

14

She'd always hated the idea. Suppose she wrote in a journal and someone found it? Suppose she wrote the truth and Jake, in his night time investigations of the house, the drawers and closets, even her purse, found the book and read about himself?

It'd do the bastard good, the voice said. *Keep the journal. Start today.*

"Maybe," Nan said again. Writing was such an effort. When it took all her energy simply to keep from falling apart, to summon a smile for the neighbors, where was there any to spare for putting words on paper?

She pushed the argument aside as Jamie dumped his books on the table.

"I don't know how you stand it, Mom."

He looked older than sixteen. There was a dark and terrible knowledge in his eyes.

Nan's heart clenched in her breast. *What have we done to this child?*

"Don't worry about me," she said. "You've got a big math exam today. Worry about that."

"Yeah." He poured milk on his cereal and helped himself liberally to the strawberries she'd put out. Then he said, "I'm staying over at Edward's tonight and maybe tomorrow. Okay?"

That meant she'd be alone with Jake all evening. All night. That meant he'd be waking her up early for sex, for "making love," as he, ludicrously, called it.

"Okay," she said. "Did you put clean clothes in your bag?"

He nodded.

"Have a good time, and don't worry about me. I'm all right." Mother and son looked at each other in complete understanding.

After he'd gone, Nan began trembling again. She was

alone with no one to talk to but herself.

She poured a third cup of coffee then went to the drawer where she kept her notebooks. Taking one out she sat down and began to write.

CHAPTER TWO

Sometimes I pray to God for a miracle. "Please, God," I say, "take Jake away. Take him now." But nothing ever happens. When I finish praying, if you can call asking for another's death praying, Jake is still there. His voice is still there, rising and falling, accusing me of things I've never even thought of doing, and making them sound so logical that I'm forced to believe that maybe I am the dreadful creature he thinks I am. The filthy woman that he married. But if I'm that awful, why did he marry me?

He tells everybody, even Jamie, that he married me to keep me from being an old maid. Then he laughs, that laugh of his that sounds like it's tearing out his throat. Me, the unwanted.

Sure, I was twenty five, and in those years if you didn't get married right out of college you were headed for spinsterhood, but I had plenty of dates. I wasn't worried about it. I even had a job I was good at. Reviewing books, films, plays for the paper. Everybody knew me. I was Nancy Alden, and what I said counted. I had opinions that people talked about. That they believed! Now nobody would believe me. I don't have any opinions. I'm not allowed to have opinions.

Why is this? What is wrong with me? Maybe nothing is. Maybe life just sucks and everybody forgot to mention it.

No. Wait. Maybe I should ask another question. What is wrong with Jake?

She put down her pen feeling guilty, as if Jake were peering over her shoulder. What a terrible thing to have written! Here she was, Nan Alden Fletcher, with a fifteen room restored colonial house, a famous husband, a lovely son, a garden shown on all the tours, more jewels than she could count, most of them in a vault at the bank because Jake bought only quality, and she had the temerity to ask what *his* problem was?

By all the standards, she had everything. She should be rejoicing instead of sitting here at her kitchen table looking and feeling like hell and wondering what was wrong with her husband.

Once, early on, she'd faced him with that question, suggesting that they seek counselling. His anger had been so terrifying that, at the last she'd relented, no, pleaded with him to calm down. He'd packed a bag and was on his way out the door. The plate with his half-eaten dinner lay smashed on the floor, and Jamie was wailing in his crib.

"Psychiatrist!" He was yelling. Spit formed at the corners of his mouth. "I'm not the one who needs a psychiatrist. It's you! You know that, don't you? You've never grown up. You still need someone to tell you everything, and when I do, you resent it. Well, no more. I'll leave. Then see how you can take care of yourself. You'll end up on the street, and I'll have Jamie. They'll lock you up. You're halfway crazy right now, and you're telling me I'm the one." His hand was on the door knob, and he was staring at her with those protruding dark eyes in which she had once seen what she thought was love.

"Please!" The word was torn out of her heart, her terror. "I didn't mean it! I was only trying to help. Please don't go. I'll . . . I'll try to be good. To be better. I didn't mean it was you. I only meant that I love you."

And so it ended. Her one attempt at freedom. Was she mad? Inept? Incapable? She didn't know. All she knew was that she was bound hand and foot to marriage with a man

18

who humiliated her, body and soul, a man she had come to fear and despise. But divorce was unthinkable. No one she knew had ever gotten a divorce or even spoken about it, and the very idea of telling Jake she wanted to leave him conjured up such frightening scenes in her mind that she knew she could never face the actuality. Although he'd never hit her, she suspected that, in one of his rages, he might, and these days his anger was so frequent, so unpredictable.

No, she had to make the best of it. And maybe someday God would hear her and take him away. The ringing telephone made her jump. What if it woke Jake up? She grabbed it before it could ring again.

"Nan?"

"Oh, Wendy! Oh, I'm glad it's you."

Wendy Moran was her best friend since fourth grade. They'd gone through high school and college together, shared every intimate fact of their lives until they'd married. Paul Moran and Jake hated each other on sight. The two women now spoke infrequently, and confined their gossip sessions to those times when both men—often as it happened—were out of town at the same time.

"Can I come over this afternoon? I have to talk to you." Wendy sounded breathless.

"Sure. After two, though. Jake went to bed late."

"Shit," Wendy said. "The things we have to go through."

Tears welled up in Nan's eyes. Life had been so simple before. So easy. She had friends and kept them. Now she had to plot, devise schemes and time frames, sometimes even lie.

"Oh, Wendy," she said. "Nobody ever said it would be like this."

When Wendy answered, she sounded as if she were speaking through clenched teeth. "Do you have any booze?"

One thing Jake insisted upon was a well-stocked bar and

wine cellar to accompany his gourmet meals. "Always," she said. "You know that. See you later."

She hung up and listened. If the ring had disturbed him, Jake would be calling. But the house was silent, breathing steadily in and out through its brick walls.

Thank God! She thought she'd like a drink now—at 8:30 in the morning. Maybe two. What was happening to her? Where would it end?

CHAPTER THREE

It was one o'clock when Jake finally got up and went to shower, for a change not calling her for a second cup of tea and a scolding.

Hurrying, she hung his pajamas in the cupboard and started to make the bed. He hated her to do that while he was still home. "Trying to get rid of me," was how he put it. But if she didn't do it now, she'd have no time later.

She was pulling up the heavy, fringed spread when Jake opened the bathroom door, crossed the room, and yanked it out of her hands.

"Rushing me out again? I've told you *not* to do that. Not to make the bed until I'm gone, but you keep on doing it. Don't you listen to anything? Don't you understand? As if this morning wasn't bad enough!" He threw the pillows on the floor and ripped off the blanket.

Nan sat down on the lumpy edge not looking at him. "Wendy's coming over. I just wanted to get it done."

"Wait till I'm gone," came the answer. "Besides, today's the day to change it. It's been three days."

The old argument. "Nobody I know changes the sheets more than once a week! My own mother doesn't!"

"Your mother," he said scornfully. "She isn't the perfect housekeeper, and neither are those friends of yours."

"They're clean!" Nan looked up then, eyes flashing.

21

"We're all clean! You know that. I'm not a dirty person."

"You're not as long as I'm watching." He tightened the bath towel around his waist. "I'll have oatmeal and some more tea. And maybe some yogurt. Bring it when it's ready. And bring a pitcher of cold milk on the side."

While the oatmeal simmered, Nan reached for her journal.

I am not dirty! she wrote in a slashing, angry hand. *I'm not! I take a bath every day. I brush my teeth. Clean my nails. I clean this goddamned house on my hands and knees, and then he comes home and finds a hair in the sink or a kleenex in a wastebasket and goes nuts. Why? Why? It isn't me. I know it isn't. But someplace inside I'm afraid that it is. Because no one ever found fault with me before. Not to this extent. Everybody always liked me. Praised me. I never had to be told how to behave, what to do. So what is it? What's wrong? And who can I ask?*

There wasn't anybody. All she had was herself, such as it was.

So figure it out for yourself, the voice said. *Regardless of what he says, you're not stupid.*

She thought about that for a minute. No, she wasn't stupid. She'd graduated from the university *cum laude*, landed a job immediately, and kept it until she married. And recently she'd had several stories accepted by good literary journals. That had given her a brief flush of achievement until Jake brought her back to earth.

"Do they pay for these?"

"Only in copies."

"Oh." He'd gone back to his own work; work that paid the bills, Jamie's tuition, Jessie, the cleaning lady, as he so often reminded her. What had she expected? That a few published poems and stories would make her his equal? Something like that.

"Hell!" she muttered, and replaced the journal under the

tea towels at the back of the drawer where she doubted he'd ever look. Then she carried the tray of oatmeal up the curving stairs.

Wendy arrived just as Jake was leaving, interrupting his list of things he wanted done in his absence.

"The medicine chest over the sink. How long since it's been cleaned?"

He'd have gone on, but caught Nan's glance over his shoulder and turned, smiling his shy, charming smile that made women want to know him better and old ladies reach to pat his cheek. Once that smile had even evoked tenderness in Nan. Sometimes, even now, when he was in a good mood, relaxed and smiling, she would find herself responding, allowing herself the hope that all that had gone before had been simply a bad dream.

"You girls have fun," he said as he stepped aside to let Wendy enter, "but don't forget about your poor husbands and their dinner." He sounded cute, almost flirtatious, a stranger Nan couldn't connect with, an actor wearing a mask and fooling the world, though his message was plain.

We are living a lie, she thought. *We are both actors.* She shivered and then looked at Wendy who was always dressed expensively and well. Today was no exception. She wore a black wool turtleneck and Calvin Klein slacks, and carried a trench coat over one shoulder. If only Jake would give her an allowance so she, too, could buy clothes like that!

She swallowed her envy. "You've lost weight!" she said. "You look fantastic! Come on in."

They both headed for the kitchen where they always sat, feeling at home around the oak table in the bay window.

"What's happening? You had something to tell me. Want a drink?" she asked.

"Bourbon on the rocks," Wendy said. "A double." She lit a cigarette. "No, just fill the damn glass to the top."

"Jesus! Will I have to drive you home like in the old days? What'll Paul say?"

"Paul!" Wendy took a slug of her drink. "Paul!" Her hands were shaking. "I just filed for a divorce from Paul!"

Nan let go of the glass she was holding. It crashed at her feet, shards flying everywhere.

"You what?" she gasped.

"You heard me." Oddly, Wendy started to laugh. "You should see yourself. You're as white as a sheet. You look worse than I feel."

Nan stepped over the pieces of glass and sat down with a thump. "Why?"

"You won't believe this," Wendy said. She was staring at her hands.

"I'll believe it if you say so."

"The son of a bitch is having an affair with his secretary. Everybody knew but me. Even Mikey knew. He said something at the dinner table that clued me in, so I followed the little crud when he said he was going back to the office. Some office! He went to her house."

Nan reached over and took a sip of Wendy's bourbon, too shocked to get up and get her own sherry. "Then what? How do you know what they did? Maybe he just took her some papers to work on."

Wendy shook her head. "I waited. I parked down the street. He was in there for hours, and when he came out, she came with him. In her *robe*. And they kissed right out on the front porch where the whole damn world could see. I went home and threw up."

"No wonder." So she wasn't the only one living a lie, living in misery, alone, uncared for. The notion stunned her.

Wendy lit a second cigarette from the dying end of her first. "It gets worse," she said. "I don't even know how to tell you."

"Just say it," Nan urged. "After this, nothing can surprise me."

"That's what you think." Wendy took a deep breath, then blurted, "That son of a bitch, that sneaking creep, that toad hasn't slept with me since before Mikey was born, that's what! Me. His own wife! I'm not good enough for him. But some dumb kid right out of typing school is."

Nan leaned back in her chair and closed her eyes trying to accept what she'd just heard. "Sixteen years!" she said then. "Sixteen years! Why didn't you say something? Tell me? For God's sake, Wendy, sixteen years!"

Wendy burst into tears, and Nan felt tears prickling her own eyes. What had happened to them both? How had they come so long, so far hiding such misery?

"He said . . . he said it was my fault. He said I just didn't arouse him anymore. And he sent me to a shrink to find out *what was the matter with me!*"

"And you believed him?" Nan could hardly get out the words.

Wendy nodded. "I did. What else was there? Who else? When your own husband says . . . things . . . well, he's right. That's what they taught us when we were kids, remember? Our mothers. Our friends. The nuns at school. The man is always right. Didn't they say that?" She pounded on the table with a clenched fist. "Didn't they?"

"Fairy tales!" Nan shot back. "That's what we were sold. A bunch of goddamn, lying, 'happily ever after' bullshit. Grace Kelly did it. So could we. Oh, Christ, we were so innocent!"

"Grace Kelly!" Wendy snorted. "Her life didn't exactly

sound like any fairy tale. And she wasn't so innocent. Not like us."

"No," Nan said softly. "Not like us. But sixteen years. What did you do?"

"I had an affair. I had two of them." Wendy tilted her chin.

"Who with?"

"Andy. And the guy across the street."

Nan was awed. "You should get an Academy Award. Honest. I never saw any of this. You always seemed so happy. You were always going out. You had time to paint. You never said a word."

"And I always felt like hell. But Paul said it was my fault, so how could I go public? I'd have had to admit . . ." she stopped and searched for words " . . . admit my own failure. My husband didn't find me attractive. I didn't know why, and he wouldn't talk about it, so how could I say anything? He was all I had." She gave a short, sharp laugh. "So I faked it. I kept up the facade. I did a good job, huh?"

She smiled through her tears, and Nan thought she'd never seen anything more dreadful than that bleary attempt at pride.

She said, "You were superb. You still are. Just look at you. Right out of *Vogue*." She reached across the table and grabbed her friend's hands, noting that they were ice cold and still trembling.

"There's *nothing* wrong with you," she said loudly, as much for herself as for Wendy. "Nothing. You always were pretty. You still are. You always were sexy!" She laughed. "Remember Bob Whatsit in college? Remember you went all the way, and I was still emotionally back in eighth grade with Heathcliff and Mr. Rochester?"

"I should've married *him,*" Wendy said glumly. "He had no complaints."

"Oh, hell, nobody normal would. I never could stand Paul, but I never said anything. I thought you loved him. He always gave me the creeps. Like he was thinking dirty thoughts."

"He probably was. But not about me."

"That's his problem. There's a name for what he did, I mean not touching you, but I can't think." Nan pushed back her chair. "Now it's my turn for a drink. Let's hang one on for old times."

Wendy held out her glass for a refill. "I'm halfway there already. But it feels good. And he won't be there when I get home."

"Where is he?"

She shrugged. "How in hell should I know? I threw him out, Gucci loafers, Brooks Brothers shirts, and all. Probably with little Louise. Did I ever tell you he made me iron his undershirts?"

Nan sat picturing it—Wendy at the ironing board folding undershirts when she should have been at her easel. "Good riddance," she said, holding up her glass. "Here's to you. Luck, love, and may the right man come soon."

"Screw men," Wendy said. "I've had enough to last me."

"That's what I'm talking about. Screwing. With a real man for God's sake, not that little nothing. I remember you from the old days."

"Yeah," Wendy said sadly. "The good old days. I wish they were still here."

"So do I," Nan said, lifting her glass and drinking deeply. "So do I."

The telephone rang, startling both women who jumped and then stared at each other, resenting the intrusion.

"Probably Jake," Nan said. "He'll know we've been drinking."

"Don't answer."

"If I don't, he'll keep calling back." Nan reached up for the receiver.

"You're there." Lottie, Jake's mother, made the two words an accusation.

"I have company." Nan did her best to conceal her annoyance with the old woman.

"You were supposed to take me shopping. There's no food in the house, and I've been waiting all day for you."

Nan closed her eyes. Surely she hadn't said today. Or had Lottie deliberately misunderstood as she did so often? "Tomorrow," she said slowly. "I do shopping on Thursdays, remember?"

Lottie's reply came back with the precision of darts, each one touching a nerve. "Wednesday, Thursday, what's the difference? I could starve to death for all you care."

"That's not true!" Nan squirmed in her chair, hating the feelings of guilt that came regardless of her innocence. "You know I wouldn't let you go hungry. But I can't leave right now. Tell me what you need, and I'll pick up something later and send Jamie down after school." Then she remembered. Jamie wasn't coming home. "No," she corrected. "I'll have to do it. Jamie won't be here."

"He's never there," came the answer. "Nobody has time for me. Never mind. I'll open a can of something. If I can find one. I'm sorry I bothered."

The phone went dead, and Nan slammed the receiver down hard.

"Who on earth was that?" Wendy wanted to know.

"Lottie. She drives me crazy. All she does is demand things, and when I can't do what she wants she accuses me of hating her."

"Well?"

Nan laughed without humor. "I didn't at first. But she

28

wants constant attention no matter what else I have to do. She pushes. *Give me! Give me!* She could phone in an order, but that's too easy. She wants *me*. She wants me to feel guilty. Guilt's her weapon, and boy does she use it! Now I have to go to the store because she says she's starving."

"That old woman would have survived in the Donner party," Wendy said. "You can't please everybody. Get selfish. It's time we both stopped doing what we're told."

Nan looked at her in amazement. "But I've always tried to do what was needed."

"Yeah. And where'd it get you? Where'd it get me?"

"I don't know."

Wendy drained her glass and set it down carefully on the table.

"Don't you think it's time we found out?"

CHAPTER FOUR

Jake looked at her across the dining room table that was now littered with his papers, manuscripts, pens and pencils. "We have to discuss what we're going to do, so don't run off to bed," he said.

Nan gathered her wits. Because of his invitation to Russia, their long-planned trip to a ranch in the Southwest was in jeopardy. Except that Nan fully intended to go and to take Jamie, regardless of any stumbling blocks Jake threw in her way. Years of dealing with his whims had taught her well. She let him start the "discussion."

"It's not a good idea for you to go by yourself," he began. "If something happened, I'd be impossible to reach. I know you've been looking forward to this, so have I, but I think we'd better just cancel. See if we can't do it in the summer instead of over spring break."

He'd given her the weapon she'd been waiting for. She folded her hands in her lap and squeezed them hard. "I know you're disappointed," she began, not looking at him. "But this Russia trip is a great chance for you. Definitely you have to go. God, it's fantastic!" She lifted her eyes and hoped they didn't betray her. "Although," she frowned, "it's a shame to disappoint Jamie. We promised him, and he's been working hard. He deserves a break. Besides . . ." she'd held her trump card for last, "our tickets aren't refundable. We'd be out all that money plus the deposit at the ranch. Jamie and I could go. We're perfectly able to do it. Then you'd only be out one ticket."

Money mattered to Jake. He held the purse strings tightly, going over the bills, the checking accounts, the grocery charges twice a month and questioning any expense that, to him, seemed unnecessary. Nan dreaded those sessions and the cross-examinations that went with them, dreaded having to explain the cost of underwear for Jamie, a pair of shoes for herself. At the thought of losing his refund, he looked like she'd punched him in the stomach.

"Damn! I forgot about the tickets!" he said. "Are you sure we can't get a refund?"

"Almost positive. But I could call in the morning."

"Do that. And if we can't . . . well, you'll have to go. That's all. I can't afford to support the airlines."

She concealed a smile. Money always won, even over her supposed safety. Free! She was almost free! Two whole weeks on a ranch, on the back of a horse, the wind in her face and the desert flowing around her!

"Don't worry," she said. "You know, something could happen right here at home. Nothing ever has. You've been taking these trips for years, and everything's been fine."

"Yes. Well . . ." he rustled some papers. The loss of his ticket still bothered him. "You could take my mother."

Take Lottie! Take that old woman who made her life worse than the hell it already was with her consuming need to possess her son! Nan sat up and squared her shoulders. "No I won't," she said enunciating every word. "I'll stay home if I have to take her. What would she do on a ranch anyhow?"

A smile actually crossed Jake's face. "It was just a thought. All right, maybe we can all go later on. But we certainly can't tell her I'm taking a trip. We've had enough accidents."

31

"And I can't handle another," Nan said, scenes from the past vivid in her mind—the phone calls at midnight from Lottie who said she was having a heart attack; the time she'd come back from taking Jake to the airport and found her mother-in-law unconscious at the foot of the porch steps, a weeping three-year-old Jamie standing guard over her body. That accident had frightened him so it had taken him years to tell of his feeling that, somehow, her fall had been his fault. And it had taken Nan days before she'd gotten him to understand his innocence.

"The last thing I told her as I left was that, under no circumstances was she to go out the back door because that step was loose," she'd reminded her son. "I told her to stay inside and let you have your nap. But no. She got you up and did exactly what I told her not to do. You were only a baby. You had nothing to do with it. Understand?"

Slowly, he'd nodded. "Why didn't she listen?" he wanted to know then, the fine points of neuroses beyond his grasp.

"Because she wants attention," she said gently. "So badly she'll hurt herself to get it. Some people are like that, and we have to live with them. You have to be nice to her. She *is* your grandmother."

He looked up then, blue eyes puzzled. "Are you like that?"

"I hope not. I really do. It's like being sick."

His response had been oddly adult for the child he still was. "I'm sorry, Mom," he'd said.

Now she looked at Jake and sighed. "I'll make up some excuse," she said. "And I won't tell her that Jamie and I are going 'til the cab's at the door. That way she won't have time to do anything about it."

He nodded, fully aware of his mother's scheming. "It'll be best."

Nan let out her breath. She felt drained, as if she'd been

running a race to save her own life. "I'm going to take a bath," she said.

He was already immersed in his work. "Just don't go to bed without telling me. I'll want something to eat. And I'll wake you later." He looked up, eyebrows raised.

"Sure." She'd known that was coming. Every victory, no matter how small, had to be paid for. This time she'd pay gladly. Her heart thumped in her breast and she nearly ran up the stairs. In her mind, she was already free.

CHAPTER FIVE

"You'll ruin your hands. Why can't you learn to wear gloves?"

Nan's mother had come in through the back gate and was watching her pull weeds from the perennial bed.

"I can't get all the roots with gloves," she explained patiently, knowing the explanation wouldn't be accepted anymore than it would be if she said she loved the dampness of the earth, the coolness of the thrusting stems.

Helen Alden held out her own perfectly manicured hands. "Nonsense. Someday you'll be a lady of leisure and wish you had beautiful hands."

Nan tossed a clump of grass into the wheelbarrow, then sat back on her heels. She and her mother were opposites in every way possible—earth and air, fire and water—a fact Nan had understood even as a toddler, but which Helen refused to grasp, just as she had never been able to comprehend that her daughter had become an adult.

With an inward grin Nan said, "What's that? Lady of leisure? It sounds like ladies of the night."

"You're impossible," came the expected response. "I'm telling you for your own good."

But she wasn't. She was, even now, attempting to shape the clay that was Nan into the mold she considered acceptable. Endlessly the battle went on—and on. Annoyed, Nan jumped to her feet, knowing that still another battle lay ahead.

"Where are you off to?" she asked, putting off the moment. "You're all dressed up."

"A luncheon date. And maybe I'll go shopping after. I've had so many dates this month I don't have anything left to wear."

Usually, when Jake went on a trip, Nan indulged herself with a shopping spree, then hid the bills and paid them off a bit at a time. Although her father had died several years before, her mother had always been free to come and go as she pleased, to have her "dates" and spend an afternoon in the stores.

The differences in their lives struck her as she headed for the house, but she wasn't about to complain because she knew what her mother's response would be. Helen had never liked Jake and, indeed, had warned her against him. "He'll drive you crazy," she'd said with all the dramatics of a fortune teller, and, as usual, Nan had done the opposite and married him anyhow.

"I'm glad you stopped by," she said, holding open the screen so Helen could enter. "I have something to tell you, and I don't want you to tell anybody else."

Helen gasped. "A baby! You're expecting a baby!"

"God forbid." Nan dropped into a kitchen chair and hid her dirty fingernails on her lap under the table top.

"What then?"

"Jake's going to Russia, and Jamie and I are going to the ranch like we planned. But Lottie mustn't know."

"You can't." Her mother glared at her. "It's too far to go by yourself, and besides, you're married."

"What does that have to do with anything?"

"What will people think? Your neighbors here. The people

you'll meet there. You'll be with strange men and no husband and they'll think you're leading them on."

Sex, Nan thought, was definitely the root of all evil and uppermost in Helen's mind. She saw men waiting to ravish her everywhere—in gas stations, supermarkets, even the church parking lot.

She said, "All you think about is sex."

Helen looked indignant. "I do not. But *they* do. *Men*. Your problem is you just don't realize when you're putting yourself in danger."

"I haven't noticed any men whipping off their pants and coming after me," Nan said with a grin.

"And I didn't bring you up to say such dreadful things. You were supposed to be a lady."

"And I'm not?"

Helen sighed as if the weight of the world were on her shoulders. "Sometimes I don't know what you are."

"Join the club," Nan said.

"You've never been like other girls. You've never confided in me."

"Better that way." If she didn't confide, she was safe. But from what? Ruefully, Nan shook her head. "Anyhow, it's decided. Jake and I talked about it, and he doesn't see anything wrong. And I *am* old enough to know how to act in public."

"I hope you don't regret this." Helen's blue eyes had turned to slate. She got up and stood looking down at her daughter whose chin was set in defiance.

"I won't," Nan said. "I'm sure. Just don't tell Lottie. Okay?"

"That woman!" Helen had disliked Lottie from the first.

"Exactly," Nan said, glad they were in agreement even over such a small matter as her mother-in-law.

"I never talk to her at all if I can help it," Helen said. She

36

paused on her way out and looked back. "Promise me you'll be careful. I'll worry about you—about my grandson, 'til you're home where you belong."

Where she belonged. But she didn't belong anywhere. "I promise," she said, and exhaled a sigh of relief when she heard the tapping of her mother's heels receding and then the click as the garden gate swung shut.

CHAPTER SIX

As the ground disappeared beneath a layer of clouds, Nan let out her breath. She felt she'd been holding it for a week, ever since she'd put Jake on his plane.

She looked at Jamie who was grinning. "We did it," she said. "We really did."

"I didn't think we would." He, too, leaned back and sighed. "I thought grandma Lottie would find out for sure, and when I came home late that night before Dad left, I thought it was all over."

"Why did you do that?" She challenged him, curious. "You *knew* he'd be furious. You know how he likes us around before he leaves."

He shrugged. "I don't know. I just get so fed up with his nagging. It's like he doesn't care about us at all. How do *you* stand it, Mom?"

It was her turn to defray the answer. "I think about something else, I guess. I go deaf, like you do."

Was it wrong, she wondered, to be so honest with a teenager? She wasn't sure, but lying to him was impossible. He'd seen too much, been on the receiving end himself for too long. Somehow it was up to her to show him the way, to assure him that he was, indeed, the intelligent, capable kid that he was, and not the useless idiot Jake made him. If she failed . . . she shuddered. She wouldn't, couldn't, fail Jamie.

"I wish he was like other fathers." Jamie was looking down into his lap. "He's never taken me to a ball game, Mom. He's never even played catch in the back yard. Gramps did all that, but he's dead, and all dad does is yell."

And she had thought that, by leaving home, she was free! "He isn't like other fathers," she said slowly. "Oh, he loves you. I know that. He just doesn't know how to show it or how to have fun. But it isn't *your* fault. Or mine. We just have to live with it."

"Why?"

Why, indeed? "Because we're a family." She took the easy way out, not wanting to burden a child with her own agonizing. "Anyway, we're on our own for two weeks. Let's just enjoy it."

"Yeah."

She'd copped out, and Jamie knew it. She rested her head on the back of the seat and closed her eyes. *Goddamn you, Jake,* she thought. *You'll not ruin our son like you ruined me.* She could almost taste her anger, like salt and bile. And her impotence, that word commonly applied to men, but which fit her to perfection.

She hadn't always been like this—terrified, stressed-out, a slave to everyone's whims. And she'd dated Jake for a year before he'd asked her to marry him. Sure, she saw how he treated others, even harassed the waitresses in the restaurants where they went to the point of tears. But to her he'd always been courteous, even gentle. How could she have known he'd change as soon as he had her married and securely in his possession? How could she have foreseen that something as trivial as a few of her hairs left in the sink would rouse him to hysteria and then to rage. "Filthy! Filthy! You're a filthy woman!" She could still hear him, still remember her own shock and the fear that followed. She, and she alone, was responsible for turning the man she loved into a screaming stranger. Her fault. And over the years her faults had multiplied, a rosary of errors, her personal Stations of the Cross.

She opened her eyes. "Jamie," she said, "let's play a game. Let's pretend he isn't there. That we never have to go back."

He looked skeptical. "Sure," he said. "If that's what you want."

"It is."

She knew she could do it. With Jake five thousand miles away she could be her Self again, the old Nan who laughed a lot, talked with confidence to people who saw nothing in her to blame; who put words together on paper and made sense; who had no ache where her heart was.

The problem was Jamie. He had no old Self. All he had was the person she and Jake had fashioned, a person as fragile inside as a bundle of twigs.

She turned away from him and looked out the window, but her tears blurred the sight of the ground far below and turned what were mountains and plains into a river of dull colored mud.

Ben Fuller entered the airport, read the list of incoming flights, and swore under his breath. A half-hour delay, and he'd left a mountain of paperwork undone to get here on time.

Running a cattle ranch wasn't easy, and taking in guests doubled the work. Not for the first time he wondered why he'd continued the business begun by his parents in the 30's when the bottom had dropped out of the cattle market.

For the same reason, he admitted to himself. To keep the ranch afloat. Guests brought in needed cash, and it was as necessary today as it had been in the Depression, more so since eating beef had become a crime.

And he, Ben Fuller, had to paste a smile on his face and welcome guests, regardless—the undisciplined kids, the smart alecks who'd seen all the western films, the women who, more often than not, ended up making a pass at him.

He wasn't interested in women. Margo had seen to that with her greed, her constant complaints and taunts, and finally her drunken chasing after every cowboy and truck driver in the county.

Well, she'd given him a son, and for that he was grateful. He loved the boy with a love that was almost an ache and that he tried to keep hidden. He'd loved Margo that way at first, given her everything including his heart. And she'd thrown it back in his face.

Remembering the last time he'd seen her, in the hospital dying, he winced. Why think about her now? It was over and done with, and he had guests to pick up. A woman and her son.

That was another thing. They were coming alone, a change of plans at the last minute she'd told him over the phone, sounding breathless and a little desperate. She hadn't mentioned her husband, simply said he wasn't coming. So what did that mean? A separation? An open marriage?

Well, he'd make the best of it, and if she came on to him, he'd be polite, and firm, and honest. "Sorry, sweetheart. I'm married to the ranch. Besides, I've got nothing to offer a woman, and that's the truth." He'd lost count of the number of times he'd said those words or a variation of them. What he had was his ranch, his son, and a head full of painful memories, nothing any woman would want.

A voice over the loud speaker announced the arrival of the flight. He sighed, tucked the newspaper he'd been staring at but not reading under his arm, and walked over to the gate.

★ ★ ★ ★ ★

"Mrs. Fletcher?"

The tall man with Indian-black hair and piercing hazel eyes removed his Stetson.

For a moment the ground seemed to lift and fall under Nan's feet, and she was afraid, not of him but of her own inabilities, for something in his eyes suggested that this man could see into her mind, into that place where the real Nan lay curled and protected from all harm.

Then she felt a great compassion in him, a warmth that enveloped both her and Jamie. She lifted her chin and put out her hand. "Nan," she said firmly. "Call me Nan."

Who had frightened her? he wondered. Who was responsible for the sadness in her dark eyes? His heart thumped out of rhythm as he shook hands and felt the slender firmness of her fingers.

"Ben Fuller. And you must be Jamie."

The boy nodded, obviously ill-at-ease in his presence, and again Ben was puzzled—at himself and at his reaction to these strangers—the tall woman with the secrets in her eyes, and her son who faced the world with such reluctance.

When he spoke again, it was with his usual politeness and the hope that he could put them both at ease. "Glad to have you at the Rocking F. I'm sorry your husband couldn't make it."

Nan smiled. "Maybe we'll all come again," she said.

Relieved to hear that, he returned her smile. "We'll do our best to show you a good time. Spring roundup starts tomorrow. You did say you could ride?"

"Since I was a kid begging rides on every old nag and plow horse in the neighborhood." Nan smiled at the memory. "I was a horse nut then and I still am."

Now this was the kind of guest he liked. He understood

her love of horses. He was the same. "It's a sickness," he said, smiling. "You're born with it. Horses are either in your blood or they're not, and God help you if they are."

"Could be worse," Nan said. "I guess you see lots who are scared to death of horses. It must be rough."

"You've said it all." He was beginning to enjoy himself. The woman wasn't at all the way he'd thought, and she actually seemed to comprehend the facts of ranch life. He turned to the boy. "How about you? Ready to bust broncs?"

Jamie looked at the ground. "I do okay."

"He's been taking lessons," Nan said. "He's pretty good if I do say so."

And as frightened of something as his mother had seemed, although now she was at ease, tilting her head to meet his eyes.

Lord, he was tall! Nan thought. And handsome. She was easy in her bones, earlier qualms gone. Here was a man who accepted people for what they were with no attempt at a makeover.

"Let's get your bags," he said abruptly. "We've got a three-hour ride ahead of us."

"Good. We live in the city, but I hate cities. I was raised in open country."

"You'll find plenty of that where we're going." Ben was leading the way through the terminal, and Nan was trotting to keep up with his long strides.

Suddenly she stopped and laughed, causing Jamie and Ben to stare.

"I can't believe I'm here," she said in response to their amazement. "It's wonderful! I've been trying to get out West since I fell in love with Roy Rogers' horse Trigger! And now here I am for two whole weeks. It's like a dream."

"Then I hope it never ends." Ben slipped a hand under her

43

elbow. "Come on, cowgirl, we have ground to cover. And what ground! You may never go back."

She pushed the thought of home far down in her mind. "I just got here," she said, hoping her distress didn't show. "Let's not talk about leaving yet."

"Maybe we'll just keep you then," he answered, and was astonished to realize he had said it.

Ten minutes later they were on the freeway headed East toward the far corner of the state where, Ben assured her, she could look out at night and not see a single light or any vestige of a city.

"And coyotes?" she asked. "Will I hear coyotes?"

"More than you ever imagined." He was concentrating on the road, which gave her a chance to study him.

That sudden leap of her heart, the movement of the earth under her feet still perplexed her. Surreptitiously she eyed his profile—straight nose, high cheek bones, a beautiful face, really.

How would it feel to touch? she wondered, and then was shocked. He was a man, like any other; bigger than most, nicer than most, but that was no reason to want to know— what was it she wanted to know? She chewed her bottom lip, confused, and turned to watch the scenery. Mountains rose on all sides, like sea waves frozen in time. Over the rocky slopes, cloud shadows painted purple flowers—the giant petunias of O'Keeffe, the darkness in the hearts of irises— and something in her, spirit or hunger, struggled and burst open and went out to meet the vastness without fear or hesitation.

"I love this!" She turned to Ben, her eyes shining. "All this wonderful, empty space!"

He glanced at her then. "You'd be surprised how many it scares off. They look at it, turn tail, and run."

"I want to run *into* it!" she exclaimed. "I want it all. Why," she stopped as a new thought came to her, "why, you could be or do anything you want out here. You can get *big* here, as big as the country. There's nothing—nobody—to say 'no'." Not even Jake. Especially not Jake.

"That's how we feel. Some people come out and think it's desolate, but it suits those of us who live here. I can't imagine living anyplace else."

"It's like coming home," she said and realized that she did, indeed, feel at home—with the man beside her and with the land that spread out as far as she could see.

Even the road seemed familiar, and the stone canyons with their towering rock walls. And when at last they turned off the highway onto a red dirt track, she leaned forward in her seat, eager to see what lay around each bend.

On either side were large pastures. Cattle grazed on tall grass the tawny color of a lion skin, and the leaves of the mesquite trees glinted green in the late afternoon.

Ahead she saw more mountains, their smooth flanks catching the light of the setting sun and glowing with a radiance that seemed to come as much from within as from the glow in the western sky, and the beauty was such that she said nothing, only stared, her hands clasped together as if in prayer.

"Alpenglow," Ben murmured, seeing her rapt attention. "It happens here just like in the Alps."

"Every night? Or is this special. Just for me?"

"It's always special. A time for looking. Thinking over the day maybe, or just giving thanks."

And she couldn't keep it—the loveliness—except in words, her own words, written in solitude and in haste.

"I wish it would stay forever," she said, her voice trembling.

Her tone surprised him with its echoes of need. She was a complex woman, he decided—sad one moment, joyful the next, reaching out with sudden passion to gather the world in her arms.

"It'll happen every night," he said gently. "Different, but the same. You'll see. And there's the ranch." He pointed into the valley that opened in front of them.

In the fading light she saw a long, low adobe house at the end of a curving drive. Behind white fences, horses raised their heads and watched their approach, eyes reflecting the headlights. Wood smoke scented the air, and she sniffed in wonder.

"Piñon," he answered before she could ask. "Lupe must've known we were nearly home and lit the fire."

"Who's Lupe?"

"She runs the ranch and me. Been here since I was a kid, and her husband, Wish, with her. She cooks, she cleans, she gives us our orders. We'd be lost without her. Especially Bay." He caught Jamie's eyes in the rear view mirror. "Bay's my son. He's looking forward to having somebody his age around for a change."

"Bay?" Jamie repeated the name as a question.

"Short for Bayard. Named for my grandfather who homesteaded here."

Jamie's curiosity was aroused. "When?" he asked.

"He came out in the 1880's. The old house is still standing. And there was a post office for awhile in the 20's. Now we use it as a kind of rec room. You'll see it tomorrow."

Ben pulled up beside a small house surrounded by oak and mesquite trees and switched off the ignition.

"You'll be staying here," he said to Nan. "But meals are in the main house. You have time to unpack and get settled before dinner."

46

She got out of the van slowly, not wanting to break the spell that seemed to hover around her like a protecting cloak. "Magic," she whispered, as much to herself as to him. "It's magic here." Then she stood and listened to the silence that was so dense it was almost tangible.

The earth was holding its breath, she thought. It was waiting, waiting, but for what? And then it came, the howl of a creature lost, followed by another and another until the night trembled with the wild chorus of hunting coyotes.

The hairs on the back of her neck tingled, and she raised her head and stood, letting the music fill her. She was aware, for the first time, of blood running through her veins, of nerve endings stretched taut, of the place within that was like a vessel, filling and pouring out, in words, in gestures.

Her intensity communicated itself to Ben who put a hand on Jamie's shoulder. "Let her be," he whispered to the boy. "She's having herself a moment." Irrationally, he wished suddenly he could be a part of what she was seeing, be the reason for the ecstasy that swept across her face.

CHAPTER SEVEN

The door to the main house was open revealing a small entrance hall with a red tile floor the color of the earth. A large Apache burden basket hung from one wall. It was filled with hats of various sizes and shapes, probably for guests who had forgotten the strength of the southwestern sun, Nan decided.

Beyond was a living room, the center of which was a rock fireplace where Lupe's fire burned with welcoming warmth. Ben was standing beside it, one elbow resting on the carved mantle.

"Here they are," he said, seeing Nan and Jamie and coming to greet them, drawing them firmly into the circle of light cast by the fire.

His arm was warm around her shoulders, and for an instant Nan felt awkward, the woman who effaced herself and watched others, giving nothing away. But Ben didn't seem to notice, and she was grateful.

He made the introductions smoothly, to the Tilsons, an elderly couple who were bird watchers; to Wish Redfern, "my foreman and right hand;" to Bay, a younger copy of his father; and to Lupe, who looked, Nan thought, like an oracle with her height and proud bearing, her bottomless dark eyes.

Nan noticed Jamie slip, silent and wraith-like, into a chair on the edge of the firelight.

"We usually meet here for a drink before dinner," Ben

said. "Or in the summer on the terrace to watch those mountains of yours."

"Of mine?" Nan emerged from the trance she'd been in.

"Sure. You looked at them. I saw you. Now they're yours."

How could he know? she wondered. How had he realized that she'd taken them in, filmed them with the camera of her eyes? She managed a chuckle. "Are you always so observant?"

"Not always," he said, and she heard a deeper meaning in his voice. "Drink?" he said then, gesturing at the bottles and glasses, the bowls of chips and salsa on top of a carved Mexican chest.

"Sherry if you have it," she said, thinking that her request was ridiculous here two hundred miles from anywhere.

He bent and reached into a cabinet and pulled out a dark bottle. "Jerez," he said. "We aim to please."

"And you succeed." She took the hand blown glass and admired the golden liquid shot through with the light of the fire. "To the Rocking F," she said.

"To a happy time," he replied, raising his own glass.

Later, lying in bed too excited to sleep, she remembered how their eyes had met and held, in friendship and in something more. Something that had to do with the blaze of the fire and the dark turnings of her bones, with that place within that received and gave back with a constancy she had never realized.

And Ben's wife? Where was she, the woman who had borne a son so like the father? A man like Ben wasn't cut out for celibacy, she knew that much. He was proud, passionate, and caring, that was obvious even to the casual observer.

Sighing, she slid down between crisp sheets that smelled of sunlight and the sweetness of juniper and closed her eyes. So many questions! So much to see and do, and who was she now, out of her element yet eager as a child? She still didn't know the answer, but her tensions seemed to have vanished, replaced by a joy that came out of the earth, out of the sight and sounds of mountains and valleys, out of the promise of words yet unspoken, the warmth in the depths of a man's eyes.

In the main house Ben was banking the fire for the night. As he bent over the smoldering logs, he was trying to solve the riddle that was Nan and Jamie.

The boy was so diffident, and his mother . . . he shook his head. She was like a will o' the wisp, here one minute, gone the next, dancing ahead like a blue flame, and vulnerable in spite of the fact that she seemed untouchable.

And he wanted to help. That was his problem. He was genetically unable to resist a plea, silent or otherwise, and Nan, though she'd not confided in him, was in need. Of what, he wasn't sure; perhaps only a shoulder to cry on, a friend to listen.

He was lost in his own thoughts when Bay came in through the kitchen, shaking his head. "He beat me at pool," he said. "Four to one."

"Guess you'll have to practice."

"Yeah. Guess I'll turn in now, though." He yawned, showing white teeth.

"What's he like?" Ben inquired, curious to learn more of the puzzle.

Bay thought for a minute, frowning. "Nice. But he said something funny."

"What?"

"He said he was glad his dad wasn't along. That if he was, he wouldn't have been allowed to stay up late just to have fun."

"Anything else?"

Bay shook his head. "Not much. He's aces at pool, though. And he's in the same grade as me. Wants to be an engineer."

Ben pulled the fire screen shut and stood staring at the coals, assimilating Bay's information and forming a picture of a rigid father, one who forbade pleasure even for himself. And for his wife who was a woman born for happiness if he'd ever seen one.

"Well," he said, "I promised her a good time so let's make sure they have one, father or no father."

"No problem."

But there was. For the first time in years he was interested in a woman. And she was married, skittish as a green colt, but possessing, he was certain, a heart as big as the country she'd embraced.

Right now she was probably asleep a few hundred feet away, worn out from travel, altitude, the complexity of her emotions, her dark hair spread across the pillow and veiling her face.

"Easy, boy," he said to himself. "You go looking for trouble, and you'll sure find it."

Nonetheless, in the morning he was going to put her on a horse and turn her loose, and he doubted she'd disappoint either of them.

CHAPTER EIGHT

Nan awoke at first light and lay listening to the fluting song of larks, the incessant burbling of a mockingbird in a tree just outside her open window.

By some miracle she had found this place with the power to heal. Already the fragments of herself were knitting together so that she felt whole again and at peace—a delicate process like the mending of old lace or the strengthening of a spider's web.

She yawned and stretched, aware of her body beneath the sheets, the strength in her long legs, the ripple of spine and shoulders.

A roundup! She was going on a roundup! At the thought, she was out of bed, shivering a little for the morning air was cold. Hastily she pulled on her robe and went to the door that opened onto a small, walled terrace. What did it look like in daylight, this ranch, this shrine to the mountain gods?

She turned in a circle, then caught her breath as the mountains to the west caught the rays of a still invisible sun and began to burn with the radiance of stained glass.

It was like being in a cathedral, she thought, half expecting to hear the surge of a mighty organ, powerful music that would shake the earth underfoot and cause the flaming clouds to disperse.

"Look!" she commanded herself. "Look and keep looking.

Hold it close. This time won't ever come again."

And so she watched while the brilliance intensified then faded, and the mountains with their cliffs and canyons, jagged crests and tumbled boulders turned back into earth, solid and uncompromising.

What she had said to Ben yesterday had been the truth. It was possible, in fact it was necessary to grow if only to survive in such surroundings. Strength, violence, grace, the lightning strikes of incomparable beauty all required a humanity that was different from anything she had been brought up to believe.

That somewhere deep down she had recognized that the falsity of her life was to her advantage now as she cast off an old skin and became acquainted with the new; as she shucked her robe, pulled on jeans, boots, and a sweater and happily went to wake Jamie and conquer the day.

But Jamie wasn't in his room. Startled, she stood in the doorway, and voices, the ghosts of her other life, assaulted her. "I *knew* you'd regret it!" "What kind of mother are you?" "All you think about is what *you* want."

But what harm could have come to Jamie here? She drew a deep breath and looked around. His bed had been slept in, the clothes he'd worn the day before were in a heap in the corner, and his jeans and boots were gone. Smiling, she shook her head. Would she never get him to clean up after himself? Well, at some point she just had to let him go and damn the consequences—as well as the voices so eager to accuse.

She walked to the main house, her boot heels stirring puffs of dust. Before she reached the door, the smells of cooking reached her—bacon, eggs, the pungency of green chilies— and the sound of laughter, Jamie's and Bay's.

If Jake were here, he'd go in ranting about the mess in Jamie's room, not caring that his friend was sitting with him at the table, and that both boys were happily scoffing down breakfast.

"You're up early," she said.

When Jamie looked up, his face was set, but seeing her smile, he relaxed. "We were brushing down horses. So you wouldn't have to."

She preferred to curry her own horse but hated to spoil his good intentions. "Service!" she said instead. "Thanks, guys."

Bay stood up. "There's food on the buffet, but Lupe will cook eggs however you want."

She noted his politeness with approval. Obviously he'd been brought up right. Ben? she wondered. Or the tireless Lupe? "Go on and eat. I'll help myself," she told him and wandered over to the long Spanish table that held chafing dishes filled with hash browns, ham and bacon, and scrambled eggs. There was a basket of warm muffins, boxes of cereal, bowls of strawberries and a pitcher of thick yellow cream.

"Do you eat like this every morning?" she asked, liberally pouring cream over her fruit.

"Mostly."

"I'll have to do a lot of riding. Or else I'll get so fat nobody will recognize me."

"You look fine to me. Doesn't she, boys?" Ben came in and helped himself to coffee.

"Flatterer." She realized that she was having fun—and at seven in the morning, the hour when she usually hid out in the kitchen and attempted to write. And now she was with a family that seemed like her own.

"Honest Ben, they call me. I always tell the truth," he said, sitting down beside her. "How'd you sleep?"

"Like a rock."

"Good." He watched her over the brim of his cup. She did

look rested, with a faint blush in her cheeks and a sparkle in her eyes that made her seem heartrendingly young.

Abruptly he pushed back his chair. "When you're through, we'll go down to the corrals."

She took a last bite of muffin. "I'm ready," she said and followed him out.

In the hall he stopped. "Not so fast, cowgirl." He reached into the Apache basket. "Can't have you getting sunstroke on your vacation. Come here."

He selected a hat and placed it gently on her head, then stepped back and studied her. "Nope. Not that one. Let's try another." It was an excuse to look at her, to touch her, but he couldn't stop himself. She looked so eager, so different from the woman he'd met at the plane.

"There," he said. "Go look at yourself." He turned her to the mirror framed in gaudy Mexican tin work on the opposite wall.

She stared at herself in the black felt hat, at him, his hands on her shoulders. In the glass their eyes met again, his probing, hers suddenly veiled. "We look like a painting," she said.

"Not American Gothic, I hope."

"God no. I hate that painting. Those two mostly dead old people stuck with each other and a pitchfork. Making the best of a bad marriage."

"And how many bad marriages have you known?" he asked, still watching her.

She shrugged. "A few. My best friend just filed for divorce, and the thing is, I never even knew she was unhappy."

"Maybe you weren't looking."

"I wasn't. But I should have been. I mean, she was my friend and going through hell, and I could've at least been there."

"Quiet desperation."

"Something like that."

"It's always better to talk to somebody," he said. "But we don't, do we?"

What was he getting at with his gentle questions, those eyes that were able to pierce through her fragile shell? "It's not easy to bare your wounds in public." She stepped away from the mirror and the warmth of his hands.

"You're right. It isn't. But it's just as hard to suffer in silence." And wasn't that what he'd done all these years—keeping quiet, going on about his business, turning a cheerful face to Bay and working himself into the ground so he could sleep at night without remembering the cruel laughter, the hate in his wife's eyes?

The contrast between that wraith and Nan's warm gaze was striking, the more so when she reached out and put a gentle hand on his arm. "We're taught that we're put on earth to work hard and pay our dues," she said slowly. "But more and more I'm thinking that's a lie. And being here, seeing all this has kind of convinced me we should be happy. I don't want to suffer. I don't want you or anybody else to suffer. And today I want to have fun!"

He, in turn, wanted to hold her, to bury his face in the hollow spot at the base of her throat where the pulse beat—quickly, in time with his own. The need itself didn't surprise him nearly as much as the intensity of it, but he held back. She was, after all, a guest. And a very-much-married stranger.

CHAPTER NINE

"I can't believe this!"

They had pulled up on the crest of a hill, and spreading out from where they sat, flowing down the slope into the valley like a golden waterfall were poppies, more than she had ever imagined, their small faces tilted to the sun, their petals fluttering in the constant breeze.

"Mom's nuts about flowers," Jamie put in. "You should see her garden."

"But nothing was ever like this!" She wanted to gather them all, hold them in her hands and against her face, learn the silken petals with her fingertips.

He'd known she would respond like this, with a passion for the land he, himself, loved; not with a momentary flash but with that part of her that embraced the earth, felt kinship with its cycles.

He said, "We had a rainy winter. The flowers are out in force. Maybe the gods knew you were coming."

Yes. The gods. The One. The many. And here for her. Reluctantly she picked up her reins. "We have work to do, and here I am gawking."

"Gawk all you want. You're having fun, remember? Anyhow, we'll split up here. All we're doing today is taking a head count of mama's and new calves."

She listened, awaiting orders. God forbid she do something wrong, injure the horse, make a fool of herself! He wouldn't look at her so kindly then.

"You and Dancer go down around that red hill." He pointed to a small cone thrusting up from the valley floor. "There's a spring on the other side, and good grass, and they like to hide out over there. Push 'em toward the corrals." He pointed again, and she followed his gesture, squinting in the sun. From the hill to the corral gate looked about two miles, maybe more. Distance, she was learning, was deceptive here.

She managed a smile in spite of her doubts and moved Dancer carefully down the side of the hill, following a narrow game trail through the waves of gold.

And then she was on the plain, the grass brushing her stirrups, the poppies dancing like a painted screen. She was alone, on horseback, in a place that had no end, a valley that ran to Mexico and beyond to where crumpled purple mountains held up the sky.

The wind sang in her ears. A covey of quail burst from under a mesquite and took flight, their wing beats loud, like clapping hands. Dancer moved smoothly, knowing his business, responsive to her every cue.

She was alone, a solitary figure moving through a wilderness of grass, sky, and red volcanic hills. "Free!" she said aloud, and the wind took the word and carried it away. "I'm free!"

But she wasn't. She had a job to do. "We'll cut around the east side," she said to Dancer, as if he could understand. "That way, when we come out, we'll be headed toward the corrals."

Pleased with her ability to make a decision on her own in a strange, nearly directionless place, she moved him into a jog, laughing although there was no one to share her delight.

A cow bawled a warning and was answered by another.

Four of them, small calves at their side, turned protective heads toward her as she rode up to the spring.

"Good morning, ladies," she said to them. "Sorry to disturb you, but we're going to take a little walk."

The biggest of the bunch, an old brindle with a twisted horn, lowered her head in a menacing gesture.

Such fierce motherhood! Nan thought, watching with admiration, realizing that, year after year, this same creature bore a calf, raised it, cared for it by herself, using horns, hooves, and the richness of milk from her own body to assure it life. Mothering, regardless of species, was the same the world over. You nurtured, protected, and loved, and the love was ingrained, a part of your flesh.

"Come on, old girl," she said. "We're not going to hurt anybody, just look at your baby. You know the routine."

The cow lifted her head and looked at her with dark, nearly iridescent eyes as if she somehow, across the barriers that separated them, understood.

"I'm talking to cows," Nan said to Dancer. "What next?"

He twitched his ears and curved his neck around to look at her, moving impatiently.

She patted his smooth shoulder. "Business, right? Okay. We'll push 'em out like in the movies."

She rode now with confidence, the cattle walking ahead. She could see the corrals, see other cattle coming out of the brush raising dust that blew away, dispersed by the wind. And when one of the calves, older than his companions, ran off, she was ready for Dancer's quick leap to head it and drive it back into the bunch.

It had been years since she'd known the oneness of rider and horse, the single-minded purpose of achievement that approached perfection. She'd forgotten the glory, the smoothness of motion, and how her body seemed all of a piece. Sex was supposed to be like this—a union of differences. But it wasn't. At least not with Jake.

She scowled. Jake and sex! She was as bad as her mother, thinking about sex out here as far away from the act of seduction and joining as was possible.

From out of the corner of her eye she saw Ben riding toward her at a lope, looking like a centaur on his tall black horse. He transitioned smoothly into a walk as he joined her.

"I did it!" Her face was glowing.

"Were you worried? I wasn't."

"Well," she said, "I'm a dude after all."

He laughed. "No you're not. If you were, I wouldn't have let you out of my sight. It's no picnic wrangling dudes, believe me. I keep a string of plugs for them or the insurance would break me."

"How'd you know I wasn't one?" She was curious and, though she hated to admit it, hungry for his praise.

He rolled his eyes. "Sweetheart," the word came out effortlessly, causing her to blush, "I've had people here, women *and* men, too weak to lift a saddle. Who mount from the wrong side, try to jump on from the rear. Who want to take off and run and sit so candy-assed they'd fall off at a walk. I watched you saddle up. I watched everything. You're not a novice, you're a horsewoman. Believe me, I can tell."

She fastened onto his figurative language. "Candy-assed, huh?"

"You bet. Now let's get this bunch corralled and have lunch. Lupe's here with the works."

Food! And approval! And from Ben! She squared her shoulders and settled more firmly in the saddle. "I'm starving," she said and hoped he didn't realize the deeper meaning in her simple response.

CHAPTER TEN

"She's a keeper!"

They were at the dinner table, Ben at the head, Nan at the foot, the rest seated in between and beaming at her as if she'd just won a marathon.

Wish was raising his glass in a toast, and Nan wished she could crawl under the table and disappear. She had done what she had done, and Ben had praised her. That was enough.

"Come on, fellas," she said. "All I did was push in a bunch of cows. You do it all the time."

Edna Tilson leaned across her plate. "What do you do at home?" she asked. "Surely you must ride a lot. Heavens! I took one look at those creatures and decided to stay on my own two feet."

Nan shook her head. "I used to. Now I . . . I just keep house. Nothing to talk about."

"She writes!" Jamie announced proudly. "My mother's a writer."

Why had he said that? Now she'd have to talk about herself to this woman with her permed hair and a coyness that reminded her, uncomfortably, of her mother. It was a trait that hid a kind of emotional greed that had always terrified her.

"What do you write? Have you published? I always wanted

to write a book. The stories I could tell you. Oh, this is so fascinating."

Edna was babbling, and Nan felt herself shrinking away from her curiosity. Writing was her private world. She swallowed. "Poems. A few. Some stories. Nothing much."

"I never met a real writer before. Will you recite for us?"

Recite. It was a poor choice of words, conjuring up memories from grade school—little girls saying poems without understanding or caring in the least.

It was innocent; Nan knew that. Yet she also sensed that Edna would fasten on her like a leech, poking, probing into that which was none of her business. It wasn't her work that was important to the woman but the birthing, and birth was a private affair between mother and child, poet and the feelings that were thought captured by language. And the agony belonged not to Edna but to herself.

"I'm sorry," she said, her voice trembling. "I haven't memorized anything."

"But you must be working on something. It's *so* inspirational here."

Nan laid down her fork. "I'm not. Really. Now please excuse me." And she fled into the night that was pierced by the rising of the moon.

She had always been this way—protective of that place where words arose. She buried her face in her hands. Could she never escape her own being, her own fears? Was her life to be one of constant protection of an act even she did not understand?

"Are you all right?" Ben was beside her. She felt his warmth, the solidity of his body curving around her like a wing.

She nodded, afraid to trust her voice.

"You're bone weary. Come on. I'll walk you over."

That was all. No questions. No prying. She marveled at the simplicity of him and let him lead her through the dazzle of moonlight.

She said, "You're very kind."

The moon touched the planes of his face, the high cheek-bones, the curve of dark brows. He put a hand on her hair, lightly, so lightly it might have been the breath of the wind, and she looked up at him in wonder.

"Sleep well." It was a whisper, no more, as fleeting as the touch of his hand, as startling as the flood of light from the darkness of sky.

"You, too," she said. "And thank you."

"For what?"

"For the loveliest day."

In the oak tree the mockingbird tilted his head and began to sing, and he did not stop until the first light of the sun spilled down the face of the mountains.

In the morning Nan was ashamed of what must have appeared as an over-reaction to a simple request. They probably thought she was a snob, or crazy.

She stepped into the shower as much to wash away her thoughts as the soreness of muscles unused to riding. She'd been called a snob before, been labeled "different" by everybody from her teachers to her peers. And she *was* different, even secretive, but not because she thought she was better than anyone else.

Of them all, only Ben seemed to understand her sudden flight from the table. Only Ben had resisted opening Pandora's box. Yet he'd touched her with such tenderness, as if she were made of brittle glass that he had no wish to break. And she had fought off the desire to lean against him, if only for a minute, savoring his gentle warmth.

Abruptly she reached and turned off the shower. What was she thinking—just because he was kind, and good, and praised her?

She dressed quickly, tying back her hair in a red scarf, then checking her face in the mirror. It was the same face she'd seen all her life, but today it was different, her eyes darker and shining with expectation, her skin faintly tanned by the sun.

"Oh, Nan," she said. "Be careful."

"Of what?" the face asked.

"Yourself," she said, "whoever you are," and stuck out her tongue at her image for good measure.

She checked Jamie's room, found him gone, and walked across the yard without pausing to look at the mountains. Ben met her at the door.

"I thought maybe you'd sleep in."

"Nope. I'm ready to ride." Best not admit to sore thighs and the ache across her shoulders.

"I'm packing salt to the Hill Pasture. It's a rough trail. You up for it?"

She met his eyes. "Yes."

"Good girl. Get some breakfast, then we'll head out."

He followed her into the dining room, curious about her behavior of the night before, her sudden retreat as if she had closed a door on them all. Well, it really wasn't his business. He didn't intrude on the privacy of others and expected to be treated the same. But nevertheless it bothered him that it had hurt—being locked out. What he wanted, he was discovering, was to be locked in with her and able to tell the rest of the world to go to hell.

The trail cut through a meadow then ascended the side of the mountain. It was narrow and rocky, with a precipitous drop-off as they went higher. Oak and juniper crowded the slopes, and the scent of pine was heavy on the air. Below them, heat waves shimmered over the valley, turning the familiar into mirage—seen, then gone in an instant.

They had pulled up to let the horses blow, and Nan was watching the ripple of air, the shapes that formed and disappeared before her eyes. "There's always a mystery," she said. "Something you see but can't quite get hold of."

"Like what?"

She rested her hands on the saddle horn. "Like those visions down there. And there's always that thing you can't find words for. You try and you try, and all you get is an approximation."

"In writing or in life?" he asked.

"Both, I guess. But you have to keep trying." She hesitated, then went on. "And I owe you an apology for last night. Running off like that. You must have thought I was nuts."

"Actually," he said, "what I thought was that Edna was being a pain in the ass."

Nan smiled wryly. "She's not alone. The world's full of people like her, but I usually try to avoid them."

"Why?"

Could she tell him? She owed him the attempt. "Because she wasn't really interested in what I've written. She wanted the source. For her it was a kind of vicarious thrill, like a peeping tom. It was a power trip. Am I making sense?"

Was she? He went back over the scene putting together what he knew. She was leaving a lot unsaid, but what she *had* said rang true. He nodded. "Sure. She's a wannabe."

"A what?"

"As in 'I wannabe an Indian.' Or in her case, a writer."

Put like that, Edna was simply pathetic and not the vampire she had thought. She giggled. "I'll have to remember that one. A wannabe. How will I face her tonight?"

"You won't have to. They're leaving this afternoon. It'll be just family for dinner."

Family. So he'd felt that, too—the simple pleasure of sitting down to a meal with those with whom you were in sync.

Later, coming down from the pasture high on the mountain, she kept her eyes on the trail but glanced with longing at the house below in a grove of oaks and cottonwoods. It was a welcoming place with its adobe arms open to whoever came—the warmth of the living room with its fireplace and leather couches, its old baskets and pottery that spoke of a history shared by all who entered through the carved front door.

She looked and she ached with a wanting that had been hers as long as she could remember. Home! Belonging to a place, a piece of earth, a family that was not the enemy in disguise.

Tears stung her eyes, but she blinked rapidly to clear them. She was a woman lost and searching but life was precious. And, as she had learned, there was always a tomorrow.

Ben had been right. Without other guests it seemed as if she and Jamie belonged to the family, and when he and Bay went off to play pool, Nan went along much to Ben's astonishment.

"You play pool?" he asked.

She responded with a giggle. "I used to. In college. And when I worked for the paper I went out with the guys sometimes. It's been years, though."

"What'd you do for the paper?" he wanted to know, his curiosity about her growing.

She giggled again, a delicious sound like flowing water. "I wrote features. Did interviews. Reviewed films. I loved it. I got to meet all kinds of interesting people and ask the questions nobody else could. And after work I'd go out with the others, and we'd eat and play pool, and talk about everything."

Those were the days! She sighed, remembering how it had been as part of a group, many of them young, most of them believing that good writing and reporting could change the world.

"Do you miss it?" he asked.

"Sometimes. Oh, maybe if I'd stayed at it I might have become cynical like some of the older staff writers, but maybe not. It kept me thinking. That's what I miss. Being in the middle of things happening. Being able to say what I think."

"There's no law about that," he said, handing her a pool cue. "The last I heard, we still had freedom of speech."

"Yeah." She chalked the tip of her stick. Little did he know! And she wasn't about to explain the circumstances of her life.

"Let the lady break," he said to the boys.

She looked at him, her eyes twinkling. "Lady! That's a good one. My mother told me no real lady ever, *ever* played pool."

"Why not?"

She drew herself up in imitation of Helen. "Because gangsters play it. Hit men. Odd balls, if you'll pardon the pun. My mother believed what she saw in all those old movies."

"And Minnesota Fats," Jamie said. "Come on, Mom. Do your stuff. How come you never told me any of this?"

"You never asked," she said, bending over the table and taking careful aim.

From where he stood, Ben admired the graceful curves of her hips, her long legs in snug jeans. How would it feel to hold her? he wondered. To have her against him? It would be so easy to do, such a simple motion.

Nan broke, then squinted down the length of the table. "Five ball in the corner pocket," she announced and proceeded to do just that.

Ben shook his head. "Jamie," he said, "your mother might play like Minnesota Fats, but she'll never look like him."

"Thank God," she said over her shoulder and missed her next shot to her disgust. "Damn! I've lost my touch!"

"You'll get it back by the time you leave," he said and saw the brightness in her face fade.

"Now what?"

"Nothing." She picked up the chalk again so she didn't have to look at him. Like a prisoner out on a weekend pass, the idea of going back was stultifying. "I'm having fun. Let's leave it at that," she said.

"My pleasure, madam." He bowed from the waist and was relieved when she grinned back at him, a conspiratorial grin as if she'd admitted him into her fun as an equal partner. And what would her husband have to say about it all? The man who would deny his son the pleasure of a game with friends, and his wife the freedom to enjoy herself?

Again, it was no business of his, except he was drawn to her, wanted to be with her, show her his world, all of it, all the time.

"Your turn." She broke into his reverie, then stood aside and watched him, thinking that this was like the old days when no one passed judgement on her and she was free to take her pleasure as it came. Except that there hadn't been a man like Ben around. If there had . . . she caught herself on the verge of a daydream. Life wasn't like that. It was hard knocks, struggle, anger, with a few golden days in between. This was one of those days. No sense dreaming when she could be living it. No sense at all.

CHAPTER ELEVEN

Dinner was over. They were relaxing around the big table talking idly about ranch business, the mare that was near her time, the places Nan and Jamie should see.

When Lupe rose to clear, Nan jumped up. "Let me help," she said. "I feel guilty sitting here while you do all the work."

The older woman shook her head. "You're a guest. Sit, please."

"I don't feel like one, though. Unless I'd be a bother."

Lupe smiled. "No bother."

"Then I'll clear." She began stacking plates.

Inside the kitchen door she stopped and stared. "What a wonderful room!" she exclaimed. "I know people who'd kill for a kitchen like this."

The floor was tile, the ceiling beamed. Bunches of herbs and red pepper ristras hung from the heavy wooden *vigas*. Windows over the large double sink and counter opened onto a vegetable garden where Nan saw rows of lettuce, green onions, clusters of broccoli, and, in one corner, a rosemary bush, its needles releasing a pungent scent.

" 'Rosemary for remembrance,' " she quoted, putting the dishes on the counter and turning to Lupe. "I have one at home. It's a special plant."

"What you want to remember?" Lupe asked. "What special thing?"

Images ran through her head—poppies dancing, the stained-glass light, cattle, horses—Ben. "All of it," she said, unwilling to confide in this woman with the secretive, onyx eyes. "You're so lucky living here. But I guess you know that."

Lupe nodded, then sat down on a kitchen stool. "Sit," she urged Nan, gesturing at its mate. And when Nan complied, she smiled the sweet smile of a beneficent saint.

"This is paradise," she said slowly. "And I am here because I followed my heart. Because I did what I had to do. It's a story, my life, like all lives are stories, as you know."

Nan hunched forward, resting her elbows on her knees. "Tell me."

"I was born far from here. In *Tierra Amarilla*. You know where that is?"

"I think." Nan was impatient, not wanting a geography lesson, only the flowing of the tale.

"So, I was born there, like my family had been born there for two hundred years, never leaving, never wanting to leave. What was there for us in cities? Noise, cars, people killing for no reason. We had our house, our fields, food on the table. And my mother and grandmother were *curanderas*. I, too, was one. It's a gift, you know. A way of seeing, and I had it. It comes, and you feel it in your hands, your heart. Maybe like writing comes for you, but don't talk about."

At Nan's startled look, she laughed. "Oh, I saw you. You and that *bruja*, that Tilson woman who wanted what you have. You did right, leaving, as you know. Anyway, I was there. I had a *novio*, a young man who wanted to marry me. Me, I wasn't so sure, but I said yes because there weren't too many men for me in the village. And then one spring, late May, there was a storm. Snow and wind coming out of the mountains so bad like it happen sometime. And there was an accident. A truck coming from Colorado turned over, and they brought the driver to the house of my parents. To my mother who put him in bed, and set his arm, and give him broth and *yerbas* to heal the wounds no one could see."

Lupe's soft voice went on. She swayed a little as if she were keeping time with the rhythm of her speech, and Nan, hypnotized, swayed, too, letting her mind follow Lupe's trail into the past.

"Me, I sit by the bed. I hold this man's hand, send life into him from my own heart. I can do this, you see. I can send the message of life and hope. How? I don't know. But he was helpless, and so much needing. So young. And handsome, too. And one day he open his eyes and I see myself in them like a *milagro*. I see I have given away my heart to this stranger, this *gringo,* and that it was meant from the beginning.

"When he was strong again, he ask me to go with him, and I say yes, because what is there left for me without a heart? Oh, they were angry, all of them, the *viejas, mi novio.* All but my mother who understood. She tell me, 'Be happy. Without love there is no connection to the earth, to life. *Vaya con Dios.'* You understand this?"

Nan's answer was a whisper. She understood only too well. Without love you shriveled like a gourd. Without love and the giving of love, you died inside where no one could see, and you walked through life waiting to be put into the ground where you deserved to be.

Lupe said, "The man, you know, was Wish. He bring me here, and here we stay, and we are happy with ourselves and with this place except for one time."

"What happened then?"

"That's another story. Not for now. For now I have said enough, and the dishes don't clean themselves."

"It's a wonderful story. I like happy endings." Nan got up reluctantly and stretched, her muscles still sore.

"Sometimes a wolf in a trap will chew off its foot to get free," Lupe said. "Because it knows the wildness of its heart."

Her words dropped like polished stones into the silence, and Nan stood still hearing the echoes, feeling their weight. "Why are you saying this?" she asked when she could speak.

"You don't like my story?" There was gentle chastising in Lupe's sideways glance.

"Yes. I did. But . . . that part about the wolf." Nan waved her hand that clutched a pile of silverware.

Lupe squeezed suds into the water with vehemence. "I see your face, so full of questions, and I try to help. That's all."

"Do you tell fortunes, too?"

"Nah! I only know what I see. What I feel. Here." She touched her full bosom. "And I see you are tired. Go to bed. Sleep. Have happy dreams."

Lupe was right. She was suffering from system overload. Too much seeing, feeling, taking in; too much exploration of her own emotions and those of others, always a complex process but made more so here where everything was new. Her exhaustion was like a cloak that covered her from head to foot and blotted out any ability she might have had to learn from Lupe's gift.

She managed a smile and laid the silver on the counter. "You're right. I suspect you always are. It's early bed for me and thank you."

"*De nada,* little one," came the answer. "It's nothing."

CHAPTER TWELVE

The knock on the door came several hours later, awakening her from a deep sleep. "What?" she called, confused and reaching for the bedside lamp. "Who is it?"

"Ben. I hate to wake you, but Glory Be is foaling, and I figured you might want to be there."

They had brought the young mare in the day before, a lovely chestnut, slender-legged, round-bellied with new life.

"I do," she said. "Hold on, and let me get dressed."

"Take your time. It'll be awhile yet." He sat down on the porch step and leaned against a post, then caught himself wondering what she looked like as she dressed. Did she wear a nightgown? Was it frilly and feminine or did it cling to her like a skin? And was she one of those women who took hours to make themselves up, keeping the man waiting impatiently? He'd bet she was quick, not wanting to miss a moment, and he congratulated himself when she pulled open the door and appeared, minus her makeup and her hair falling loose around her shoulders but lovely nonetheless.

"Is it right?" she asked then. "Should we be there watching?"

He laid a hand on her shoulder. "I bred her, now I have to be there. It's her first. She's young and I may need to help. Hold her hand, so to speak, and make sure nothing goes wrong."

"You would do that," she said. "You're that kind of man."

He looked down at her curiously. "Meaning?"

"Considerate. Thoughtful. Worried about everybody, even an animal."

"She has feelings the same as we do. And she'll be frightened. Anybody would do the same."

"No," she said. "Anybody would not." She had been in labor for hours with Jamie, alone in a room with her pain until almost the end. Jake had wanted nothing to do with the birth. "You're on your own," he said. "Men have fainted watching that," as if it were a gruesome act instead of the giving of life, as if women hadn't died in the process, or screamed, or fainted themselves from the doing.

The barn was dim, the foaling pen lit only by a single light over the wide aisle. The mare, the same golden color as the straw, seemed calm enough, although sweat had foamed and dried on her blond hide, and her nostrils were distended as she gasped for breath.

She moaned and heaved as a spasm shook her, and Nan felt the bone-cracking pain in her own body, the force of thrusting life that could not be stopped. But how different this birth was from her own, Ben holding Glory Be's head with gentle hands, murmuring love and support, and Wish standing by to help if needed.

"Push, Glory!" she heard herself cry. "Push, girl. It'll be all right."

Ben looked up, struck by her compassion. "She's doing fine. Better than you. Don't worry."

"I hate not being able to help." She took a deep breath of the night air that flowed through the open door but didn't obliterate the odors of birth and blood.

Far away a coyote howled, an eerie wailing that curled around the mountains, drifted for miles on the subtle air. And as if in response the mare screamed, rose to her knees and screamed again, her neck arching, and her backbone, until it seemed it would cut through the fine skin, emerged white and gleaming and curved like a knife.

Nan screamed, too, but it came out a whimper, and what was born was a sack that glistened, a chrysalis bursting with life, with head, neck, hooves that came suddenly free and lay shimmering in the golden straw.

Nan knelt down and stretched out her hands, afraid to touch the tiny creature, yet wanting to take him into her arms. "Look at him! He's like a little butterfly. A baby Monarch."

Ben moved and knelt beside her, his arm around her shoulders. "I knew you'd want to be here. It's a fine thing to see."

She agreed. The evening seemed holy in retrospect; holy and filled with hope and the joyousness of a new life. Even her own labor seemed blessed now, a miraculous link in a chain that stretched to the beginning of time.

"Reckon you just named him," Wish said from the other side of the stall where he was offering the mare a pail of water. "Monarch he is. He's even the right color."

She was leaning against Ben, beyond caring what he thought of her actions. "He is!" she exclaimed as the tiny foal, nudged by his mother, struggled to stand, his bright bay body gleaming. "He is. And I'm glad. Now I've left something behind. Made my mark."

Her hair was tousled, her face flushed. Looking at her, Ben knew her joy and felt his heart turn over. "You'll always leave a mark," he said, his voice unsteady. And then, because he didn't want to be alone in the darkness of his own house he added, "Want coffee? Lupe always leaves a pot on after dinner."

How could she sleep after such an event? How go back to

her bed, empty and cold? "I'd love some."

"And maybe a brandy. We'll toast Monarch."

"Toast Glory Be. She's the one who did all the work."

He laughed. "You're right. She did. Women have it hard. I feel sorry for them."

How unlike Jake he was! Jake! He was always there, lurking in her mind. She couldn't get rid of him, try though she did. Talk about leaving a mark! He'd carved his sign all through her as surely as if he'd wielded a knife. She set her shoulders and walked toward the barn door.

He followed, wondering what he'd said that had turned her into that other Nan, the woman who stood rigid, waiting for a blow. "Did I say something wrong?" he asked. "If I did, it was by accident."

"You said everything right." She smiled to reassure him. "Most men don't even think about what women go through. You're not like that."

And she, in turn, was different from all the rest, appreciative of the person he liked to think he was. "Am I? That's good to hear."

"You're kind," she said. "And you're nice and not afraid to show it."

He took her arm and steered her toward the back door, the inevitable comparison between her and others giving him the courage to speak. "My wife didn't think I was so kind," he said.

It was so unexpected that she stopped and turned to stare at him, squinting to see his face in the dark. "Your wife?"

When he answered his voice was flat, unemotional. "I was married once. Together we had Bay, and I thought we were happy. But she didn't like it here, hated me and made that clear. She probably never loved me at all if I want to be honest about it."

"How could she not?"

He smiled, but his eyes, she saw, were haunted. "I tried so hard. Tried to give her what I thought she wanted, but it wasn't ever enough. Maybe she didn't *know* what she wanted. She never said. Never talked to me at all. Just walked out when Bay was eight. No explanation, no nothing. Not even goodbye."

"And now?"

"She's dead. A botched abortion."

Nan's heart gave a lurch. "Yours?" And she prayed that it wasn't, prayed that this man had never known that kind of despair.

"No. She was sleeping with every cowboy and drifter in the country. I never touched her after she left. Couldn't. I couldn't stand the hatred in her face."

"I'm so sorry," Nan whispered, wishing she could take away his pain and knowing that she couldn't.

He was quiet a minute, reflecting. When had Margo ever commiserated, and in such a tender way? Finally he said, "It's done. And there hasn't been anybody since."

She thought she misunderstood. Women probably came after him in swarms, and he was, without doubt, a passionate and caring man. "Nobody?" she asked. "Why not?"

"She took it out of me. I failed with her, why try again with somebody else and make a worse mess?"

She was filled with anger—for him, for herself, for everyone whose faith had been destroyed, whose innocence had been the cause of destruction. "You wouldn't fail," she said, wanting to explain him to himself. "It was probably all her fault anyhow, so why blame yourself? I hope she's in hell," she added vehemently.

"If there is one. I always thought it was here on earth."

"Oh, there is," she said. "There has to be, only not here.

There has to be a special place for cruelty like that. For her. For . . ." she stopped before she said Jake's name.

He caught her hesitation. "For who else?"

She was tired of her burden of secrets, of never telling, always protecting the man she'd married, tired of wearing a falsely happy face so the world wouldn't know what really went on between them. Her tears spurted out with her answer. "For Jake. For the man I married for better or worse. And that wicked old lady who's his mother!" Then she snapped her mouth shut, shocked by the tears flowing unchecked down her cheeks.

"Whoa!" He put his hands on her shoulders and pulled her close, felt her trembling like a scared colt.

She fought the urge to put her arms around him and hold on. They should see her now, all of them—her mother, Lottie, Jake, even Wendy—in the embrace of a stranger.

At the thought her tears turned to laughter, and Ben, sensing hysteria, tightened his hands. "Let's go get that coffee. And the brandy. Seems like we could both use some."

"Y . . . yes," she agreed, sniffing, wishing she had a handkerchief. Her mother always carried one, lace-edged, ironed, folded into a neat square. At that she laughed harder. Ridiculous the things one thought of under stress. Ladies always had handkerchiefs, and here she was, obviously no lady, wiping her nose on her sleeve.

"I'm okay." She took a ragged breath. "Really."

He opened the door to the kitchen and switched on the light illuminating Lupe's domain. The temple of the oracle, Nan thought, where you went and had your questions answered with riddles, and left feeling blessed.

Ben took out mugs from the cupboard and the jug of real cream that always sat on the top shelf of the refrigerator.

When he'd poured the coffee he said, "Do you want to talk about it?" He hoped she did, hoped she had come to trust him.

She was a creature curled in the depths of a shell, walled in but pulsing with the need for light. Was it possible to eradicate years of silence, stand naked, imperfections and all, before this man she hardly knew? "Maybe," she said, her voice small.

Was she going to disappear again after her astonishing admission? Pull down the shade and hide behind it, so that what was there was the ghost of Nan masquerading as a person? Not if he could prevent it. "Come on," he said. "The brandy is in the living room. A shot will do us both good." And maybe break down that wall she seemed to create at will.

She followed him and sat down in the corner of the big leather couch, watching as he stirred the fire then poured two snifters of brandy. But she wasn't prepared for his question.

"Are you afraid of me?" He stood there, one dark brow raised.

"Afraid?" What could she tell him? She was afraid of her own yearnings. "Why?" she countered, stalling for time.

"Because you're squeezed into the corner of the couch like you think I'm going to rape you." He handed her a glass, then sat beside her. "You don't have to worry. I told you. I haven't been with a woman in almost ten years. Margo did a job on me. Might as well have used a knife."

What did he mean? That he was impotent? She shook her head. He was masculinity personified, sitting there with the fire creating an aura around his head, and his eyes reflecting the flames. Sad eyes, she realized. And lonely. As lonely as she was.

"Life seems to have treated us both badly," she said, not wanting to delve into his private demons uninvited.

"We've got our sons. Maybe that's reward enough."

But it wasn't. Jamie would grow up and leave and then she'd be alone with Jake following orders as she'd always done, scribbling stories and poems in odd moments, burrowing deeper into her own flesh. She shook her head. "Their lives are theirs. Don't we get a chance? Ever?"

"Good question. And I can't answer it. I figured I'd had my chance and blew it. I never met anyone I wanted enough to try again. There's a limit to the times I can throw my heart over the fence, and once was enough for me. Then you came along."

Of course he hadn't meant it the way it sounded. "What do I have to do with it?" she asked, steeling herself for the rejection she was sure would follow.

"Everything. You took me by surprise. I thought you were just another woman who wanted to come out here, no strings attached, screw a cowboy and then go home and boast about it."

She was shocked. "Me?" she choked out, feeling the beginnings of anger. "I never thought of any such thing!"

He chuckled. "Of course not. You're a woman with love written all over that secret face of yours. Yes, you try to hide it, but you don't. At least not from me. I think I've been waiting for you all my life, and now here you are. I don't want to lose you, but the question is, how do you feel, and what are we going to do about it?"

It was the longest declaration he'd ever made, and having made it, he felt naked, waiting to be ridiculed. He didn't look at her. Couldn't. Instead he stared into his glass at the dark swirling of the cognac and waited.

How slowly the world moved! How tentative the steps of the dance between man and woman! She heard the crackling of the fire, his unsteady breathing, the silence of the barrier mountains outside as she examined the meaning of what he'd said word by word, the whole a gift as precious as life.

He had laid his heart with its doubts and imperfections in her lap, an act of courage that she understood for what it was, for she was the same, battle-scarred and wounded, defenseless in the face of possibility.

Scenes from the past played themselves out; scenes of anger, her own fear, cringing away from Jake's words as if they were blows to her physical self, as if they drew blood, shattered her bones. What pleasure there? What kindness?

Again she looked at Ben with an emotion that was almost awe, seeing his face in profile against the fire, a proud face yet easily hurt; a man's face filled with strength and an unexpected sweetness.

"Ah, Ben," she said, finding her own courage at last. "I didn't expect anything like this to happen, either. Not ever. I didn't even know I was waiting and now I can't believe I've found you."

His expression didn't change. "You're sure," he said, feeling his way with caution, leaving her an out if, woman-like, she changed her mind.

She knew his confusion as if it were her own. Oh, he was wary—like a dog that had been beaten too often; like herself, wanting but afraid to reach and take.

"Yes," she said, then folded her hands in her lap lest they betray her and move to touch him. Touching was for later. For now it was the exchange of hearts that was important.

"Who scared you?" he asked suddenly. "Who robbed you? Somebody did, and whoever it was, I'd like to kill them."

It was Ben asking. Ben who knew her through osmosis, who opened doors she had never realized were there and encouraged her, whose hands were gentle, who understood the trauma and the joy of birthing, and who would never, she

81

knew, seek to take that which was hers. She was, therefore, free to give it.

Later, alone, she would examine the happiness that flooded her with her insight, the release from the cell she had occupied for as long as she could remember. But his question needed to be answered, as much for herself as for him.

"I'm a woman," she began, choosing her words with care. "And I was a child, a little girl, in the days before women were much of anything except housewives and mothers. Women, especially my own mother, were afraid of everything then. They expected to be ostracized for mistakes, speaking out of turn. So I was brought up to efface myself, to always do what was expected, and never say what I thought. Maybe never to think at all, because men weren't supposed to like smart women or being contradicted. And when you tried to talk to a woman, even a teacher, about anything serious, they acted like you were committing a crime. So I was also taught guilt. And shame because I was different. It's hard to explain, but that's the way it was. I was guilty of sins I would never commit because I was female and human. But I asked questions. I threatened the social order of the convent school, of my mother's view of the world. And then I'd be punished. Humiliated. I escaped by writing. The person who writes is me, but nobody knew that. I made my own world and lived there, and it was a safe place. Happy. And when I met Jake I didn't realize that he didn't give a damn about who I was or what I did."

She stopped and sipped her brandy, trying to find a way to bring to life the man she married so that the man she loved would see. "Jake didn't care if I wrote. Even now, he calls it my little hobby, because he's not interested in me or my mind, only in how well I can serve him. He wanted a wife who wouldn't disgrace him socially. Who'd serve him, fill all his needs. I was the perfect victim. I'd been trained to obedience like a dog that comes when it's called, pees when it's told to. I gave in to him from the first because nobody had ever yelled at me the way he did, so I was sure I was at fault. What else could I think? I was raised to know I was guilty. I'm sorry now that I didn't stand up for myself, but it's too late. He won't listen to me, and he's angry and yelling most of the time. So am I scared? Yes. I never know what's going to set him off, or when, or how horrible it'll be, what I'll be accused of.

"Now I'm worried about Jamie. It's just as bad for him, maybe worse. Jake expects his son to be perfect, but he's only a child and doesn't understand. How can he, when I didn't for years? I have to be there for him, but my marriage is a farce. It's a nightmare. American Gothic with a vengeance. You're the only person I've ever told." She gave a small smile. "That's it in a nutshell. Now you know."

He pulled her into his arms. "I'd like to kill the son of a bitch," he growled, and she felt the violence beneath his gentleness, the purity of a masculine fire that burned on her behalf.

The realization came with the whip-lash of a desire so intense she thought she might die of it. She moved her hands to learn his bones, somehow delicate for all his strength, and she raised her mouth to meet the warmth of his without hesitation.

"Ah, Ben," she whispered. "Ah, Ben. I love you so."

Later, lying sleepless, she replayed the time that followed—the kisses that burned into her soul, the ease with which they had arrived at such a knowing.

He hadn't said he loved her, but she knew. She got up and went to the window, stared out at the mountains, black beneath a dazzle of stars, at the moon, far to the west but spilling silver across the fields, the quivering leaves of the cottonwoods. Everything seemed a miracle, freshly made, painted with a shimmering brush.

"I love you," she said into the night, and her words spun away like the magical song of the mockingbird that began, at that moment, to sing.

In the main house Ben heard the music and stopped pacing the floor to listen. He had done what he had sworn never to do. He had fallen in love, and with a woman married to someone else, making him no better than those who had hung around Margo in the early days. With one exception, he admitted, with his usual honesty. None of Margo's so-called admirers had been in love. They'd been looking for quick thrills, cheap sex, a one-night stand.

What he felt for Nan was so different any comparison at all was obscene. For years he had existed without hope, subli-mating his energies in ranch work and the raising of his son, and pretending that was how he wanted it.

And then, without warning, there she was—his fantasy made flesh, a woman with no expectations, no guile, only that pathetic dignity she held onto with such determination, and that capacity for joy that had wrung his heart from the first.

"I love you," she had said.

And he hadn't answered. He didn't believe in tempting fate, in raising her hopes—or his own. She was married. She lived 2000 miles away. What use was love or the desire that had stirred in him for the first time in years as she came so willingly into his arms?

It was madness, all of it; crazy to believe any good could come of a love with so many barriers to be crossed. She loved him. His fault for breaking his silence and the promises to himself. Whatever happened now, he was responsible. Who-ever got hurt, it was because of him. And he didn't want her hurt, would die to keep her safe—from the world, from that monster Jake, from his own foolishness.

Love, no matter the circumstances, was terrifying. You walked the knife-edge between ecstasy and agony, praying not to fall, shielding your heart and the heart of your lover with all the puny devices given you. With luck, you succeeded. So far, he'd had precious little of that.

He sighed and crossed the room to the window. Her light was out. Was she asleep, or was she lying awake, battling the deceptive tendrils of their lives?

"I love you, too," he said, and the wind took his words and carried them away—to the mountains, to the bird high in the branch, who stole them and made them a symphony.

CHAPTER THIRTEEN

No one was in the dining room, and only Nan's place was set. She had overslept, and when she woke had lain in bed a long time, astonished to find herself rested and with a lightness of heart she couldn't remember ever feeling. She might have been a child again with an entire day before her. A day in which she would see Ben, perhaps ride with him and say all the things she'd not said the night before.

Now she stared at the empty room bewildered. In the kitchen she heard Lupe humming to herself.

"Can I come in?" she asked, stopping at the door.

Lupe's dark braid swung as she turned. "Sure! Come in. Have some coffee. Ben and Bay, and that boy of yours went off to town. Ben say to let you sleep." She scanned Nan's face. "So. You saw the colt born. And named him, too."

Nan nodded, digesting the fact that Ben had left without seeing her. Had he had second thoughts? Regrets? Had she made a fool of herself like those women he despised?

She swallowed hard and managed a smile. "Monarch. He's beautiful. It all was. The whole thing made me think. About everything," she added.

Lupe pointed at the round table by the window. "Eat here with me. Tell me about what you thought. It's good to talk."

"Is it?" Her defenses raised, Nan sat down slowly.

The older woman chuckled. "You don't trust no one. Not

me. Not yourself. But nobody here will hurt you. You want eggs?"

The sudden switch caught Nan off guard. "What?" she said, then laughed. "If it's no bother. I usually don't eat much for breakfast."

"And get skinny. Does your husband like to hold bones?"

Jake. Strangely, she'd not thought of him once since last night. "He never said. At least he never complained." But then, he wouldn't. Not about that. In his good moods, he even said he loved her. But what did that mean? Surely he didn't feel the way she had felt in Ben's arms.

"Did Ben say when he'd be back?"

"Before dinner. Don't worry."

Damn the woman! She was able to read minds. "I'm not," she said. "I just wondered."

But Lupe wouldn't be put off. "I see how it is with you," she said. "And I remember when this was a happy place. Before *she* came. He tell you about her?"

"Margo?"

"Yes. A bad woman, but Ben, he was young. Hot-blooded. Who ever told a young man anything? Nobody." She answered her own question as she put a plate of eggs and toast on the table. "When she left, I hope it all would go back the way it was, but no. When she left, she take a piece of Ben's heart."

"He didn't hate her?" Nan asked. "I would have."

Lupe shook her head. "He blame himself. He die a little inside."

Nan poked at the eggs and followed the flow of her thoughts. When she spoke, it was slowly. "Maybe . . . maybe we all carry little deaths inside," she said. "Life is like that. Chipping away at us until we're somebody else and can't get back to who we were."

Lupe grimaced. "You're too young to believe that. Why you think I tell you about the wolf?"

"I don't know. Why?"

"Ask yourself," came the elusive response.

The woman was impossible! "I'm tired of asking," Nan said crossly. "All you do is talk in riddles."

"You want everything easy. Nothing worth having is easy."

"That's what they all say."

Lupe reached across the table and patted her hand. "Answers come when you're ready. Not before."

"Like poems."

"Maybe. I don't know about that. But today, maybe you take a walk up the mountain."

Now she was planning her day! Everyone had always planned for her. But Lupe's hand was comforting and filled with a gentle strength. Irrationally, Nan wanted to lay her head on the woman's full bosom and make what amounted to a confession. She wanted forgiveness, but for what? For loving Ben when she was tied to another? For her own confusion? Or was her burden of sin older than that, a weight she had carried so long she'd forgotten it?

"All right," she agreed. "I'll take a walk."

"And I pack a lunch." Lupe stood up looking victorious. "Lots to see from up there. The day will pass."

It sounded like a promise, or a blessing. Nan smiled at her. With luck the day would pass quickly and Ben would be home. But before that, she had some sorting out to do.

The trail wound through a field, crossed a wash filled with boulders, then headed up toward a sheer face of rock a thousand feet high and nearly vertical. The path became a broad lip above another sheer drop down the side of the mountain.

Unused to the altitude, Nan stopped to catch her breath, and for the first time looked across the valley below. The immensity, the sweep of color, the shimmer of heat waves and light, struck her full force. She sat down on a rock and stared.

All her life she had dreamed of such a place, and now it was there in a reality that was almost painful, a beauty that clutched at her, demanded a response.

What to do? What order to make out of the chaos of her life? What to do about Ben who, though she'd known him only a few days, tore at her heart as no man had ever done? Could she really go back to Jake and live as though nothing had changed?

Her problems seemed insurmountable. Asking Jake for a divorce was out of the question. He'd eradicate her, and he'd never let her forget. At the thought, she felt her stomach tighten. Over the years Jake had sapped her confidence, demolished her strength, and she had permitted it, had actually come to believe she was nothing and nobody without him.

She got up and moved along the ledge toward a cluster of trees. It seemed a secret place, a refuge, and it lured her with the promise of discovery.

Parting the branches, she stepped into a small glade. At her left was a cave that penetrated deep into the core of the mountain. To her right was a shoulder-high rock, hollowed in the middle and forming a bowl filled with the water that fell from overhead with a sound like glass striking glass. Again her body responded to the magic of place. Someone had lived here! Someone had called this home!

Through the trees she could see the eastern mountains, a maze of peaks, canyons, cliffs. The valley lay sun-washed and vibrant, in bands of green, gold, the red of earth, the purple of cloud shadow. The dripping spring, the rustle of leaves intensified the silence. Around her was peace and a great happiness as if someone had loved and left their mark.

And then, lifting her head, she saw the paintings, rude sketches on the face of the cliff—a ripple of water, the hooves of deer, a spiral twining inward, and a woman, arms outstretched, dancing.

Of course it had been a woman! Of course a woman had been here and left her marks, tangible and intangible. Lacking the ability to write, she had painted herself and her world onto the rock, and although she was gone perhaps a thousand years, a part of her remained and would remain until wind, water, and time erased her.

Gently Nan reached out and traced the figure. "I'm here," she whispered. "I know you. You were like me, loving the world and trying to keep it."

She saw herself as she had been, reaching out for what seemed to be the overwhelming loveliness of field, forest, sky with a wanting so huge it terrified. She was three years old, and the concept of change was threatening her entire being.

Tomorrow, nothing she saw today would be the same. Tomorrow, the leaves would turn color and fall, the sunset clouds, as brilliant as birds, would have changed shape and flown.

She lay on her small bed saying the words that flooded up inside; words that made sense out of what she saw and needed, so desperately, to keep. Words were magic. Spoken, the images danced in her head where she could keep them safe—sky, water, the painted wings of birds above the trees.

Elated with discovery, she fell slowly into sleep, and echoes of her chant wove themselves into her dreams.

Nan stared down the tunnel of years more frightened than she had ever been. It was a memory, no more, she told herself. A fragment out of time. And yet her heart was beating so that she could hardly breathe, and the terror she felt was real and not imagined. She closed her eyes, and the scene played out as if it were happening again.

There was company for dinner, a man and a woman she did not know. After coffee, her mother stood up, the candle flames on the table reflecting in her glasses, hiding her eyes. There was the dance of light, the mouth opening, closing, speaking her words. *Hers!*

"No! No!" A whimper, unheard. A scream out of her silence.

Her mother's mouth moved again. "Poetry! Sheer poetry! And out of the mouth of a babe." Her hands moved, rubbed her arms. "Oh, I have goose flesh!" The paper she held fell to the floor, and Nan watched it fall as if it were herself, snatched away, stolen, trashed.

The terror that claimed her was more hideous than even the demons she saw sometimes in the night. She was powerless, helpless, exposed to them all, to strangers who stared at her, whose mouths curved in foolish and threatening smiles; to her mother who had taken her soul.

Nan shuddered. It had been rape. Violation. And it had repeated over the years, Helen revealing how she'd crouched outside the door and taken her daughter's ecstasy for her own, and reading the poems over and over until they were meaningless.

The result had been a sealing off of self. Gradually, layer by layer, she had vanished behind a barrier of her own making. Gradually the child called Nan had disappeared and become another—a brittle shell, a puppet separated from her own reality.

No wonder Jake had the power to frighten her! It was Helen's power handed over, and she not knowing, perhaps not caring until too late. Shaken, she wrapped her arms around her knees for comfort. All those years living a lie. All the words not written or, worse, dashed off with a falsity that made her sick.

"You don't trust no one." Lupe's words filtered back. Of course she didn't. From the cradle caution had inhabited her bones. Trust, and learn humiliation. Expose your heart and have it shattered.

"I love you," she'd said to Ben, and where was he now? He'd gone off, probably sickened over her display of emotion.

She wished she could go home, but she had no home. All she had was herself—violated child, wretched wife, and something else. What was it? She turned and saw the paintings on the rock, the lasting signature of a woman who, like her, had sought to hold the world, but who then had reached out her arms and danced.

CHAPTER FOURTEEN

Ben pulled off the highway onto the ranch road and turned to Jamie. "Want to drive?" he asked.

"I. . . ."

Desire and shock showed on the boy's face. He had no confidence in himself at all, Ben thought. In fact, he was painful to watch, with his quick intelligence and the doubting probably put there by his father. Nan's husband—he corrected himself with a frown.

"Slide over." He got out and walked to the passenger side. "You've been telling me all about the engine. Now you can see what it feels like."

Grinning, Jamie took the wheel and sat listening to the deep throb of the motor. Then he said, "You mean it?"

"Drive." Ben pulled his hat down over his eyes and leaned back.

"Floorboard it!" Bay urged.

"Is that what you do?" Ben sat up slowly and looked at his son whose merriment subsided.

"I was joking, Dad. You know that."

"That's a relief." He closed his eyes again, wondering if Nan would be there to see her son drive in. She'd said she loved him, but had she meant it, or had it simply been a phrase mouthed in the midst of passion, a polite form of permission for her actions?

She didn't seem that kind of woman, but what did he know about her really? That her marriage was unhappy, that she fascinated him because of the way her mind worked and her emotions followed, and that he wanted her with an almost constant ache.

What was love, anyhow? He wasn't sure he knew or even wanted to find out. He hadn't been able to face her this morning, but now they were almost home, and she'd be there waiting the way he'd always wanted his wife to wait. But this was Nan. She was bound to someone else, and he had no excuse for his behavior of the night before except that he had spoken the truth. He could not bear to lose her, to never see or talk to her again.

Jamie pulled up, and there she was on the porch, her hands on the railing, laughing as she caught sight of her son but with an emotion Ben couldn't identify shadowing her face.

"Did you have a fun day?" She spoke to Jamie, not sure how to approach Ben, because who was she now—the passionate woman of the previous night, or the child, violated? Perhaps she had made a mistake saying she loved him. Perhaps she had played the fool.

"Great!" Jamie's eyes sparkled. "Ben let me drive in from the highway."

She looked at him then, confusion plain in her eyes. "Thanks," she said.

"For what? He did fine, and it was good for him."

"For giving him the chance."

"What did you do?" he asked. "Sleep late, I hope."

He seemed interested enough, she thought, or maybe he was simply being polite, treating her as he would a guest. She struggled with her desire to run and hide.

"I did sleep in," she said cautiously, feeling her way back to the intimacy of the night before. "Then I . . . I went up the

94

mountain." Could she tell him? Share the pain of her discovery even though she might be mistaken about what she thought was love? "I saw the rock paintings."

"And felt the magic?"

"You've felt it, too?"

He nodded. "It's a special place. I went there all the time as a kid. Sometimes now I just go to think. Or maybe just to let thinking go."

"Yes," she said. "That's the way it is. You kind of float out over the valley. Only, only I remembered things. I saw them like they were happening again." She wrapped her arms around herself, knowing that telling him of her experience was opening the door into her world, the door that she had kept locked out of fear.

"It seems I've been acting a part so long I'm not sure which part is me or who's the real Nan. Maybe no part." She watched his face as she spoke, searching for signs of patronage.

Was this her way out of a difficult situation? he wondered. If so, better to know than hang on looking like a damn fool. "Are you apologizing for last night?" he asked, his voice harsh.

"No! That was real." How to make him understand? She took a deep breath and floundered on. "What I remembered has nothing to do with you—with us. Or maybe it does in a round about way."

"Tell me."

She glanced around. The boys had disappeared. She and Ben were alone, and the mountains had begun to burn—crimson, rose, purple in the hollows of their flanks. Their massive fortitude gave her courage.

She told him, leaving nothing out. When she finished, she spread her hands. "That's it. I hid from that time on. I hid so well, I even fooled myself. Until you. Now you see me as I am. Exposed." Then she waited, head bowed, her neck gleaming white in the gathering dusk.

"Poor kid," he said. "Poor little girl. And the worst part is, your mother must have loved you very much."

"Maybe." She was relieved he hadn't focused on her own vulnerability. But that was like him, to take the broad view and not the narrow. "Or maybe," she went on, "maybe she simply wanted to possess. Like that Tilson woman ready to suck out my soul. Lupe called her a witch. It's hard to say what to call my mother. She's always been so different from me. Oh," she straightened up and looked at him, "I'm not blaming her for all my mistakes. At least not from here on. Now I know. Now it's up to me to fix myself."

She grinned crookedly. "It's pretty easy to shift the blame. Everybody does it—blame their parents for their own actions, but that's just an excuse to keep on doing the same dumb things like a kid. At some point we have to be responsible for ourselves. At least I think we do."

Ben chuckled suddenly, and she looked at him with irritation. "What's so funny?" she demanded.

"Not you," he said. "And not what you were telling me. I just had a silly thought. A picture of you in pieces like a pizza. Everybody grabbing what they wanted and putting on different toppings until what you were to begin with disappeared and nobody knew what they had. I know it's ridiculous, but still . . ."

It made so much sense that she laughed with him. "Actually, that's a dandy simile. I'll have to remember it. I've thought the same thing, only not quite like that. How everybody wants a piece of me like I'm divisible."

"Or like the whole poses a threat. Ever thought that?"

"No," she answered slowly. "I never did. I guess I never

saw myself as a threat to anybody."

"Look again." He was deadly serious. Even a heart as big as hers had its limits. "I've been watching you since you came. You're smart, honest, and you have a voice, and when you use it, you make a point. And the point usually cuts away all the crap and hits home."

"From journalism, I guess," she said. "A long time ago Jake told me I was too rational for a woman. He made it sound like a crime."

He snorted. "And what's that supposed to mean?"

"I guess that women aren't supposed to think. Me, especially."

"But you do, so you're a threat to his way of life."

"Something like that. And I guess I've always let myself be used because it's easy and because that's the way I am. And that way they leave me alone and in peace for awhile."

"And that's all you want? Peace at any price?"

She frowned. "Put that way it sounds like a cop-out."

"Think about it," he said, and then, seeing her face fall, was filled with remorse. He was as bad as the rest, making demands, asking her for decisions he had no right to ask, putting her on the defensive when all he'd really wanted was to help.

He reached out and pulled her close. She was fine-boned, like a bird, and her head came just to his shoulder. Exposed, she'd said, yet oddly her fear made him the more vulnerable.

"If this is what happens when I leave you alone, I'd better not do it again," he murmured. "It sounds like you had a hell of a hard day."

"Better now." Her voice was muffled. "I wish we never had to leave each other."

And the agony was that he wished it, too.

CHAPTER FIFTEEN

Dinner was a green chili stew redolent of spices and peppers and served in a hand-painted Mexican tureen that dominated the center of the table.

"You're an artist," Nan said to Lupe. "This is an edible still-life."

Lupe accepted the praise seriously. "A meal should please the eyes, the nose, the mouth, no?"

"It should, yes," Nan agreed.

Cooking was one of her passions, but would Jake appreciate this simple yet gratifying dinner—stew, golden cornbread and pats of real butter, a fruit salad in its own colorful bowl? Probably not, she answered herself. He was rigidly formal and always correct, while she loved the expressions of earth—rustic pottery, the fruits of the garden, green chilies and meat pungent in a hand-painted bowl. Her connection had always been to the natural world, except she had shut herself away, lost touch with all that she loved. And the result was that she had become no one. That was what she was when she married—a cracked vase, a carnival mask that hid only emptiness.

She sighed. Unraveling her wrong turnings was going to be neither simple nor joyous. By her actions she would hurt both herself and those accustomed to her diffidence.

Ben watched her, fascinated by the way her face reflected

her thoughts. She thought she hid behind a mask, but to him she was transparent, scarred but unbreakable, a piece of Damascus steel.

He said, "You should see some real cliff dwellings before you go, if you think what you saw today was spectacular."

Her eyes met his across the table. "Where are they?"

"Back in the mountains. Rough country. It's an overnight trip with horses."

"Can we go?"

He turned to Lupe. "We're not expecting any guests this week, are we?"

She shook her head. "No. You take her. Wish and me, we keep the boys busy here."

Go alone? Just she and Ben? Nan's heart jumped so wildly she put her hand on her breast to calm it.

"You really want to?" His eyes seemed to penetrate her skull.

"I . . ." Of course she wanted. Her hesitation was the old Nan, attempting to repossess what she had lost. "Yes," she said shortly. "Yes, I do."

"Good." He controlled his own delight. "We'll take tomorrow to get ready, sort out the camping gear. Then head out early next morning."

She was going off on an adventure, into the wilderness with the man she loved, and be damned to the rest of them—mothers, husbands, sons. Right or wrong she would go, and if all that she had for the rest of her life was a memory, at least she'd know that once she'd been alive, had loved from the depths of herself.

Unconsciously she straightened in her chair. "I'm ready," she said, feeling that she was, indeed, ready for anything.

It was a dream that would surely end—a dream of turquoise sky, scented air, the smooth motion of a horse, the intangible thread that bound her to Ben who rode at her side.

They crossed the valley and turned into the narrow mouth of a canyon. Ocotillo bloomed on its steep walls, fountains of flowers red as cock's combs or the crests of cardinals, and around them the silence was loud.

She said, "The absence of noise is noisy."

Ben laughed. She had a way of uttering truths that made the familiar new. "Will you write about all this?" he asked.

She thought, still caught in the dream. "I might. Not about us. We're private. But about the others—Lupe, Wish, Monarch being born—I think so. I can't plan what comes, though. It's more like I wait until the voice starts." She smiled, impishly. "I know that sounds crazy, but that's how it happens, at least with me. The words—or the picture of them—won't let me alone 'til I write them down."

"The muse?"

"I don't know. I've never been sure exactly what *is* the muse. Whether it's a person or just a moment of unity with the world. For me, it's seeing something, the making of a connection between myself and earth, or an idea and a person."

"Will you write to me? Send me what you've done?"

There was the dream's end. She knew it had to come, the tearing away, the snapping of the thread. "Yes," she said, blinking back tears. "You know I will. I don't know how I'm going to go on without at least writing to you."

"We'll manage." He reached out and laid his hand on her thigh. "I promise."

She wished she had not spoken, ruined the silence with the specter of parting.

They went up and up, the world falling behind, the land around them a maze of rock carved into spires and shapes like people. *Like the statues on Gothic cathedrals,* she thought, and the mountain, itself, was a place of worship.

She saw everything with a poignancy that increased her seeing, knowing that when loneliness came, as it would, she could relive this time with vivid memories.

They crossed a stream, narrow in its wide bed and singing to itself. Looking down, she saw the sky reflected, the splintered rocks, and her own face, pale in the shadow of her hat.

Ben pulled up on the bank. "Nearly there. The Forest Service has an old corral where we can leave the horses. Hungry?"

She had forgotten her body in her state of wonder. "Yes," she said. "I sure am."

They unsaddled, turned the horses loose, and ate the lunch Lupe had packed with such care—chicken sandwiches, apples, a thermos of coffee. Nan stretched out on the grass and watched the tops of the pines moving in the wind.

"Nothing seems complicated here," she murmured, her voice echoing the hum of branches. "It's like nothing exists but this place and us in it."

"That's one of the reasons I wanted to bring you," he admitted. "I thought we needed some time by ourselves."

"I wish I never had to leave. I wish we could just ride off and disappear."

"We could," he said. "But then you might regret it. You have a lot of thinking to do."

She sat up suddenly. "Not now! Not here! This is our time, let's not waste it talking about *that*."

"The world is too much with us," he quoted, knowing there would be days when he'd miss her in his bones, and the emptiness of his life would weigh on him like a shroud. He held out his hand. "Let's go see the caves."

They crossed a small dry wash where the sand was sculpted by the feet of quail, the oval paw prints of rabbits.

"A busy street," she observed, smiling and taking note of the thick cover, red-stemmed manzanita with tiny white flowers, the looping of wild grape vines strung from tree to tree. "Whoever lived here had it all."

"Paradise," he said. "Yet they left it. Nobody knows why for sure. I've always thought it was an epidemic. Some illness they couldn't understand and didn't know how to treat. Otherwise, why go? No one else came in their place, so it's just as they left it. Nobody even comes here except the Forest Service and me once in awhile." He took her elbow. "Look there."

She followed his gaze upward to the caves under an overhang of pink rock; a dozen of them, side by side behind the remains of what had once been a wall. Empty now, they still vibrated with life as if whoever lived in them had left only for a day.

She looked, then closed her eyes and listened for the sound of voices, the clatter of civilization—running feet, the laughter of women and children, the scrape of stone on stone as someone ground corn.

What she heard was silence, broken once by the descending fluting of a wren high overhead. What she heard was the pulsing of time—past, present, future—captured and held in the amber light of afternoon.

Here she would leave her heart. Here it would be safe until—if—she returned. She moved and buried her face in Ben's chest. "Hold me," she whispered. "Don't let go."

"Never." And he promised himself he'd make his words come true.

CHAPTER SIXTEEN

Hopes, wishes, words—what were they compared to the explosion of stars in the night sky? Puny things, Nan thought, finite dreams limited by one's own mortality. You ran your race, dreamed, struggled, achieved or lost, and then you were gone, swallowed up by eternity.

They had climbed up to the dwellings on rude steps cut into stone, worn by usage and uncountable days of wind and rain. They had stood where the ancients stood, people the same as they; seen the smoke-blackened walls, the rude drawings—deer, lions, spirals like patterns of thought—and Nan had found a pottery shard.

She held it now in her hand. It was curved, the side of a bowl, and it fit her palm as if it had been born there, a part of her.

"Some things last," she said. "I'm glad."

Ben didn't respond, and she looked across the fire at him, found him serious, almost withdrawn, and she was frightened by his remoteness.

"What's the matter?"

He flicked a glance at her but didn't answer immediately. "Like I said, you have a lot of thinking to do, and I want you to be careful. I also want you to know that what I said the other night, I feel is going to last, but I don't want you hurt because of it."

She sighed, wishing he hadn't brought it up. "I don't know what I'll do, or how," she said. "I won't 'til I'm back there. I'm the one who's going to hurt people, and I've always tried not to hurt anybody. My mistake." She laughed bitterly. "I was always told that selfishness was the ultimate sin. But I'm beginning to think that was a lie like all the rest. An excuse to cover up all the misery. But if I'm not happy, how can I possibly make others happy?"

"Good question. You can't. Like you said, you have to be responsible for yourself first. But don't fool yourself into believing it's easy. They'll fight you at every turn. Individuality is a threat. The fact that you write and take it seriously is a threat. To Jake. To his mother and yours and God knows who else. Like those rock paintings we saw—words, ideas can last forever. Think about that."

"I don't have to. It all goes back to what I said about wanting to possess. Maybe they do it in the name of love, but that's not love. It's closer to hate. Or fear," she added, frowning over the idea. "They want what I have because they lack something and are afraid. And I accepted that because I wasn't aware of what was happening. Now I am. Now comes the hard part. Can I change? Can I fight them all?"

"Absolutely. You're tougher than you know." And she was, he thought. All those years of hiding had given her a discipline she didn't recognize for what it was—a survival technique, a determination to hold on whatever the odds.

"Whatever I do," she said slowly, "I have to do for me. Not for us. Not because of us. Not because I love you, but because it's necessary. Does that sound awful?" She hoped it didn't. If she hurt him, if he pulled away from her, she'd drown in her regret.

"You're a wise woman." He pulled her close, touched by her doubting. "You're wise, courageous, and lovely, and the only thing that'll make me angry is to see you get lost again, to have to stand by helpless and watch those monsters ruin you when you have so much to give."

His praise rang like a prayer. No one had ever told her such things. No one, she decided, had ever cared enough. "I love you," she said.

Could he say it? Could he break down his own barrier and admit the depth of his emotions? He struggled with his caution, his needs and hers. Always it came back to her, the woman he'd waited for, often in despair.

"I love you, too," he said and felt exhaustion as if he had fought a mighty battle and emerged the victor. "I love you with all my heart."

PART TWO

The front door opens. Sunlight pours into the hall and strikes fire from the Venetian glass mirror in its gilded frame.

I stand in the house of a stranger—a woman I knew once, slightly, and I stare at her things in the rooms she created and cared for because she had nothing else. The Scottish refectory table with its silver bowl and candlesticks; the Chinese Export chairs carved with dragons and peonies, each a work of art; the old rugs from the East, red, blue, cream, faded apricot, gleaming on polished floors.

I touch the cold marble top of the hall table, see myself in the glass on the wall. I am as hesitant as a Gothic heroine come into the manor house. I am Jane Eyre in Thornfield Hall. I am Cathy of the moors, hunting for her soul. I am Cinderella in the ashes, weeping.

"Is he coming, Sister Anne?"

"Soon."

"But not yet. Please God, not yet."

There is time to drape myself in my disguise, assume old habits, re-learn the many rooms of this house that was, once, my security.

Now it seems a prison. Now the walls close in. I cannot see the sky. I will not wake in Ben's arms surrounded by the immensity of his love.

I am another Nan. Why am I here?

CHAPTER SEVENTEEN

The phone rang as Nan stood staring at herself in the mirror. It sounded like a buzz saw and shattered what composure she had left.

Jamie ran past her to answer and then called, "It's Grandma Lottie."

So it was to start again as soon as she walked through the door. There would be no chance to be alone, to gather the remnants of self, paint her face, practice smiling.

"So you're home. Finally." No welcome in those words. She was the sinner, the accused.

"Yes," she said and waited.

"Did you ever stop to think what it's like being left here without my family? Being lied to like I'm a crazy person? Jake always going off someplace. Why does he have to do that when he knows I'm alone here? And you. You could have stayed home. I'll tell you something. I tried to commit suicide last night."

Nan closed her eyes and struggled with sudden nausea. This was her reality, what she'd lived through, suffered over because she believed in the family.

She said, "You what?" not wanting to believe.

"You heard me. I stuffed rags under the doors and turned on the gas."

Her nausea and confusion were wiped out by anger. Lottie

had planned it, intending that she arrive and find a mad-house, that she be annihilated by guilt and remorse. Once, such a tactic would have succeeded. Now she allowed her fury to surface.

"How dare you," she said, her voice icy. "How dare you do such a selfish, inconsiderate act? You're a wicked old woman, thinking only about yourself. You could have blown up your whole building. You. All by yourself, and for what? To get back at your son for doing what his job requires? To get back at me?" She paused and took a breath. "I'll tell *you* something. If you ever try anything so crazy again we'll put you in a home to keep you safe, and that's a promise."

Lottie was silent a long while. Then she said, cautiously, "I guess I didn't think."

"Well you'd better start. You'd better take a good long look at yourself. Always having accidents, always mad at me because I'm too busy taking care of your son and your grandson to have much time to spare. And he is going to hit the roof when he hears about this."

"You're going to tell him?" Lottie sounded frightened.

Nan smiled grimly. "Don't you think he'd have found out if your guilt trip had worked? What a way to welcome him home."

"I only wanted . . ." Lottie left her sentence unfinished.

"What?"

"You always push me aside." The old woman's voice cracked with what sounded like true anguish. "You act like I'm not here."

That was partly true, Nan admitted, feeling a twinge of guilt. "Look," she said, "we have our lives. You can't always be included. Jake can't take you on his business trips, for heaven's sake. He doesn't even take me. If you'd think about that and be happy for him instead of feeling sorry for yourself, you might feel better."

"When is my son coming home?"

She hadn't listened, Nan thought. Hadn't wanted to hear anything that smacked of the truth. "In a few days. And if there are any more accidents or suicide attempts between now and then, we'll have to do what I said. Put you where you'll be watched just to keep you safe. Do you understand?"

Lottie didn't answer. Nan pictured her at her desk, lower lip pushed out in a childish pout that was exactly like Jake's when he didn't get his way. "Answer me," she ordered.

"All right!" Lottie snapped.

"Good. Now, I'm going grocery shopping tomorrow and I'll pick you up about eleven. And we won't ever mention this again. Is eleven a good time?"

"It doesn't matter."

Nan's patience snapped. "I have to go. I just walked in when you called. Be good now, and I'll see you in the morning."

Lottie mumbled something, and Nan hung up, her hands trembling.

She was alone in this place that had become foreign, its language one she neither spoke nor understood, its rules contrary to those she believed. Here there were no kind words, no warmth, no welcome, only accusations and a fierce, destructive hunger.

"Oh, Ben," she whispered, and the sound of his name brought tears, a sense of loss so huge she felt she was dying.

Automatically she opened the back door and went out into the garden. The light pierced her; a car horn in the street blared and she winced, unused to the noise of the city. Where was peace? Where the silence she had so loved? Where was Ben?

111

The phone rang again and she stumbled up the steps to answer.

"You're safe," he said.

She couldn't speak. She was buried alive and struggling for release.

From two thousand miles away he could sense her pain and cursed himself for letting her go. "Nan?"

"I'm here. I don't want to be here. I don't belong anymore."

"If you ever did."

"I don't know what to do." She clung to the sound of his voice.

"Get out before they kill you." His harshness masked his concern. For two cents he'd get on a plane and kidnap her.

"Help me," she said.

She was desperate. Her plea ripped through him like a knife. "Easy." He tried to calm her with his voice carried through the thinness of a wire. "I'm here, and I haven't changed my mind. We're not going to lose each other. But you have to save yourself. I can't do it for you."

He was right. And she'd just taken the first step, telling Lottie the truth for once. She lifted her chin. "Wait'll I tell you what just happened," she said.

When she hung up, she felt lighter. He was there, and he loved her. She'd given in to her misery and probably would again many times, but she was going to dig her way out of her own grave.

Once again she went into the garden where she knelt by a bed of fragrant early lilies and let her memories rise.

CHAPTER EIGHTEEN

She wanted Wendy. Over the years, when she had needed to talk, she had gone to Wendy—friend, sister, equal in the pursuit of life, love, and the creation of something more than either. Painting and writing had drawn them together as children. If they were different from the rest, together they explored their similarities, each a sounding board for the other.

"Can you come over?" she asked.

"What's the matter?"

"Everything."

"Oh boy. Can you come here? Mikey's in bed with a bad cold."

"I'll be there."

Jake was supposed to call, but that didn't matter now. What mattered was talking to one who understood and hurled no invectives. Being with Wendy was better than ruminating over one's neuroses with a psychiatrist, and her back porch was a paradise. Honeysuckle climbed lattices beyond the screens, the pool glimmered invitingly day or night, and the wicker furniture was made for sprawling, the exchanges of confidences between two women each of whom trusted the other.

Nan fled to Wendy as she had all through high school and college, through failed romances and parental disagreements, as Wendy had come to her for the same reasons.

Wendy met her at the door. "You sounded like you'd been hit by a truck. Are you all right?"

"I met someone," Nan blurted, relieved simply to be able to say it.

"I wondered when that would happen," Wendy said, leading the way to the porch.

Nan was stunned. "Why? How could you?"

"I'll tell you a secret I kept to myself for a long time. I was scared to say anything, so don't be mad."

"Of course not."

"The day you got married, I was in the car with you on the way to church. And I looked at you, and you seemed like you weren't there. Like you were somebody else, and it scared me because I thought . . . I *knew* you weren't in love with Jake. You'd made up your mind, and you were going through with it. Leaving home, getting away from your mother. And God knows, nobody could blame you for that. But it scared me so much I couldn't say anything. Maybe I should have."

"I *was* somebody else," Nan said softly, her voice like the mourning of a dove. "I've been somebody else for years and years, and now I don't know what to do."

Wendy picked up a bottle from the ice bucket on the table. "Have some wine," she said. "It's a nice dry white. Italian. You'll like it. Then tell me everything. I promise not to interrupt."

Nan sipped the wine in its fluted glass and nodded. "Good," she approved. "I'll have to get some. Where were we?"

"At your wedding. You weren't you."

"I wasn't, either. But I thought I loved Jake. And then . . ." She was seeing down the years, the happenings made more poignant by the shock of loving Ben, by the scent of honeysuckle in the still air. "Then he changed. It was like he pulled

114

off a mask and showed himself as soon as he had me. He was a stranger I didn't know, and didn't like. He screamed at me for everything, so I saw myself as this awful person who caused her husband to turn into a maniac. By the time we came back from Europe, he possessed me. Totally. And that was what he intended to do all along. He said six months would get me away from my mother's influence, and at the time I thought that was wonderful. Well, he was right. It did. Except that from then on, I was his creature."

Wendy shuddered. "That's the most horrible story I ever heard. It's like some kind of monster fairy tale. And you never said anything."

"I was afraid." And she had been. Still was. Afraid of taking a step without permission, speaking out of turn for fear of the reprisal that went on and on, brutal words that demolished her being. "I'm afraid," she repeated. "Of everything. I'm afraid to trust my own judgement. How can I? Everything I've done for years has been wrong. Now how can I trust loving the man I met, or even believe he is what he seems? Talk is cheap. I made a horrible mistake once. Now I'm not sure I even know what love is."

Wendy lit a cigarette, leaned back on her chaise, and exhaled. "Who is this man?" she wanted to know. "Does he have a name? Is he gorgeous, rich, or what?"

"His name's Ben Fuller. He owns the ranch. And it happened as soon as I saw him in the airport only I didn't know it. It happened for him the same way. And that's part of the problem. The whole thing is like a soap opera."

Wendy watched the smoke rising, flowing out through the screen. Then she said, "The body doesn't lie. You can fool your mind, you can pull blinders over your eyes and your brain, but the body knows. I'm not talking cheap sex here. I mean total response that blows you away. Did you sleep with him?" She snorted. "Listen to me. I sound like we're still in college. But seriously, what did your body tell you?"

Nan laughed. It was such a relief to be sitting here with no one to judge her. "I didn't," she said, her voice musical as she recalled the almost unbearable sweetness of the recent past. "We spent a night camping out, but we didn't do anything except hold each other. We woke up that way and . . . and I thought I'd die I wanted him so badly. But he wouldn't. He said . . . he said it would just make it harder on me when I left. I guess he was right, but I'd have done it anyhow and be damned."

Wendy watched her, seeing her luminous eyes, the radiance in her face. "He sounds like a saint," she said.

"He's honest and kind, and the most unselfish person I ever met. And he's been hurt, too. I think he's more afraid of this than I am. But if my body doesn't lie, I want him down to my toes, so there!" Tears pricked behind her eyes. Quickly she emptied her glass before she broke down completely.

Wendy looked steadily at her. "We all have scars," she said. "But you've got a real problem. You're in love. For the first time in your life. I've known you more than thirty years, but I've never heard you talk like this, and I've certainly never seen that look on your face."

"It shows?" Startled, Nan put her hands to her cheeks.

"To me it does. The others won't notice. Jake certainly won't. He's too wrapped up in himself. I mean, how could you possibly be involved with another man when you have *him?*" Wendy laughed bitterly. "In case you want to know, I never liked him. Always yapping at you like some nasty little terrier, was what I thought. But you never complained, and now I'm thinking he's worse than that. He's some kind of blood-sucking vampire. The question is, what are you going to do?"

"I don't know!" Nan's cry was filled with anguish.

Wendy lit another cigarette from the end of her own, then held it out. "Here. Take it. Smoke it. Hold it. You need it."

"Jake made me quit!"

"Jake, Jake, Jake! Screw Jake! We're talking about what's important. Take the damn thing and listen to me."

"What?"

"Get a lawyer. I'll give you the name of the woman I used. She's wonderful. Go see her, and find out what your options are."

"Oh, God," Nan said. "I can't. If I ask him for a divorce he'll ruin me. He'll say it was my fault. He'll lock me up like he said he would. And then there's Jamie. What'll it do to him?"

"Probably no worse than what's already been done," Wendy snapped. "And as for locking you up, this isn't the fourteenth century you know. You have rights. Think about it."

"I have."

"And?"

"And nothing. I'm not ready. Everything happened too fast. I feel like I'm in the middle of the ocean and can't swim. I don't want to be here, I don't want Jake, I'm afraid to trust my own instincts, so where does that leave me?"

"Limbo," came the answer. "I've been there. But it's just a way station. Take your time, you don't have to do everything tomorrow."

"Jake's coming home the day after."

Wendy sighed. "Quit being so literal. You survived this long, there's no reason you can't go on a little longer. Or you can just walk out. Raid your bank account, and take all that gorgeous jewelry. Take the silverware and the paintings." She grinned suddenly. "Call a moving company and take the

117

whole damned house. It's a museum."

Nan poured another glass of wine and stared into the golden liquid, her eyes wide. Whatever Wendy did, she always landed on her feet. "You're so practical. I dream, and you invest. I never thought about the silver."

"Well you'd better start. Go see my lawyer, and whatever you do, remember, I was the original wimp, and I did it. So can you. Call me any time. One of the nicest things about living alone is that my time is my own. I'm here for you when you need me."

"Like always." Nan swallowed hard. "I wish I'd been able to do the same for you."

Wendy shrugged. "Maybe your turn will come. Who knows? Anyhow, that's what friends are for."

That night Nan dreamed she was running through a landscape dotted with juniper trees. She was being chased by an unseen hunter, running for her life, and for the life of the child in her womb that weighed her down, slowed her stride, stole her breath.

Behind her came the man she couldn't see. She only knew that he was running easily and would shortly overtake her. Ahead was a hill and a steep drop-off. Trees spread their branches in the valley below, and she thought that if she jumped, they would break her fall.

The cliff was sheer, the branches fragile things that snapped under her weight. She hit the ground full force and lay there panting, her blood and the blood of the lost child staining the sand.

And then she heard the voice. "You had to lose the child in you," it said. "And now you have. And now you've found me and I will be with you the rest of your life."

Then the man gathered her up. She was in his arms; she

felt the beat of his heart, the encompassing warmth of a love such as she had never imagined, and she clung to him with all the strength in her battered body.

"Love, love," she cried out and woke, swept with a joy as radiant as the first light of the sun on the mountain.

She was a creation of stained-glass, a cloud pierced by a single golden ray of hope, the mockingbird throwing its soul into the moonlight.

She was alive. Whole. Flooded with visions and the emotions she had denied herself because of a childish terror.

She scrambled out of bed and headed downstairs to write to Ben. What she said didn't matter as much as the need to share the happiness of discovery. As she poured a cup of coffee, the telephone began to ring.

CHAPTER NINETEEN

"Is everything all right? Where were you last night? I called, and I called, and got no answer." Jake sounded far away, but his irritation was immediate.

Even from Frankfurt he had the power to make her cringe. "I was at Wendy's," she whispered.

"That's what you do? Come home and go off again? I send you on a vacation, and you can't stay home five minutes when I'm going to call?"

"I . . . I forgot." The lie came easily. She was used to lying.

"Forgot!" His next words were lost in the bleep of the satellite, and she was grateful. "Tomorrow. You'll be there?"

"Yes," she said quietly. "I'll be there. I have your flight number."

"You sound different."

She cringed again but said, "It's a bad connection."

"Oh. Well, I'll hang up. Is Jessie there?"

"She's coming in a bit."

Jessie was her right hand, her savior, her black madonna who had raised Jamie from infancy and taught her the basics of keeping house that she'd never learned from Helen. Jessie was tall, wide hipped, and moved like a Florida panther, all power and grace, and Nan loved her though she doubted Jessie realized how much.

"Make sure she cleans under the bed," Jake said, and Nan

stifled a laugh, being well acquainted with his obsession. Her first act on coming home from a trip was always to sweep under the bed.

After she hung up, she stood looking at the telephone wishing she could tear it off the wall, bury it in the garden, never have to hear it ring again. But then she couldn't talk to Ben. Then she'd be cut off from her lifeline, living proof that she hadn't dreamed the whole thing.

Her dream! What had it meant? She sat and sipped her coffee, feeling again her devastation over her dream miscarriage, her sudden sweep of joy as her pursuer lifted her in his arms. Was it Ben? She hadn't seen his face. But if it wasn't Ben, who was it? In any case, it had been an important dream containing a message. She would have to decipher the symbols, ponder them, write down the whole so as not to forget.

Turning, she pulled her notebook out of the drawer, but before she could put down a word, the telephone rang again.

"Welcome home!" Helen sang the words like a cheerful robin.

Instantly Nan was on guard. Helen had radar where she was concerned. "Thanks," she said.

"How was it? I'm dying to hear."

I'll bet, Nan thought but said, "It was great. We rode roundups and Ben let Jamie practice driving the ranch truck."

"Ben?" Helen fastened on the name.

Freudian slip, she said to herself with a grin. "He owns the place."

"How old is he?"

"Now don't start," Nan said. "He's a perfectly nice man."

"Is there something you want to tell me?" Helen asked sweetly.

Soon she'd begin with coy innuendos, digging, prying, listening for an indication of her daughter's fall from grace, and hungry for any proof of emotion. Why? Nan wondered. Why this preoccupation with the feelings of another?

"We just had lots of fun," she managed to say. "Now we're back safe and you can relax."

But Helen wasn't to be put off. "I'm coming over."

Too soon! Nan shook her head. "I won't be here. I have to go get groceries and take Lottie."

"And no time for me."

She was supposed to feel guilty. That was the code. Only now she was aware of the many-sided manipulation. As Ben had warned, they all wanted a piece of her, a fragment they could call their own.

"Look," she said slowly, searching for diplomacy. "Jake's coming home tomorrow, Jessie's coming today, and there's no food in the house. We had a great time, but the party's over. I'll call you later."

"I hope so," came the dour response.

Jessie was coming up the back steps, her huge black leather purse containing her apron and her house shoes bumping the railing. The day had begun. There would be no letter written, and the muse, buffeted, intruded upon, had vanished like her dream.

Somehow she got through the ordeal of maneuvering Lottie in and out of the car, not easy with the older woman's broken hip and cane, and into and out of the supermarket. She carried all the groceries in while Lottie held the elevator, then got them into the apartment and onto the kitchen counter.

"Do you need help putting this away?" She was still the dutiful daughter, respectful of her elders, even though she felt that slowly, inevitably, she was smothering in the airless room with the windows tightly closed, the blinds drawn to keep the sunlight from fading the furniture.

"You want to go," Lottie said.

"Well . . . Jessie's there. I should make her lunch. And give her a hand."

"I'll manage. What time does Jake get in?"

That's all she was interested in. Her son. Proof of her existence, child of her womb. Son who owed her not only his birth but his every breath thereafter. She didn't feel that way about Jamie. In fact, she tried to be the opposite, giving him freedom, urging him on in spite of his father's protests. What *was* it with these mothers who couldn't let go?

She pushed her hair away from her face, felt perspiration trickling down her cheeks. "Late afternoon. I'll make sure he calls you."

"Are you going to tell him?" Lottie's eyes, huge and dark brown, seemed to be pleading with her.

"I might. But maybe you should."

"It was a silly thing." Lottie clasped her hands on the crook of her cane. "I just felt . . . lost."

"We all do at some point. But turning on the gas won't help. We just have to keep trying because living is better than the alternative. At least that's what I think."

"But you're young." It was an accusation.

"Sure," she said. "But life isn't easy for me, either."

"Jake," Lottie said. "I often wondered how you put up with him. He wants so much all the time."

Speechless, Nan stared at her. And what did Lottie want, what exchange of confidences that could be used against her? She wasn't about to be sucked into a game where she was in the middle and could only lose.

"Don't worry about me," she said. "I'm fine. But I have to go." And then she was running down the hall toward the elevator hoping Lottie wouldn't come after her with more questions she didn't want to think about or answer.

As she pulled up in front of the house, Jessie swooped down on the car and grabbed as many grocery bags as she could handle.

"You gonna work yourself to death," she grumbled. "Right here in this house. And runnin' that old lady's errands don't help."

Jessie had hated Lottie from the time she'd tried to force Jamie to eat and burned his mouth. He'd screamed, Jessie snatched him out of his chair, and stood glaring. "I rocked this baby in my arms," she said fiercely. "Ain't nobody gonna hurt him. Not you, not nobody."

Nan chuckled, remembering. Then she said, "I have to keep an eye on her. She turned on the gas and tried to kill herself while I was gone."

"Too bad it didn't work."

"Shame on you," she said, laughing.

"Shame on her. Puttin' you through that. If she was mine, I'd tell her."

"I did."

"Well that's something. You got to stand up for yourself, honey, 'cause if you don't, she'll drag you down with her. I know that kind. I bet she didn't listen much, did she?"

"How come you know so much?" Nan asked.

"I been around," Jessie said. "I've seen how people act."

She was emptying bags, stacking the contents on the table, and Nan was putting away, marveling as she always did at the rhythm of their hands, black and white, working side by side without comment.

The way it should be, she thought. Two women bound by friendship, by a loyalty that needed no explanation.

But Jessie's hands suddenly fluttered down and lay motionless, and when she looked up Nan saw, to her horror, that Jessie was crying.

"My God, what's the matter?" she asked.

The woman didn't answer, simply wept, a flood of crystal tears running down her dark cheeks and onto her bosom. Nan opened her arms, and Jessie came into them, and for a moment neither spoke.

"It's all right," Nan murmured as she would to an injured child, to any woman who wept as this one, soundlessly, out of bitter anguish. "It's all right."

"It ain't." Jessie's words were blurred. "That no good man what lives with me took up with that bitch next door. I come home last night, and they got me locked out. Out! My own house, and I can't get in." Her shoulders shook. "He call the police and tell them I'm crazy, and they want to take me away. Me. I been good to that man all this time. That's where it get you—all this doin' for somebody. You be poundin' on your own door, and them inside laughin', and you with no place to go."

"You should have come here."

Jessie snorted. "And how that look? Me in a police car on this fancy street."

"I don't give a damn how things look," Nan said fiercely. "You're my friend."

The whole world was in misery. Everyone, black, white, red, was busy cutting out someone's heart, performing clitorectomies on the innocent, so that what was left was a race of the mutilated—women doing their chores by rote; children, unloved, roaming the streets; men like Ben shocked into silence.

Suddenly she was crying, too, for the first time since leaving him, and it was good to let it out with Jessie who would never speak of it, who understood without being given a reason.

"Honey," she said, "don't cry. You just spoil that pretty face."

"I can't help it."

"Sure you can." She wiped her own face with her apron. "Sure you can. Here we are like a couple raggedy ass babies, and this whole house to clean before *he* come home. What'll he think, he find dust under the bed?"

"I don't give a damn what he thinks, either," she said. Dust wasn't important compared to human feelings.

"You best not let him know that," Jessie said. "You know how he go on. Him and that old lady."

"Do him good." She struggled with her tears another minute, knowing Jessie was right. "I'm okay," she said then, wiping her eyes. "You okay?"

"I been better."

"Me, too," she said sadly. "Maybe lunch will help. I'll make tuna salad."

Jessie started folding bags, smoothing the creases, stacking them in a neat pile. "Put in lots of eggs."

Late that night, with Jamie in bed and the back door open letting in the scents of earth, grass, the flowering chestnut tree, she sat at the table in the kitchen writing to Ben. The words flowed as her tears had done, so swiftly her hand could not keep pace.

And when she had finished, when she had sealed the envelope and hidden it in her purse, the words still came, so that she returned to the table, opened her notebook, and began to write the story that she needed to tell.

CHAPTER TWENTY

Is he coming, Sister Anne?

Yes.

The lines from the fairy tale repeated as Nan checked the house. How true those old tales were! In that story each room contained the body of one of Bluebeard's wives. Here, every room held an echo of her own presence, ghosts of the past that whispered of things she had said, done, thought, often in fear.

A bowl of flowers sat on the hall table, and the grapes that Jake liked overflowed the silver bowl in the dining room. The mail was sorted into folders, bills in one, correspondence in another. The bathrooms sparkled, crisp sheets were on the bed, and a plump chicken stuffed with wild rice sat ready to go in the oven.

"Done," she whispered, with a sigh of exhaustion. "Let him come," and went to change out of her jeans before going to the airport.

Why was she doing this, wearing herself out for a man she no longer loved, possibly had never loved? she wondered as she put on lipstick. Why kill herself when she knew he would come home and find fault?

But maybe not, she answered herself. Maybe this time would be different. Maybe he'd praise her, say how wonderful the house looked. Just once she wanted to hear him say it, to have done something right. She frowned at the logic that eluded her. Obviously Jake's praise was necessary to her, but why? She saw her reflection in the mirror—grim-faced and unsmiling, a far cry from the woman she had been only days before. He had the power to change her entire person, to erase the glow from her eyes.

Power. The key word. By withholding praise he ensured that in her own eyes she remained the woman of no value, the wife dependent on him for her very existence, the child who could do nothing right, like Jamie. Dear God, why hadn't she ever seen this before? The child! She had to lose the child, that violated, cowering three year old who lived in her body. She had to rip it out, tear it loose, and bleed and bleed.

Horrified, she turned and ran into Jamie's room. "Sure you don't want to come with me?"

"I'll stay here."

She wished she could. But at least, driving alone, she would have time to think. "There's a pot of soup on the stove," she said. "And stuff for sandwiches. You can eat whenever. We'll probably eat late." And Jamie would be spared having to sit at the table being cross-examined. The routine never varied, as they both knew.

"See you." She gave him a hug and went slowly down the stairs, avoiding the step that creaked out of habit.

In a few hours he would be walking off the plane, coming toward her. He would smile as he located her in the crowd. And what would she do, who would she be, which Nan of all the many?

Her hands were trembling as she started the car and backed slowly out of the driveway.

Traffic was light. She cut across town and headed South on the parkway. Driving always relaxed her, and some of her apprehension dissipated as she concentrated on the road.

"Lose the child." It made perfect sense now that she was calmer. The hard part would be doing it. She'd need to be aware of the reasons not only behind her own actions but of everyone concerned, and she doubted that was possible.

Surely all those who, up 'til now had dominated her life hadn't sat down and plotted their behavior. And Jake, with his fear of self-knowledge and psychiatry hadn't demonically made the decision to rule her every thought. Yet it had happened, and with her permission, quietly given, but given, nonetheless. Compliance, silence implied consent, and she had been, always, the obedient child, her own desires buried deep.

"Oh, boy!" she exclaimed. "This is a total mess!" Because once you understood what was wrong, you had to try to fix it. But when she'd told Ben she had to take responsibility for herself, she hadn't known the half of it. And where did he fit into this complex maze? He'd made no reference at all to any kind of shared future.

She bit her lip, wondering if the brief magic of their love could be counted on, but it was too late to start worrying. Somehow she had arrived at the airport, so lost in thought she couldn't remember how. The terminal rose in front of her, solid, grey, filled with travelers, probably most of them with overwhelming problems of their own.

A car pulled out of a space, and she backed in expertly, then sat, her fingers gripping the wheel. In a few minutes Jake would be coming toward her. Jake. Her husband. Father of her child. Fighting apprehension, she got out, locked the car, inserted quarters into the parking meter, and went inside to meet him.

He came toward her smiling, weighted down by his carry-on bag and briefcase, and she remembered how it had been when they'd been dating, and meeting him at the airport was a daring and sophisticated thing to do. Sometimes she had packed a picnic, the exotic food Jake loved—Greek olives, grape leaves, French bread, cheese, a bottle of white wine in a cooler. Or, if the flight was late, they'd simply go to a restaurant or Jake's apartment and cook a simple pasta before falling onto the bed and making love.

But that, she reminded herself, was then, when Jake, too, was another person, witty, intelligent, solicitous of her feelings; when she had been eager and passionate, ready to marry, and he had been equally as passionate, filled with praise of her eyes, her hair, even her arms. "Greek goddess," he'd called her then. "Nan of the almond eyes."

Now she forced a welcoming smile and submitted to his kiss, noticing how she held her body away from his, fearing intimacy.

The body doesn't lie.

Fortunately, he didn't notice, just asked, "Are you parked far away?"

She shook her head. "Not very."

"Good. How's everything at the house?"

"Fine," she said. "Jessie came yesterday."

"Any problems with my mother?"

She sighed, debating with herself, then blurted out the truth. "She tried to kill herself."

They had been walking toward the baggage claim, but Jake stopped and stared at her, his expression grim. "When did this happen?"

"I guess the night before I got back. When I walked in, the phone was ringing like she couldn't wait to tell me."

"And you couldn't wait, either. What a welcome home!"

She straightened her shoulders. "You asked."

"Yes. Well. It's a great thing to get hit with after flying a few thousand miles."

"That's what I thought." She picked up his briefcase and started walking. "She's your mother, but I'm the one who has to deal with her. At some point, you're going to have to have a serious talk. She turned on the gas, Jake. Think about that."

"Not now." He was watching the carousel as if the sight of the bags could erase what he'd just heard. "Why don't you go get the car and meet me out front?"

If she walked slowly, she'd have a few minutes to herself. "Okay," she said.

"Take the carry-on." He pushed it toward her with one foot. "But be careful. There's a couple bottles of Russian vodka inside."

On the way home they talked easily, out of habit, Jake telling stories of his trip, Nan listening, even laughing, all the while amazed at the world she had helped to create. She had been as unaware of what was happening as he, and they had lived like two fish in a bowl, blinking, breathing, holding on because that was all that stood between them and disaster. Jake demanded, and she agreed. There was a word for this, but she couldn't think of it, could only concentrate on driving and the drone of Jake's voice.

Finally she said, "I told Lottie you'd call."

He pushed his glasses higher on his nose. "Did she say why she did it?"

"Only that you had no business going away, and I had less."

"Doesn't she realize . . . ?"

"No," Nan said. "She just wants. Everything. All the time. And I'm not sure that what you say will make any difference."

Just like us, she thought. *All the logic, all the words ever spoken can't, now, make a difference.*

With a sigh she pulled up at the front door, dreading the evening ahead.

As soon as Jamie came down the stairs, she turned guard dog, alert and on the defensive.

Jake put out his hand, and Jamie shook it, not meeting his father's eyes.

"Hi," he said. "How was your trip?"

Jake glared at him. "Speak up! You're always mumbling. Can't you speak to your father so he can understand you?"

Jamie winced, then a look of rebellion crossed his face, coupled with a flash of what seemed to Nan to be hatred.

"HOW WAS YOUR TRIP?" he shouted, loud enough to be heard across the street, and this time he looked squarely at Jake, refusing to back down.

"That's right! Start before I get in the door. Don't you dare yell at your father like that! Go up to your room, and it better be neat by the time I get there. I suppose your mother let you get away with living like a pig while I was gone."

Without warning, Nan began to scream, a high-pitched keening that startled them all, and that seemed to come all the way out of her womb.

"What's the matter? Stop that noise and tell me what's the matter." Jake appeared to be in shock.

But she couldn't stop. Broken, split into fragments, her cries continued.

He grabbed her shoulders and shook her, his face inches from hers, and she saw herself reflected in his glasses, wild-eyed, her mouth open. She was a madwoman mourning the destruction of her life and that of her child, and this man, this husband, had no idea of what he had done.

"You're the matter!" she choked out. "Coming home and attacking us. Brutalizing your own child. We're supposed to

132

be a family." A sob cut her off before she could say more.

"Don't take his side!" Jake snapped. "He has to learn."

"What? What does he have to learn?"

"To show respect for his father."

She wanted to laugh, but had enough wits left to realize she was on the verge of an hysterical breakdown.

"Respect?" she said. "Respect? You'll be lucky if he doesn't murder you in your bed some day. And if he doesn't, I might!"

He let go of her so roughly she fell against the wall, and when he answered, his voice was thick with rage. "You want to be a family? Fine. Be it without me and see how you like it!" Then he turned and left, slamming the door.

"Mom?" Jamie touched her arm. "You okay?" He was, she saw, terrified. Her outburst had threatened the only security he had.

She hugged him, noticing that he was taller than she was, almost, but not quite, a man. "I'll be all right. Don't worry."

"Is Dad . . . you think he'll come back?"

"Yes," she said, sure that Jake would never give up the pleasure of home, at least not without a far worse fight. "He probably went to his office."

"What if he doesn't?"

"Would that bother you?"

He frowned. "I don't know. He is my father and all. But I wish . . . I wish he was like Ben."

She held him tighter, not wanting him to see her face. "So do I," she whispered. "Oh, baby, so do I."

CHAPTER TWENTY-ONE

"Mom?"

It was nearly ten o'clock, and Nan, exhausted and jittery, was sitting at the kitchen table wondering what would happen next.

"What, honey?"

Jamie stood in the door in his pajamas. "Is it my fault?"

She'd been writing to Ben, a frantic letter because she needed to talk to someone and, as usual, searching for the words to explain. She put down her pen.

"Not really," she said, gesturing at a chair. "You reacted, and I don't blame you. You were trying to do the right thing and instead you got jumped. I know how it is."

When he didn't answer, she went on. "We've always taught you to be respectful and talk nicely, so in a way you did something you shouldn't have. But you're growing up. You're not a child, and you want not to be treated like one. And rightly. You've never given us a moment's trouble, and you deserve our respect, too." She stopped to make sure he understood, saw his eyes, very blue, watching her.

"Your father's a difficult person. It's hard to know what he expects. How to please him. We both know that. I'm not making his apologies, understand. I don't think the way he acted was right, either. I'm simply stating the obvious. And I don't want you to feel guilty, whatever happens. You acted the way you felt, and that's not a bad thing as long as you don't make it a habit."

He grinned. "Like somebody we know."

"Sort of." She looked at the clock, wondering if she'd been wrong and this time Jake wasn't coming back.

Jamie said, "Can I ask you something?"

"Sure."

"What's with you and Ben?"

She hoped her shock didn't show. Had she said or done anything to betray her feelings. "Nothing I'm ashamed of. Why?"

"I wondered. You seemed like somebody else around him."

"Is that good or bad?"

"Good. It was good. You were fun. Now we're here and you're like you always are. Kind of . . . *brown*."

"Brown?" She raised her eyebrows.

"Yeah," he said, squirming. "Like you're some kind of ghost."

He was closer to the truth than he knew. "Well," she said, "I'll have to do something about that. Maybe think red. Now I think you'd better get to bed. And don't worry. He'll be home and we'll go on like always."

"Cool," he said, the irony in his tone cutting like a knife. He got up and came around to hug her. "Are you going to wait up?"

"For awhile."

After he'd gone back upstairs, she finished her letter, five pages on both sides, then, as if that had been only a prelude, she began a poem that had been haunting her all day, and then another. When she finished she put them in the drawer. In the morning she'd look at them with a fresh eye, type them out, look again. She wished she had someone she could share them with, another writer, another poet who could give her an educated opinion. As always, however, all she had was herself.

In the morning Jake would be home. Or would he? She looked again at the clock. Nearly midnight. He was punishing her, she knew, hoping she'd be frantic with worry, overcome with guilt. But no more.

Leaving the hall light on, she went up the stairs, pausing briefly on the landing to look out into the branches of the big elm tree, its new leaves glinting in the light from the street.

So filled with promise, she thought. *So sure that summer will come.*

If a tree could hope, why couldn't she?

At two o'clock, still awake, she heard the door open and close, heard him mount the stairs. He switched on the light beside the bed, and she opened her eyes and looked at him.

"You could've waited up," he said.

No apology there. No regrets.

"Where were you?"

"My mother's. Then I went to the office."

"What did she have to say?"

He took off his jacket and tie and hung them on the chair. "Not much. I asked her to dinner on Friday so we can both talk to her. Is there anything to eat right now?"

"Chicken. In the fridge," she said, knowing she was expected to get up and put it on the table. Instead she lay still and closed her eyes waiting for him to ask.

He didn't disappoint. "If you put it out for me, I'll just help myself," he said. "I'd like to get out of these clothes and take a shower first."

She weighed her options. She could do as he asked or refuse. If the former, he'd eat, then come to bed. If the latter, he'd explode and rage until she gave in and did it anyhow.

"I'll leave it in the dining room," she said. "You'll have to put it away."

At least he hadn't mentioned love making. At least she'd been spared that for the night. When finally she got back into bed, she gritted her teeth as a precaution against talking in her sleep, calling out for Ben who was so far away.

Ben hadn't slept well. He kept thinking he heard her repeating his name over and over like a mantra. He was here, she was there, and they were both helpless. He went to breakfast early and found Lupe setting the table.

She smiled, then saw the darkness like a pall around him. "The coffee is ready," she said.

"Maybe that'll wake me up."

"You didn't sleep?" Her voice was gentle.

"Not much."

"She will come back."

Not for the first time he wondered how she knew about things never spoken, how she had the uncanny knack of going straight to the heart of trouble.

"It'll take a miracle," he said.

She shrugged. "Even miracles take time. You think they just happen? You think God snaps His fingers and flowers bloom in the desert? Have patience."

"For how long?"

"As long as it takes," she said severely. "You want everything now, like a baby, but you know better."

Her eyes were twinkling, belying her words, and suddenly he laughed. "Damn it, Lupe, sometimes I think you're a witch. I wish I could believe like you do."

"Believe," she said. "Believe she will come. She needs all our help. Yours, mine, her own wishing. She needs to know you will wait."

Wait! And four days seemed like a year! He missed her laughter, the warmth of her hands, and the way she looked at him, her brown eyes shining with love. He couldn't have been mistaken, and yet now it all seemed an impossible dream, a sweetness from long ago, a poignant interlude in a life of hard work and longing.

"I'm going over to the old homestead," he told Lupe. "I won't be back 'til supper."

The house, built by his grandparents out of native stone, still stood on the banks of French Jack Creek. At some point a prospector, an old Frenchman, had panned the creek looking for gold. Whether or not he'd found it, no one knew, but he'd left his name behind and a hint of mystery as well.

He dismounted, tied his horse to an old hitching post, then walked around to the front of the house. The door had been missing for years, probably stolen for firewood, but the walls were intact, and the big fireplace with its wide stone hearth stood like a monument to the woman who had labored there—cooking meals in a cast iron kettle, heating wash water, rocking a squalling infant in tired arms.

Theirs had been a life devoid of convenience, a life of labor and hardship, yet they'd survived, put their mark on the land and in his blood. They hadn't been quitters anymore than his parents were, than he was.

Often he'd thought about fixing up the old place, having a hideaway of his own, and now, as he looked around, he saw that it could be done, and that the big main room overlooking the creek had a charm undiminished by cobwebs, pack rats' nests, and years.

He wondered what Nan would think of the place with its echoes of history, the curling of the creek around stones.

The roof was mostly gone, and the plumbing non-existent, but the old well was a good one, still being used to pump water into the next pasture.

It was a project to keep him busy, something to dream on, and he wouldn't tell her. Not yet. Wouldn't offer her a place of her own until she gave him reason to hope.

He went outside, checked the foundation, and found a rosebush clinging with tenacity to the wall, a few tiny flowers reaching toward the sun. Grandma Libby had been a fierce gardener, he remembered, nurturing her plants whenever she had a spare moment. Like Nan, her eyes reflecting the dance of golden poppies, reaching out for the flame-tip of ocotillo flowers with a kind of hunger.

It all came back to Nan. But now he had a project. Happily, he mounted his horse, his head filled with plans. And if they came to nothing? his common sense asked.

"Believe," Lupe had said.

So he would. There was nothing else he could do.

CHAPTER TWENTY-TWO

The house was filled with the scent of roasting meat, and Jamie sniffed as he came in and dumped his books on the kitchen table. "Who's coming?" he asked Nan.

"Grandma Lottie."

His face fell. "Can I eat early?"

"No you cannot," she said sternly. "You'll wash up, change your shirt, and eat with us. Then you're excused. We have to talk to her."

"Good luck."

"Thanks. We'll need it." She checked the leg of lamb, Lottie's favorite, then dipped a spoon into the pot of watercress soup. "Ummm," she approved. "It's good. Want a taste?"

He shook his head. "How come you're going to all this trouble?"

To her, cooking was no trouble. It was a kind of passion like writing or gardening. It was the chance to make something out of nothing, to create a salad bowl that was a visual treat, a soup that lingered on the tongue like a good wine. And it took her mind off her problems that seemed to mount with every passing day.

Just this morning she'd let Jake make love to her. He'd been passionate and quick, and she lay there trying not to cry out, enduring his kisses, his hands on her breasts with an emotion that amounted to terror. How could she do this for the rest of her life? It was like prostitution, selling her body for the sake of security, for peace and order, a dishonest act, even an immoral one.

"No!" she'd wanted to say. "No!" Instead she sealed her lips, shut her eyes, and, at the last, faked her orgasm convincingly.

"I missed you," Jake said.

With her eyes still shut she answered him. "Me, too." And he was satisfied.

Now she turned to Jamie. "Cooking is fun," she said. "Go wash up. Dad's bringing Grandma home with him."

As usual, Lottie was dressed to the teeth and glittering with jewels. During dinner she was on her best behavior, asking Jamie questions about the ranch and Jake about Russia as if nothing had happened during his absence.

Just as Nan was serving coffee and dessert, the phone rang. "For you," she said to Jake, then followed him out of the room. "Try not to stay on too long, will you? We need to talk to her."

"I'll try," he said.

She seated herself again and cast around for a neutral topic. "That's a gorgeous necklace," she began, admiring Lottie's hammered 18-karat gold collar that gleamed in the candlelight.

Lottie raised a hand and touched it fondly. "It'll be yours when I die."

"Oh, please," Nan said, annoyed. "That's not what I meant, and you know it."

"I know you're just waiting. Both of you."

Nan was getting desperate. Where was Jake? "Please try not to think like that. To be so depressed." She leaned her elbows on the table. "We care about you. You don't know how much we worry."

Lottie was quiet a minute, then looked at Nan, her eyes filled with tears.

"Don't cry, Lottie," she said. "For heaven's sake, what's there to cry about?"

"I want you to love me!" Lottie slammed her hand down on the table so hard her bracelets jangled. "I want somebody to love me."

In spite of herself, Nan was touched. "Poor thing," she said. "We love you. You know that. You also know that you just can't have everything your way. Life isn't like that."

Lottie glared at her, tears in the corners of her eyes. "What do you know about life?" she said bitterly. "You and that mother of yours, always living in this little town, always protected. Always cared for. I know about it. I know my own mother didn't love me. She sent me away. I only saw her once before when my father brought me here. And I tried to make up for it with Jake. I tried so hard. And what happens? I come here to live, and he leaves. Every other month he's going someplace. Leaving me. And he doesn't even say goodbye, just lets you say it for him. Now he's on the phone, talking like I'm not even here, and you sit there hoping I'll go soon. So I will." She stood up, tottering a little from too much wine.

Nan reached out and took her hand. "Don't go. At least not yet. Wait'll Jake gets through, then we'll drive you. It's too late for you to walk."

"I'm used to it."

"Oh, hell!" With a suddenness that astonished her, Nan lost her temper. "Stop feeling sorry for yourself. Stop working the guilt trip on us. There's lots worse off than you. You don't know what your mother felt, or why she did what she did. You were too young to know. She . . ." Nan stopped, wanting a name, a face to give to the woman, Jake's grandmother. "What was her name? Your mother?"

Lottie stared at her as if she were seeing someone else, someone far away, a face out of the past, but when her answer came, it was a shocking one. "I don't know," she said.

"You don't know your mother's name?"

She shook her head still looking vague. "I don't. That's the truth. My father hated her so much he wouldn't talk about her, even when I was old enough to want to know. But what I know is enough. She didn't want me. Nobody's ever wanted me really. Even Jake's father." Her voice caught on a sob.

"That's not true!" Nan wasn't sure if it was or wasn't, but wanted to reassure the woman. "How can you say that?"

"I can say it. Because I know. Now get my coat. I want to go home."

The ride to Lottie's was a short one. Neither woman spoke until Nan pulled up at the entrance to the building and helped her mother-in-law out of the car.

It was like handling a bird, she thought, taking hold of Lottie's elbow—like holding some feathered, jeweled creature whose substance was simply a handful of fragile bones.

On impulse, she put her arms around Lottie's shoulders and hugged her. "Now be good," she said as if talking to a child. "And sleep well. We love you, and that's what you have to remember."

The fact that she didn't love her seemed unimportant. Lies came easily to one who always worried about the feelings of others.

Unexpectedly, Lottie returned the hug. "You're a good girl," she said. "And dinner was delicious. Have Jake call me."

"I will," Nan promised. "I'm sorry about that phone call, but you have to understand. Jake's work comes first, before you or me. That's just how it is."

"I didn't raise him that way."

But she had. She had so structured his life that he'd taken refuge in himself and had never come out.

Not the sins of the fathers, Nan thought as she drove away, but the sins of the mothers, those women who struggled for any semblance of love, and who sought recompense from their children for what had been denied them. To many, love was seen as a duty. Payment for past wrongs. But how could a child, or even an adult, repair the damage done in other generations? How could she, herself, be expected to stitch up wounds she hardly understood?

Lost in thought, she took the long way home, then circled her block once, twice. She didn't *want* to go home, didn't belong there. What she wanted was to point the car West and drive through the night, through the next day and the next until she reached Ben and safety. For she, too, wanted love, needed it, had taken a wrong path in her search.

"Call your mother," she said to Jake as she came in the house.

As usual, he was at the table, his papers piled around him, the remains of dinner pushed aside.

He completed writing a sentence before looking up. "What does she want?"

"Damn it!" Nan threw her keys on the hall table. "She wants *you!* She wants you to pay some attention to her! You invite her to dinner and then you go off and talk on the phone like she's not here. I'm used to it, but she can't understand. Meanwhile, you leave me to deal with her, and I have enough problems. Now go call her."

He stared, surprised by her outburst, but all he said was, "Bring me the portable phone."

"Get it yourself!" she snapped. "I have this mess to clear up."

"Now wait a minute. I'm in the middle of something important, and you come in and start shouting. The least you could do . . ."

But she cut him off. "Don't make it my fault. She's not *my* mother. And if you think your work is more important than her suicide, then I can't help you." She could feel anger building, a tension in the muscles of her throat. "My mother at least knows what *her* mother's name was."

"What are you talking about?"

She walked further into the room. "You . . . we . . . have a problem," she said, then told him the rest.

When she finished he shrugged. "My grandmother was insane. She died in an asylum somewhere. My grandfather took Lottie and left, and as far as I know they never saw her again, probably just as well."

"That makes it right?" She wanted to shake him, to wipe the bland expression off his face.

"No. But my mother's always been like this. She drove my father crazy. Hell, she drove me crazy. Always wanting her way, always picking at something. You remember how she was with Jamie and his toilet training. How all she could talk about was how she'd trained me when I was eight months old. Well, now she's starting all over on something else."

"But you can't pretend she isn't here because she is. And if she kills herself it'll be on your head, not mine." Nan threw her jacket on a chair and began stacking plates, banging them together without regard for the delicate bone china.

"Just one dish!" Jake's voice rose an octave. "I've told you and told you. Carry one at a time or you'll chip them."

Possessions. Always possessions came first. They were the way in which he defined himself, and she was the servant who saw to their perfection. As usual, they had wandered away from the initial topic.

"I'll bring you the phone," she said, then saw the maneuverings by which she had been brought to obedience. In order for him to do as she asked, she first had to do what he had requested.

Did one human being ever understand another or even see deeply into self? Or was life nothing more than a series of manipulations, war games, sorties onto the battle ground without forethought or plan?

She shivered as she collected the plates, careful now not to damage them. Somewhere lay the answers to all her questions, but she didn't know where.

CHAPTER TWENTY-THREE

Nan heard the garden gate click shut and quickly bundled the tablet and her letter to Ben into the drawer. It had to be Helen who always came in the back, probably because that way she wouldn't have to talk to Jake if he were home. And Helen would go straight to her writing as if drawn by a magnet, hoping to find . . . what? Some display of emotion, the key to her daughter's mind to which she had been denied access? Nan sighed and prepared herself for interrogation.

"You never called back so I just decided to stop in," Helen said from the back door.

"I've had my hands full."

"With what?"

"Lottie for one thing."

"Spare me." Helen sat down. "I want to know about you. Your vacation."

Nan busied herself at the sink. With her back turned she wouldn't have to face her mother's penetrating gaze. "It was great. Gorgeous weather, the best horses I've ever ridden, and really nice people."

"Who's this Ben you mentioned?" Once on the scent, Helen could be counted on to stay for the kill.

"I told you. He owns the place. His grandparents came out and homesteaded it. Now there's a lovely house and guest cottages and about twenty thousand acres to look at. It's a dream."

"Is he handsome?" Helen had turned girlish, inviting confidences.

Nan shrugged. "I guess."

"How old is he?"

"I didn't ask." Taking a breath, she turned around. "And you can quit fishing. Nothing happened. He's a nice guy, he has a son Jamie's age and they got along like gangbusters. We all did. Now can we change the subject?"

"Don't get huffy with me," was the response. "Methinks you're protesting too much. Like you're guilty."

"Well, I'm not." She hoped her face wasn't red. How good it would be to be able to confide, ask advice, speak rationally. But it wasn't possible. She said, "You're all dressed up. Where're you going?"

"To lunch with Martha." Helen touched her hair under her wide-brimmed hat. "I just came from the beauty parlor." She frowned then and looked puzzled. "While I was under the dryer I was reading a magazine. And I . . . I came across a word I've never heard before. Maybe you know what it is."

Nan dropped into a chair opposite, relieved that the heat was off. "What word?"

Helen moved uneasily. "It . . . it was in an article about men. And women. What they do in bed. And it kept referring to something called . . . called orgasm. Have *you* ever heard about such a thing?" She turned her eyes, blue and innocent as a child's, to Nan.

How to answer? How to conceal shock, anguish, dismay? This was her mother sitting here asking questions she should have had answers for years ago. This was her mother turned child before her eyes, pleading for knowledge denied her by a conspiracy of years of silence.

"Yes," she said cautiously. "I know the word." Then she waited.

"I wondered." Helen's voice was a whisper. "Have you ever . . . ?"

Nan swallowed. Talking to Jamie about the facts of life had been simple compared to this insight into her parents' life, this secret she did not want to hear. "Yes," she said. "And so did you probably. You just didn't know there was a name for it."

"Oh." Helen relaxed. "Oh. Of course. It . . . it's only a word after all. Isn't it?"

But words had invisible meanings. They had echoes and associations, regardless of the fact that they were, simply, sounds attached to tangible objects, physical acts.

"Yes," she agreed gently. "It's only a word." Then she sat back and heard the silence between them, punctuated by the steady beating of her heart.

Somewhere there was a thread that connected the present to the past, that made sense of all that was happening and would happen. She had only to find it.

She said, "Lottie can't remember her mother's name."

Helen stiffened. "There's no similarity between that woman and me. None."

But Nan persisted. "Jake says she never even *saw* her mother. That her father took her away. What was your mother's name? My grandmother?" She was curious about the woman she'd never known, a woman who had died in childbirth when her own daughter was only five.

"Nadine," Helen said firmly. "Her name was Nadine. And I . . . I remember she had a blue dress the same color as her eyes."

"What else?" Nan strained to see the woman who had been, until now, merely a ghost, a faded image in an old photograph.

"Well," Helen paused. "We had a garden. Herbs. And

149

vegetables. And there were white peonies along the fence. A bowl of them once on the kitchen table. I guess she must have picked them, or maybe I did. But I can still see them there . . . so white, so fragrant. See her at the stove cooking something." She spread her hands. "I was so little when she died. I have scenes I remember, but if she said anything to me it's gone. Even the sound of her voice. It was a long time ago. And there wasn't anybody for me until I met your father. Until *you* were born."

And became the center of her universe, the child who by extension became the mother, the repository of all the love never given.

Lose the child.

And become what?

"It looks like we're all a bunch of mistakes," she said with an attempt at humor. "A crazy quilt without a pattern."

When Helen answered it was with indignation. "Oh no," she said. "It's not like that at all. Because of you."

"Me?"

"Yes. Because you're smart enough to see things as they are and do something about it."

"And you don't?"

"I was a different generation. And I didn't have anybody to tell me things so I just did the best I could. I was always afraid I was doing the wrong thing, so most of the time I just kept quiet. Now I have regrets, but it's too late."

"About what?" Nan was curious and, in spite of herself, filled with pity for this white-haired woman, her mother, who was looking at her with sadness in her eyes.

But Helen had said enough. She smiled. "Oh, just things I would have done differently if I'd known. But no use crying over spilt milk. I'd better get going or Martha will think I had an accident and call the police. She's such a worry-wart."

After she had gone, Nan sat a long time at the table seeing the bowl of white peonies, the shadow figure in the blue dress, the women neither she, nor Lottie, nor her mother had ever known.

Wrong turnings compounded themselves, and innocence became evil. She could continue to walk blindly, stumbling and feeling her way, or she could take charge, search out a new path leading from the dark wood into sunlight.

She stood and went to the telephone. When Wendy answered she said, "It's me. Give me the name and number of your lawyer."

CHAPTER TWENTY-FOUR

Even with the name of Leona McGivern safely written down, she couldn't bring herself to make an appointment. The very act of walking into a lawyer's office and telling her story was terrifying. What if she were seen? What if Jake found out? She was waiting for a reason, an act of cruelty, a major upheaval in a sea of wrongs to which she could point and say to Jake, "*You did that.* You brought me to this."

But oddly they had entered into one of those periods of calm that, in the past, had always given her false hope. *Maybe he's changed,* she would think. *Maybe it won't happen again.* And then she would breathe freely for awhile, go about her chores with a lighter heart.

She wrote a story about the white peonies, the image of which had haunted her, and when she finished and read it through, she was satisfied, both with the story and the message that it carried—the world of women searching for strength with no one to guide them.

Without misgivings, she put it in an envelope and sent it off to a magazine, then went back to work on another story, letting her words and thoughts pour out almost as fast as she could write.

She was only vaguely aware that she was drawing a roadmap of her own life, illuminating experiences, acting out possibilities, erecting guide posts to point the way out of the maze in which she had lived for so long. And she was doing it with Ben's constant and unflagging encouragement.

He opened each of her letters as if it were a gift, read her stories over and over and marveled that this woman loved him—a cattleman as far removed from her world as she was from his. He read, then impatient for the sound of her voice, called her, always early in the morning when he knew Jake would be asleep.

Except, good as it was to talk to her, he always hung up feeling more frustrated than ever. She seemed to have fallen into complacency, writing stories, shouldering her duties, going on as usual, while he cursed himself for his doubts and helplessness, lived with his longing.

Maybe he *would* have to kidnap her, do something to stir her into action before they were both too old to enjoy life, before she forgot him entirely and sank under the weight of a loveless marriage.

"I have the name and number of a lawyer," she told him.

"Have you made an appointment?"

"Not yet." She pictured him, frowning, wanting her as she wanted him. But she felt paralyzed, unable to make any motion toward freedom.

"Damn it! Why not?" He hated running in place, though he'd done it himself for years. "Just go find out your options. Don't operate in the dark."

She said, "I'm scared. I am, and can't help it. Can you understand?"

Her fear was almost tangible. He could feel it, hear it, and wished he could reach out and hold her. "I just don't want you used, or punished, or hurt. That's all," he said.

"I know." She blinked back tears. "I'm doing the best I can."

"You're not doing anything but writing stories."

That sounded like an accusation, the last thing she needed. "I have to," she said firmly. "I have to write them. Do you think they're any good?"

They were hers and as such, precious. But he knew they were more than that. "I want you to listen to me," he began. "Because what I say is the truth. These are more than good. You're one of the best. You're writing literature. What I want for you is to see you keep on writing, to be free to do it, not to be mopping up after that old lady who ought to be locked up, not carrying breakfast on a tray to that husband of yours. I want to see you let loose, your face lit up like it was when you looked at the mountains, at the flowers, at . . ."

She cut him off. "At you."

He remembered, could still see the brilliance in her eyes, the passion that was so much a part of her hidden in their depths. "You need to get out of there," he said.

"Please wait for me! Promise."

He laughed. "I'm not going anywhere. Only I warn you. I'll come back and steal you if necessary."

"I wish you would."

But that would make it easy. That way she might have regrets and someday blame him. "Take all the time you need," he said. "You know how to find me."

But she wanted to see his face, touch and be touched, talk without fear of interruption. She wanted an end to doubting, the clear, hard bite of reality.

She closed her eyes. "I know," she whispered. "And I'll be there. Someday."

When she hung up she visualized again the horror of asking Jake for a divorce. The resultant images made her tremble. He'd shout, denigrate her, reduce her to a blob of fears, a woman unable to do anything without help, the woman that she already was. She was a coward, and she had always hated cowards.

Damn it! Ben was right. The least she could do was find out her options. Gritting her teeth, she punched in the number of the lawyer's office, the number she had memorized and carried in her head for a month. Then she made an appointment for the following afternoon.

She was actually gasping for breath by the time she parked the car, her heart pounding so hard she thought for a moment she was going to faint. What if she met someone she or Jake knew? How would she explain being in a part of town where she never went? What if they asked her where she was going?

She leaned her head on the steering wheel and fought for control. "Stop it!" she said to herself. "Stop this right now!" Forcing slow, deep breaths, she willed her hands to stop shaking.

The waiting area in Leona McGivern's office was empty. The receptionist looked up and smiled. "Mrs. Fletcher? She'll be back in a few minutes. Make yourself comfortable. Like a cup of coffee?"

Nan hadn't been able to eat all day. "No thanks."

Cautiously she sat on the edge of a couch and looked around. She had never been in a lawyer's office before, had no idea what one should look like. Here the furnishings were few but expensive, the rug on the wall an old Navaho, and in a bookcase stood a row of Kachinas that she recognized from her trip to the ranch.

She got up to take a closer look. Warrior Woman, Butterfly Woman, Crow Mother, Snow Maiden. They seemed old and familiar friends, a contact, however small, with Ben.

"I only collect the women." The voice came from behind her, and she turned to see a small, well-dressed woman with a pair of grey eyes that seemed to bore into her brain.

"Leona McGivern," the woman said, putting out her hand.

"Nan Fletcher. Why only women?"

"Because we're at the root of everything. Never mind the hoop dancers and the big show. These gals grow crops, bring rain, defend the home. That's what I want to make clear to my women clients. That they're important whether they know it or not." She walked over to a door. "Don't get me wrong. I'm not a man-hater. Far from it. Come in and sit down. I'll be just another minute."

Nan sat and forced herself to relax. For the first time in months she felt that she was no longer fighting on her own.

Leona sat down behind her desk. "Now," she said, focusing her grey eyes on Nan's face, "how can I help you?"

Where to begin? How to make her see without seeming the fool she knew she was? "I think . . . I think I want a divorce," she said.

"You think? You're not sure?"

In her mind Nan saw a door partially open. Beyond it, fields of yellow grass, the sky, a piercing blue, mountains like her own bones jutting out of earth, and Ben. Always Ben. Without hesitation, she pushed the door wide.

"I'm sure," she said. "I just don't know how."

"Tell me." Leona sounded more like a psychiatrist than a lawyer.

Nan looked down at her hands clasped in her lap, the white knuckles, the leaping of her pulse. "I've been married eighteen years," she said. "And it seems Jake's been screaming at me the whole time. And at our son Jamie. He's seventeen, and he doesn't know what it's like to have a real father."

Once she started, her words poured out. "I don't get any sleep. Maybe four hours a night because Jake gives me so much to do. And if I forget, I hear about it. Over and over. If I forget to clean the broiler after dinner, he wakes me at four in the morning and yells until I get up and do it, just to have some peace. If he finds water spots on a glass, it's the same thing. If the basement's not picked up. I know this sounds crazy, but please believe me. Please!" She looked at Leona and saw horror on the woman's face. "He even wakes Jamie and makes him go clean up things. Jamie's a nice kid. There's nothing bad in him, but Jake acts like he's a criminal, and I'm afraid for him. Afraid of what we're doing to him." She stopped, her breath coming so fast she was dizzy again.

"Take it easy," Leona said. "You have plenty of time."

Nan bit her lip. When the room stopped whirling, she went on. "Jake says I'm filthy. He says I'm too stupid to live without his help, that I'd have been an old maid if it wasn't for him. But none of those things are true. I had a life! I traded it in for him. He says all these bad things I do are because I don't love him. I don't. That's true. But he killed it. He killed it trying to make me into something I'm not. I don't do anything to hurt him. I keep trying. Just once, I'd like some praise for something. So I try harder, but it's never enough. All I'm doing is killing myself because I think someday I'll please him, and it'll get better. But it never does, and I can't live like that anymore. And . . ." She hesitated, not knowing if she should tell about Ben, even to this woman who seemed to be on her side. Was she to be trusted?

She studied Leona whose face gave nothing away. Then she decided to risk it. "I met somebody. He's kind and decent, and I love him. He says he loves me. All I want is a chance to be happy. To be normal. Jake says I'm crazy and he could have me locked up, but he's projecting. He's the one. I know it, but he won't listen. I was a writer before. I'd like to be one again if I'm good enough, but I'm not sure of that anymore. I'm not sure of anything because he's scared me so bad. I'm like a slave. A prisoner locked in my own house. And all I want is to be free." Exhausted, she sat back in her chair and waited.

Leona was silent a minute. Then she said, "You realize that this is abuse."

"Abuse?" Nan was startled.

"Of course. It's psychological abuse, but it's probably as common as physical abuse, just harder to prove. He's never hit you or your son has he?"

If he'd hit her, Nan knew she would have left him then and there. "No," she said. "Just words. Damnation. No visible marks."

"Except inside," Leona snapped, her eyes narrowing. "He's worn you down. Erased you. This is the kind of thing that's not talked about. Yet. But some people turn others into non-people, usually to fill some lack in themselves or to hide their own fears. It's a tragedy for both sides. How did you find me?"

"Wendy Moran. She's been my best friend for years. And then Ben made sure I talked to you. To find out my options. I mean, will I be penniless? Homeless? I'm afraid of everything, but I'll feel better once I know."

"What about this Ben?" Leona asked. "What does he do?"

"He's a rancher. I met him last spring, and it just happened. I wasn't looking for anybody. I thought it was too late for that, if I even thought at all."

"Has he discussed marriage?"

Nan shook her head. "No. And that . . . that scares me, too. How can I trust myself? Or him? I made a bad choice once, can I be trusted to make a better one? But maybe that's not important. What's important is getting me out before . . .

158

before I die. Ben's the one who urged me to see you. I . . . I was afraid."

"No need," Leona said. "It's a good thing you came." She scribbled on her legal pad. "How soon do you want to file?"

God, was she going to have to do this right away? She leaned across the desk. "I'm not ready. Can you understand? There are things I have to think about. How to tell Jake, or even if I tell him. I've been thinking of maybe just running away and taking Jamie. But I don't know where to go or if I'll have any money. I mean, it's not just me involved, and I'm trying to do all the thinking for everybody."

Leona stopped writing. "Don't take too long," she advised. "Like you said, it'll only get worse. But in this state we have equitable property distribution. That means that after eighteen years you are entitled to at least half of all assets. You won't be broke, and as soon as you file we can get you monthly support. Maybe not what you've been used to but enough to live on. How does that sound?"

"Better than I thought," Nan said with a crooked smile. "I guess Ben was right. It's good to know my options."

"Always." Leona smiled back. "Now, while you're thinking it over there are things I want you to do. Get your own postal box, your own bank account, your own credit cards. That's important. Without credit you'll be helpless until we reach some kind of agreement. Do you understand?"

Nan nodded. Her own credit card! Bank account! After all these years of scrimping she could get clothes for herself and Jamie! She could take control of a life she hadn't even known she had.

"And," Leona went on, "get a physical. Get your teeth and eyes and everything else checked and let his insurance pay. Keep yourself healthy."

"You make it sound easy."

"It's not. It's never easy. Not in cases like yours. He'll try to get you back. He'll try anything. Without you, he's lost control over his world, and that can be dangerous. Believe me, I've seen it more times than I've wanted to. He might, in an extreme case, turn violent."

Nan shook her head. "Not Jake."

"Don't say that." Leona's eyes looked like diamond drills, hard and grey. "It does happen. But don't worry too much. Just keep in touch with me. And try not to be scared. I know you are, but forget it. Do what you have to do to save yourself."

It sounded simple, but of course it wasn't. Except that now she knew things she hadn't thought about; now the door had opened onto freedom. Abruptly she reached into her purse. "I brought some bank statements and our last income tax forms," she said. "I thought you might need them."

"Good thinking. Let's copy them before you leave. You're already over the hump, you just haven't realized it." Leona grinned suddenly, and for a moment she looked mischievous, almost girlish, and Nan felt a vast weight lift from her shoulders.

"Maybe you're right," she said. "Thank you so much."

On her way out she paused in front of the bookcase and took a last look at Warrior Woman, bow in hand, arrow at the ready. "Someday I'll be you," she vowed, and went lightly down the steps to the street.

CHAPTER TWENTY-FIVE

Wendy opened the door, took one look at Nan, and pulled her inside. "What's the matter? You're white as a sheet."

Nan leaned against her for a moment, wanting nothing more than to collapse. "I went to the lawyer."

"Come on in and tell me." Wendy had a paint brush stuck in her hair above her ear, and her face and striped jersey were spattered with color.

Even in her daze, Nan appreciated the contrast between them and laughed. "I may look like a sheet, but you look like a perennial border," she said.

Wendy swiped at her face, leaving a smear of green. "I've been working. I sold two paintings the other day. To the bank."

Nan was awed. "Let me touch you. You're the only painter I know who's ever sold anything. How much?"

"Six thousand." Wendy's eyes sparkled. "You'll make money, too, once you get rid of asshole and get a chance to really work. What did Leona say?"

"That I've been abused. Isn't it funny, I always thought abuse meant physical violence, but now I'm beginning to see that words can be just as bad. Mind rape can be as devastating as the other kind."

Half in jest, Wendy said, "I'd kill for a good rape. There isn't a man in town who knows anything, even how to kiss.

You're lucky you found one, because I can't."

In spite of herself, Nan chuckled. Being with Wendy always seemed to simplify matters. "Trouble?" she asked.

Wendy rolled her eyes. "I wish! I went out with Joe Deal the other night—remember him? The gallery owner? Well, when we got back we sat on the couch and I thought we'd neck a little and see what else happened. Then he kissed me." She stopped and rubbed her cheek, leaving another paint smear.

"And. . . ." Nan prompted.

"And it was like kissing a pickle. Like kissing Mikey, for God's sake! He had his lips so tight shut I'd have needed a crowbar to pry them open. So I said, 'You have to open your mouth when you kiss, Joe,' and showed him what I meant." She waved her hands in the air as if trying to erase the memory. "He's forty five years old and kisses like my maiden aunt. And after I said that, he got up and left. Obviously, he didn't want to learn. So here I am. Alone, as usual. Painting my heart out, because that's all there is to do."

"So life after divorce isn't exactly a picnic?"

"Well." Wendy took a bottle of wine out of the refrigerator and poured two glasses. "Well, at least there's nobody around telling me anymore. At least my mind's my own. Oh," she stopped, grinning. "Then there's Howard."

"Who's he?"

"He lives next door. Very much married, but he obviously doesn't think so. He's been coming over, bringing me presents. This wine, for example." She sipped at it. "Good, too. Anyhow, the other day he came in. I was unloading the dishwasher, and he unzips his pants and pulls out little precious and puts it right in my hand."

"He what?"

"You heard me. He sticks his hickey in my hand and looks

at me like he's a cocker spaniel. I said, 'Put it away, Howard. That doesn't impress me.' "

"What'd he say?"

"Nothing. He just stood there with those big brown eyes glued to my face. So I told him that wasn't the way a seduction was supposed to be. I said maybe we should go upstairs and lie on the bed and kiss a little. Have a little foreplay. God help us, he looked like he'd never heard the word! And then I said that just exposing himself, putting his tool in my hand wasn't a real turn-on. He left, too." She sighed and took another sip of wine.

Nan choked with laugher. Wendy's love life had always been so wild compared with her own. "Good riddance," she said. "Who needs it?"

"I do. I'd like a man. I'd like some sex. A good fuck. I've been cheated, and all I get is these guys who think their equipment is their gift to women."

"Like we have penis envy."

"Freud sucked," Wendy said. "They all suck. Did you file, or what?"

Her abrupt change of subject caught Nan unaware. "File? Oh. No. Not yet. I have to figure out how to do it. To tell him."

"Just don't wait 'til you're too old to get a life. If there is such a thing," she added with a hint of sarcasm. "You have that lovely man out there, but he might not wait forever."

"Just what I needed to hear," Nan said, fighting down the panic that was never far from the surface.

"You do." Wendy looked fierce. "Because no matter what, you have to get out. Just do it. Then worry."

Wendy's advice was still ringing in her ears when Jake, at dinner, said, "I've been thinking about our vacation."

Nan's stomach turned over. She put down her fork. Vacations to Jake meant sex, frequent sorties to the bedroom, quickies whenever he could manage them that usually left her unsatisfied and feeling as if she'd been used.

When she didn't answer, he went on. "Since you liked that ranch so much, I thought we'd all go back. Maybe in August. You think they have room?"

She closed her eyes and fought for control. Ben. And Jake. And herself in the middle trying not to betray what she felt. The image was horrid. Her mouth was dry, as if it were stuffed with cardboard.

"I . . ." she began, then stopped, the desire to see Ben again overwhelming her judgement.

"Why don't you call up and see?" Jake said, not noticing her confusion.

"Now?" She opened her eyes and looked down at her plate.

"Why not? That way at least we'll know where we are. Can make our plans."

It was, she realized, a chance to call Ben, an excuse she needn't lie about when Jake went over the phone bills. She pushed back her chair, hoping her legs would hold her up. "All right," she said, and went quickly down the hall to the kitchen phone.

"It's me," she said when he answered.

"What's wrong? Are you all right?" She sounded so unlike herself, so unsure.

She laughed, a wisp of sound, and pictured him in his study—the book-lined walls, the colorful Navaho rugs and baskets. "I'm fine. Jake asked me to call."

"What in hell for?"

"To find out if you've got room for us in August."

As she had, he imagined it. Nan with her husband, the

man he detested without ever having met, the monster who had the woman he loved thoroughly beaten down.

"Good Lord," he said finally. "Can you handle it?"

"I don't know. I guess. It's a chance to see you again. Can *you* handle it?"

He made an instant decision. Let her see the two of them side by side. Let her judge and compare. "Yes," he said. "I sure can. Though I've never been in a situation like it."

"Me, neither." She laughed again. "I went to the lawyer today."

"What'd she say?"

"Lots. That I won't be desperate for money, for one thing. And that I'm a victim. I've been abused. And never knew it."

"And now you do."

"Well . . . well, I'm still kind of shocked. I never thought of it like that. I guess I was too much the victim to even realize what was happening."

How many women were there like her? he wondered. How many of them had he met, those guests who came on to him for some kind of reassurance, some semblance of love, caught in marriages without caring, trapped as he had been?

He said, "We'll manage all right. It's a chance to be together. How's the kid?"

"Fine. So far. I know he's itching to get back out there."

"No chance you'll leave Jake before then?"

She knew he'd ask that, knew his need as well as she knew her own. "I'm waiting for something. The right time. The . . ." she stopped, searching for the word that would explain. "The catalyst. I can't explain more. I only know what I have to do. Don't be angry."

He wasn't. Some part of him, the part that understood her deepest fears and hungers, knew she had to make her own way. She was calling the shots. He had to let her.

CHAPTER TWENTY-SIX

An accident on the freeway had slowed traffic to a crawl, and by the time he drove up to the airport Ben was cursing under his breath. Letters, hurried phone calls helped fill the emptiness she'd left in her wake, but he needed to see her again, ride beside her and hear her laughter ring out, even if she was accompanied by her husband.

That thought sobered him. He'd been brought up to accept the permanence of marriage, his own and everyone else's, yet now he was faced with a dilemma he'd never imagined. In the language of the Ten Commandments, he coveted another man's wife, he was a sinner, and worse, he was urging her to sin along with him. But, he didn't feel guilty at all and that was the real problem.

The sight of Nan, in jeans and boots and thinner than he remembered, wiped his thoughts out of his mind. She was here, and she was worried, probably wondering if something had happened. He resisted tooting the horn as he caught sight of Jake in a western hat that dwarfed him. It had to be Jake, he thought. No one else could possibly look like that, an angry little insect pacing back and forth around a pile of luggage— four steps and turn, four steps and turn—the mechanical motions of a wind-up toy.

"Good Christ!" he said, then repeated himself. "Good Christ!" Any doubts about the wisdom of loving Nan disap-

166

peared as he watched the little group, Nan and Jamie to one side, Jake center-stage, irritation evident in every gesture.

He'd pictured him in his imagination as a tweedy, professorial type, tall, probably well-mannered, but this! He fought down his emotion as he pulled up alongside and got out.

"Sorry I'm late," he said, looking at Nan and resisting the imperceptible movement of her body toward him with difficulty. "There was an accident."

"Are you all right?" Even behind sunglasses, her eyes were worried.

"Right as rain. It's good to see you." He forced himself to turn to Jake, hand extended. "Ben Fuller," he said. "Glad you could make it," and wondered if he sounded as phony as he felt.

"We were wondering what happened." Jake made it sound like an accusation, even as he put out his own hand.

"A truck and trailer overturned," Ben said. "Folded up like an accordion." That ought to give the critter something to think about! Then he turned to Jamie whose face gave nothing away. "Hi, pal. You ready to ride?"

"I guess."

It was like talking to a ghost and not the kid he'd known. No need to ask why. The reason was standing at his elbow issuing orders.

"Let's get going. I'd like to get there before dark. Jamie, give Mr. Fuller a hand with these bags."

"Ben," Ben said.

"What?" Jake looked up startled.

"The name's just Ben. None of this 'mister' stuff."

Jake smiled. "Western style, I guess."

"We call it being friendly." He lifted the suitcases into the back of the van and risked a glance at Nan who seemed to be fighting laughter. Suddenly he wanted to roar and beat his chest, to gather her up and run, where didn't matter just so long as he could hold her in his arms, keep her safe, love her to distraction.

"Easy, old son," he said to himself. "Your day's coming." Then he turned to find his irritation made worse by the sight of Jake in the front seat. Just as well, he decided. This way he could look at her in the mirror, feast his eyes, and no one the wiser.

He checked. She had taken off her sunglasses and was watching him with a passion that burned him like a brand and reminded him that his new jeans were too tight.

"Easy," he cautioned himself again, then forced his eyes away and headed for home.

Nan sat back and let the men's voices flow around her, let the sweep of valley and mountain move past in a blur. Nothing had changed—not Ben, not the way she felt. She loved him, not by design or choice but simply because she had found him, recognized him in a twist of fate.

She closed her eyes. In the front seat Jake's voice rose and fell as he talked about the history of the country they were moving through, listing dates, giving the names of those infamous Apaches whose spirits still resonated after more than a hundred years. She shouldn't have agreed to come. Having to listen to him was mortifying for her and, unwittingly, for Jake. He was making fools of all of them, Ben included.

Jamie nudged her. "Why's he talking so much? Why's he have that phony accent?"

She grimaced, hoping Ben wouldn't notice but knowing that he would. "Because he thinks he's being western. He wants to impress Ben."

"Weird!"

"Shhh," she cautioned.

Jamie cocked one eyebrow. "Geez. Ben'll think we're all like that."

"No he won't. He knows better."

Jamie squirmed. "Can't you make him stop?"

She wanted to stay inside the cocoon she'd spun, but she leaned forward. "How's Monarch?" she asked.

Ben's eyes glinted wickedly as they met hers. "He's weaned, halter broke, used to being fussed over. And growing like a weed. You'll love him."

"I already do. I'm his step-mamma. I remember the night he was born."

Ben cleared his throat. "Yes," he said. "So do I. That was quite a night."

"What happened? Who's Monarch?" Diverted from his own topic, Jake demanded to be included.

"The colt I saw being born," Nan said. "I told you."

"Oh. That." By his tone he indicated his lack of interest, and Nan wanted to throttle him.

For a moment she studied him as if he were a stranger, a man she didn't know, a man who was making his unwanted presence felt by everyone, and she realized with shock that not once had he ever touched her deeply, never would; that rather than bringing them together, marriage had increased the distance between them until, looking at him now was like peering the wrong way through a telescope, seeing him small, far away, unable to reach her at all.

She moved her hand so that she was touching Ben's shoulder and felt the swift response of his body. "How's Lupe?" she asked. "I missed her."

"She missed you, too. Right now she's probably cooking up a storm in your honor. And I practically had to hog-tie Bay to keep him from coming along when he had chores to do," Ben said to Jamie, realizing that the kid was being ignored.

To his horror, Jamie glanced at Jake before he answered, as if he were asking permission to speak.

He'd heard the term "dysfunctional family" without really understanding the meaning. Now he began to see and didn't like what he saw one bit. They were all tied in a knot, unable to extricate themselves, and Nan, his Nan whom he loved with a love greater than anything he'd ever felt, was in the middle and helpless.

Bay, Lupe and Wish came out to meet them, and Nan went into Lupe's arms as she hadn't been able to go into Ben's.

"You came back," Lupe said.

"I couldn't stay away."

"And getting skinnier than before." Lupe patted her cheek, then muttered, "So that's him."

At that Nan turned and caught Jake watching the reunion with an expression she could only describe as wistful, as if he, too, wished to be welcomed with open arms.

Guiltily, still acting the good wife as she had always done, she beckoned to him. "Come meet Lupe. She's the best cook and the wisest woman in the world."

He stepped forward obediently, smiling his best smile, and Nan took the opportunity to stand beside Ben.

"I made it," she said, looking up at the face she loved.

He nodded. "You did at that, but be careful. Right now you're looking at me like I'm dessert, and he isn't blind."

She was walking a tight rope and would be for the coming weeks, always on guard. Why had she agreed to this torture? She hadn't slept with Ben, but she might as well have. Loving him to the exclusion of all others amounted to the same thing. She sighed.

"Where are we staying?"

"As far away from me as possible. Come on. I'll take you over."

They hadn't gone far when Jake joined them. "Where's Jamie?" he demanded. "Just because it's vacation doesn't mean he can run off."

"Relax. Loosen up, pardner." Ben sounded amused. "That's what vacations are about."

"Boys that age need discipline. You can't just let them run wild," Jake retorted.

Ben dropped the subject. "Here we are." He opened the door and reached for the light, illuminating a living room and fireplace. Two doors led to the bedrooms, and Nan, stepping into the largest, saw the twin beds and allowed herself a grim smile, knowing from experience what would happen.

Behind her Jake was saying, "This is really nice. Now I know why Nan couldn't stop talking about the place. It's not at all what I expected."

"Thanks." Ben preceded him into the room and deposited a suitcase on the luggage rack.

"Oh." Jake surveyed the room, then, smiling said, "You wouldn't mind if we push these beds together, would you? Like you said, this is vacation. And this poor girl works hard."

He seemed unaware of what he was saying, Nan thought. But she'd heard it all before. How hard she worked, and how decent it was of Jake to give her a rest. She turned away and heard Ben say, "In that case maybe she'd like a room up at the house."

Her laughter erupted and broke the tension. Both men laughed with her, although Ben looked stricken, his fists balled in his jacket pockets.

"So what's the schedule?" Jake wanted to know. "When do we get to ride?"

"First thing in the morning," Ben said, making a mental

note to give him the worst of the string. "And dinner's at six. Nan knows. We wanted to keep her last time. We all fell in love with her."

She shot him a warning look which he ignored.

"If you need anything, just yell. Drinks are on the terrace before dinner."

"Nice guy," Jake said when he was gone. "A real Western type."

Nan nodded, uncomfortable but not knowing what to do.

"Let's unpack and get these beds pushed together."

She made up her mind in an instant. "Later. I want to go see Monarch."

"Can't it wait?"

"No," she said firmly, pushing out her chin. "I'm going now," and was out the door following Ben's trail.

"Don't come near me," he said, his jaws clenched. "Don't even look at me."

"Why?"

"Because he's probably watching us through the window, that's why. And because if you so much as touch me, I'll grab you and kiss you 'til you faint. Pushing the beds together! You and that self-serving, pompous little prick! You should have left him years ago."

"Now you see."

He turned on her, his hands still buried in his pockets. "What I don't see is why you're taking so long. Why you're stringing me. What do you want, the best of both worlds? Him and your cushy life and me to hold your hand when you feel bad? If that's true, you can forget it."

His words came at her like bullets, each one more painful than the last, and she hunched her shoulders trying to shield herself. "No," she agonized. "That's not the way it is at all. You *don't* see, do you? You don't understand."

"Understand what? That you prefer life with that . . . that wind-up toy? That you're scared of him? Don't tell me that because I won't believe you. Poke him, and he'd collapse like a balloon. Now do me a favor and stay away from me, or you'll find yourself in real trouble."

He left her standing in the path trembling. This was what came of loving! This bitter recrimination, this sense of belonging nowhere. She drew a ragged breath. She was here alone, with no place to go, no one to talk to. If she went back to the room, Jake would see her tears, and she certainly wasn't about to run after Ben.

She wanted to hide, to lick her wounds and regain some semblance of self. Without thinking she went to the corral where Monarch stood, head high, nostrils flaring, watching her with curious eyes.

"Oh, baby," she whispered when he approached and sniffed at her hand. "Oh, baby, it's all such a mess."

Then she put her head down on her arms and wept.

Ben had known the moment he opened his mouth that he shouldn't, but the shock of seeing her again and meeting Jake had overwhelmed him. Already he despised the little man, his arrogance, his assumption that he was better than all the rest. How could she stay with such a person?

He went in the back way, slamming the door, and was met by a furious Lupe.

"What did you do?" she demanded, hands on her hips. "What did you say to her? Look!" She dragged him to the window through which they could see Nan, her head bowed.

"This is how you were taught? To make women cry? To make *this* woman cry? I am shamed for you."

"I . . . I . . . it was *him!*" Ben got out, feeling the child as he always did when faced with a scolding from her. "He made me lose my temper! But I wouldn't hurt her for anything."

"It wasn't him. It was you. He's bad enough. He make my heart feel like a stone, but how you think she feel now, eh?"

"Rotten," Ben said. "Like me."

She pushed him toward the door. "Go back. Tell her your tongue ran away from you like a crazy horse. Tell her you are only a man, and men are foolish. And maybe she forgive you if you're lucky. If not," she spread her hands, "then you will have much time to regret your foolishness."

She was right. As usual. Gathering his courage, he went back out through the garden.

CHAPTER TWENTY-SEVEN

"Nan."

She had heard him coming and steeled herself against being hurt again. "Go away."

He looked down at the white nape of her neck, at her small shoulders shaken with sobbing. He had done this to her, taken her happiness then left her alone. He said, "I didn't mean it."

But he had, she was sure. To him, she was like all the rest. What she felt meant nothing. For whatever purpose, he had used her, then tossed her aside.

"Please," she said, her face still buried in her arms, "just go."

"I can't." He reached out and put his hands on her shoulders, felt their tension under his fingers. "I shot off my mouth because I couldn't stand seeing you with him. I thought I knew you, but around him you're somebody else, and I'd like to kill him for doing that. To you *and* to Jamie. Hell, the kid's like a shadow! He doesn't even open his mouth without permission. It isn't right, but there's not much I can do. It's your business. That's what made me angry. To have to stand around and watch you being erased."

"I told you," she whispered. "I thought you'd understand."

"I'm trying. But it's damned hard. If it was me, I'd just

walk out. That's the way I am."

"I'm not you," she said. "Now it's all ruined, and I had a surprise for you."

"Tell me."

She shook her head, then straightened and faced him, eyes filled with tears. "It doesn't matter now."

Was he going to lose her after all, have her slip away like a woman seen in a dream? He tightened his grip. "It's only ruined if you let it," he said fiercely, knowing he'd have to humble himself, and knowing that humility wasn't his strong suit. He had a choice—to stay or to walk away and spend the rest of his life regretting his own pride. Faced with the emptiness of years, he made up his mind.

"I took it out on you," he said, "and I shouldn't have. I've been here counting the days 'til you came, and then the first thing I saw was *him* pacing around like some toy soldier while you stood there looking so damn lonely, so beautiful. All I wanted was you, but you were forbidden. And it got so bad I turned on you, made you feel like hell, and I'm sorry. That's all I can say except forgive me. It won't happen again."

She had been watching his face as he spoke, reading his struggle. Now she reached up and touched his cheek, laid her palm against it. He was a proud man, and his speech had cost him. Now the choice was hers—to forgive or to pull away—hardly a choice at all as she visualized the rest of her life.

"It's all right," she said with a hint of a smile. "Only let's never fight again. I don't think I could survive another one."

He turned his head and kissed her hand, then, with a swiftness that caught her by surprise, kissed her mouth with hard almost frantic lips. He was branding her, she thought, giving herself up to him without caution, stamping her with his mark, burning through her flesh to her soul.

"Nan! Nan! Where are you?" Jake's voice shattered the moment.

Abruptly Ben let her go, cursing himself, Jake, his need for this woman whose hunger equaled his own. "Here." He pulled a bandanna from his pocket. "Wipe your face. Then git!" And was amazed at her transformation as, before his eyes, the light went out of her and the woman he knew and loved disappeared.

"Coming!" she called in answer, then moved slowly away around the corner of the barn.

He heard Jake, questioning, petulant. "Where were you? You shouldn't have left me like that. You shouldn't be running around in a strange place by yourself."

Not wanting to hear more, he walked swiftly through the garden back to the house.

CHAPTER TWENTY-EIGHT

A week passed without incident. Ben was beginning to think he'd imagined that first day, as Jake fit quietly into the routine and handled his horse with competence. Maybe he'd misjudged the guy, he thought. Maybe Nan had been exaggerating to suit her purpose. With a frown, recalling her distress, he dismissed that idea. Besides, there was Jamie's attitude. He hadn't wanted to take a hike after lunch with his father, in fact he'd looked terrified when the two set off for the mountains.

Ben had almost intervened, but realized it wasn't any of his business and that he could spend the afternoon alone with Nan.

Father and son had barely hit the trail when he said to her, "Come on. There's something I want you to see."

"What?" Her face was shining.

"A surprise. And speaking of that, you said you had one for me."

She nodded. "It's a secret. At least, you're the only one I'm going to tell. Remember that story I wrote about the white peonies?"

"Sure do."

Her smile swept her face. "Well, I sold it. To a magazine for twelve hundred dollars. I pulled out all the stops, and wrote what I felt, and it worked. And I put the money into my new bank account that nobody knows about."

"You put your heart into it," he said, as proud of her accomplishment as if he'd written the story himself. "I felt it when I read the thing. Damn, I'm proud of you." He pulled her close and kissed her. She tasted sweet like raspberries or the scent of lemon blossoms.

Reluctantly he stepped away, looking down at her, his heart in his eyes. "Come on. We'll take the truck to my surprise. It's quicker."

"Where are we going?"

"You'll see."

He had been working steadily on the old house. The tile floor was laid, the new roof was finished, a tin roof because to him the sound of rain on a tin roof was the sweetest music in the world.

The winding dirt road was one Nan had never been on, but as she looked out the window the terrain seemed vaguely familiar—the clumps of oak rising out of tall grass and red earth, the hill that sloped gently upward. And then, with a sickening lurch of her stomach, she recognized the landscape of her dream, the path she had taken as she ran, attempting escape.

She glanced at Ben, his hawk face, the black hair falling over his forehead, and heard again the words of her pursuer. "Now I've found you and I'll be with you the rest of your life."

Of course it had been Ben. She'd felt so complete with the stranger, the way she felt now, loved, secure in herself and in him. He accepted her for what she was, and she did likewise, and each filled the emptiness of the other so that together they became a one-ness.

As a child she had simply been passed from one home to another, had gone from mother to husband and meekly accepted what followed. Now she was struggling for womanhood, giving birth to herself, assuming responsibility for her own life, and the birth was hard, the labor agonizing.

So much to learn! So many thoughts to follow to conclusion before she took the final leap off the cliff and into his arms.

"Almost there." He reached out and laid his hand on her thigh, and she responded to his touch with a warmth that spread through her body like sunlight.

Should she tell him? Speak her dream or keep it for another time? Not yet, she decided. She'd keep the mystery to herself until she had sorted out the roadblocks that lay in her path. Until she had, in actuality, lost the child and could come to him as a woman, strong enough to carry her own burdens.

Ben pulled up in the clearing and watched her as she studied the house—its blue-painted window frames and door, the yellow rose, pruned and blooming on a trellis alongside.

To her it seemed a magic house, a fairy dwelling tucked away among the trees with the creek chuckling somewhere in the distance. She got out of the truck and opened her arms as if to take it in.

"Whose is it?" she whispered.

"Mine. Yours if you want it."

"Mine?" The word came out on a breath.

"I kept seeing you here. I'd be working and it was like you were in the room with me writing, thinking, staring out like you do." He took her hand. "Come on."

Inside she heard the silence like a welcome, saw the fireplace with logs already laid, two chairs beside it. It was a room waiting to be brought to life, lived in, worked in, filled with love.

"Whose is it really?" she asked, afraid to break the spell.

"The old homestead. I fixed it up. And like I said, it's yours any time you want."

A place of her own. She'd never had that, never owned anything at all. She wrote and dreamed and read at her kitchen table, that small territory bounded by sink, stove, the tools that defined her to others if not to herself.

Speechless, she walked to the window that overlooked the creek. A pair of jays took noisy flight as she pushed it open, and from back in the hills thunder rumbled.

"Is it going to rain?"

"Probably. It's the season for it. Wait'll you hear it on the roof."

She turned to face him. By contrast with the sunlight, the room seemed dark. "Are you serious about this?" she asked.

"About what?"

"This place. Being mine."

He nodded. "I thought you could write here. Hide out and dream your dreams."

She put her hands out again as if she were embracing the room, a gesture that touched him as deeply as the joy in her eyes.

"Nobody ever. . . ." her voice broke. "How can I thank you?"

"None needed." The look on her face was enough.

"Oh yes," she said. "Oh yes, it's needed," and threw her arms around him. "Hold me. Hold me and don't let me go."

He wished he didn't have to. She fit so easily into his embrace, her head resting on his shoulder. Someday she'd be here to stay, no matter what he had to do. Someday.

Overhead, the thunder growled, and through the open window came the unforgettable scent of rain, a sweetness like old wood smoke threaded by dried grasses.

"Listen," he said, as the shower began.

Together they heard the drumming on the roof, and Nan, secure in his arms, closed her eyes and absorbed the moment—the peace, the tenderness, the sound and haunting fragrance of a summer storm.

They were at dinner when it happened. Without warning, and perhaps because instinctively he feared Nan's happiness, Jake put down his fork and spoke to Jamie across the table.

"Do you have on an undershirt?"

Nan's heart thumped in her breast. *Not here,* she wanted to shout, knowing from past scenes what would happen. *Not now!*

Jamie laid down his own fork and issued a challenge. "No!"

"How many times do I have to tell you that a gentleman always wears an undershirt? Answer me. No son of mine comes to the table without one. Just because we're not home doesn't mean you can get away with something, understand? You're as bad as your mother. You never listen, never do what you're told. Now go back to the room and get one. And wash up. I bet you forgot. Have you washed your neck since we got back? Let me see your fingernails."

Jamie, his face scarlet, bolted from the room, and Nan rose to follow.

"Sit down!" Jake's voice was shrill. "He's old enough to understand what he's done and not be babied. He should know better than to embarrass me in front of others."

"Embarrass *you?*" Nan got out. "What about him?" She was conscious of the fact that everybody was staring, shocked into silence. This was her punishment for her perfect day, for the happiness that had been bubbling inside her. She left running, found Jamie in his room throwing things.

"Baby," she said and reached for him.

"I'm not your baby!" He tossed a boot against the wall. "I'm not his son. I hate him!"

"He didn't mean . . ."

He turned on her, rage and humiliation scarring his face. "Bullshit! Bullshit, Mom! He did mean it. And in front of my friends. In front of Ben!" He pushed past her and ran out, slamming the door.

Through her tears, she surveyed the wreck of his room. He'd torn the covers off the bed, heaved the mattress on the floor. Clothes lay everywhere, as they'd fallen. She was trembling too badly to pick anything up. *He didn't mean it.* But of course he had. Somehow he'd felt his control lessening and had flaunted his dominance without consideration for anyone but himself.

She went out. The last colors of sunset stained the sky, and she realized she'd not had the time to look at anything since they'd arrived. Being with Jake blotted out all thought, any semblance of the person she was. And Jamie? Where was he?

Suddenly frightened, she ran down the path toward the barn. "Jamie?" she called and heard the word swallowed up in shadow.

"Jamie?"

Nothing stirred. No answer came. Where had he gone?

Ben came out the back, saw her, and came toward her. "That was quite a scene," he said, anger rasping in his throat.

"He's gone." She looked up at him. "He ran off."

"Do you blame him?"

She shook her head, her own humiliation making her mute.

"That son of a bitch is never coming here again no matter what," he said. "He'll destroy both of you, if he hasn't already. The kid is a time bomb waiting to go off, as I guess you know."

She was trembling so violently, she could hardly stand, and he put a hand on her arm. "Go on in the kitchen," he said more gently. "Lupe's there. I'll find Jamie. Don't worry."

"I can't help it! I failed him like I always do."

In the dark she looked fragile, an aspen leaf tossed in the wind. "I'll find him," he repeated. "If it takes all night. Go on now."

Obediently she left, stumbling once, and made her way to the kitchen. Lupe opened the door and took her into her arms without a word.

She was a child again, safe, protected, wrapped in loving arms. But no! She had to lose the child. Slowly she pushed herself away and walked toward the living room where Jake was pacing the floor. She stood watching him a minute, fighting down terror and rage. Then she said, "How could you? How could you have shamed your own son?"

His head snapped up. "Don't you talk to me like that. I'm not the one who lets him go around like some street kid."

It was uncanny how he could turn the blame! Once, she'd have cringed. Now she advanced toward him. "That's hardly the point," she said. "The point is you embarrassed your son in public. The point is, he's run away because of you. The point is, you don't give a shit about anybody but yourself."

"And none of this would have happened if you'd brought him up right."

She laughed, mockingly. "It's not me, it's you. We're a family. We're supposed to care for each other not be doing some crazy one-upmanship all the time, and in front of other people. I don't give a shit about blame right now. Our son is *gone*. He's run away. Can you get that through your head?"

Jake's eyes bulged behind his glasses, and his breath came fast. "Don't tell me I'm crazy," he muttered. "Don't you dare!"

Back to that, she thought, but this time she wasn't cowed. "If the shoe fits," she snapped.

He came toward her, and for the first time she was frightened of him—of the scarcely restrained violence in his movements. She moved behind a chair. "We should be out looking for him instead of fighting," she said. "Ben's already gone."

"Ben!" he snarled. "Everybody's cowboy hero!"

Suddenly she understood. He was jealous. And Leona had been right. Their marriage was built on the struggle for power. When Jake lost control over her, over Jamie, he lost himself, too, became a three year old in a temper tantrum, and dangerous because he was an adult and capable of inflicting damage.

She chose her next words carefully. "Let's just go out and look around, okay?"

"He's in the kitchen with Lupe." Ben walked in dwarfing Jake and barely containing his anger. He had to be civil when all he wanted was to deck the son of a bitch and see him squirm.

"Is he all right?" Nan moved toward him.

"Physically, yes." He gave them both a hard look. "He was on the road to town. I had a hell of a time getting him to come back. I suggest you leave him here for tonight. Let him wind down a bit. Then talk to him rationally, if you can."

"That's not necessary," Jake said.

Ben put his fists in his pockets. Christ! It was getting to be a habit when he was around Jake. "I think it is." He nodded to Nan and left, his boot heels striking the floor with force.

"What the hell!" Jake started after him.

Nan, visualizing the two men in a power battle, said quickly, "Leave him here. It's all right. I'm going to bed."

"Don't go to sleep."

Horrified, she stopped. He meant it! He wanted her! She swallowed the bile that rose in her throat, then saw, with a clarity that startled, that it wasn't sex that he wanted but the reinstatement of his command over her. He wanted to hold her down, thrust himself into her privacy, wipe out her thoughts.

"Not tonight." Her words came out like stones. "If you come near me tonight, you'll have to rape me, and I'll scream."

"Nan . . ." He stretched out a hand, suddenly pleading, his face wiped free of anger.

"You heard me."

He came after her. In the room he watched as she pushed the beds apart. "You can't do that!" he said, sounding frightened. "We're married."

"If that's what you want to call it." She went into the bathroom and closed the door.

"But I love you," he called, and stumbled back as she opened it.

"You wouldn't know love if it jumped up and bit you," she snapped, her face inches from his. Then she slammed the door again and locked it.

She heard him pacing, heard the creak as, finally, he sat down, took off his boots and tossed them on the floor. As she had done so often, she wished he'd die, keel over from a heart attack and vanish from her life.

In the mirror, her face seemed that of a stranger, hard, unforgiving, her jaw set, her eyes dark and as unfathomable as Lupe's. Jake wasn't about to die. The ball was in her court, and whatever happened was up to her.

He was kissing her ear. His hand was on her breast, and he was aroused.

Nan stiffened, tried to move away, but he held her tightly, his fingers turned to steel.

"You're hurting me," she said through clenched teeth.

"Stop fighting. Relax." He blew into her ear. "Come on, Nan, you know you want it. Don't act like this. It's not right. I'm your husband."

"And what am I?" she shot back. "Your concubine?"

He squeezed her breast again, hard, and she stifled a cry. It was a nightmare. Soon she'd wake up and the mockingbird would be singing, the sun burning away darkness. She'd be alone, curled around herself like an unborn child.

"Don't play games with me." She heard desperation in his voice, and the beginning of anger. "I need you."

And if she didn't give in, he'd keep at her until she did. He'd call her a bad woman who didn't love him, and her guilt at hearing the truth would be her undoing. If she didn't give in, he'd turn the week into hell, making more irrational scenes, lashing out at all of them, even Ben, and she'd be in the middle tearing herself apart. Like a spoiled, brutal child, he wanted her for himself.

Swiftly she turned to him, her eyes tight shut. "Okay," she said and lay rigid, waiting.

"Touch me." It was a command. "Act like you want me." He searched for her hand, found it, brought it to himself.

What she wanted was for him to die, or to die herself. If he cut out her heart it would be no worse than the shame of this act, this forced groping that denied her will, eradicated her soul.

"Harder!" It was another order.

She pressed her lips together, blotted out consciousness. Soon it would be over. Soon.

He moved then, pushed into her, and found quick release, while she lay turned to stone.

187

"Did you?" he wanted to know, smiling now, sure of himself.

She moved her head, a gesture he took as assent.

"That's my girl." He got up then, went to the shower to remove all traces of his passion.

She lay trembling, knowing that she would never feel clean again.

CHAPTER TWENTY-NINE

Somehow they got through the last days at the ranch. Somehow she was able to tear herself away from the man she loved without showing a hint of her descent into the bleakness of hell. Somehow, she, Jake, and Jamie went on never referring to what had happened, hardly speaking at all.

Jamie went back to school for his senior year. Jake returned to his usual schedule, often not getting up until midafternoon. And Nan, once again in her kitchen, wrote obsessively, finishing one story and beginning another, defining herself by a growing body of work that she sent out with the feeling that she was tossing a note in a bottle into an infinite sea. Would someone find her message and respond?

Her pile of rejections grew. Her sales were few but enough to give impetus to her desire. And her bank account was growing. Grimly she wrote on, recreating her world.

Without warning, stress took its toll. She was in bed watching scarlet flowers float on the walls. Poppies, peonies, zinnias with shaggy petals, hundreds of them swayed, danced, faded then returned, reaching toward the ceiling.

They hurt her eyes, pounded in her head. She was hot, then cold, so cold she couldn't move. She was dying, the marrow of her bones turning to ice.

Ben. She wanted Ben with a ferocity that stabbed with each breath, but he wasn't there. He was at the other end of a telephone wire and she couldn't move to reach the phone.

She wanted. Delirious, she clung to herself, willing the flowers away, willing Ben's voice, wanting to weep, but no tears came. They had been burned away. What was left was pain. She was a cinder, and it was cold without the fire. So cold.

"Ben! Ben!"

"Nan!"

Jake stood beside the bed looking down at her. "Get up," he said. "We'll have dinner. I'll make a fire, and you'll feel better."

Fire. Ice. She would never feel better. She wanted to tell him, but her throat hurt, and her chest, wrapped in bands of steel. "Can't," she whispered. "Can't get up."

He put a hand on her shoulder and shook her, shattering the flowers into dazzling fragments. "Come on. You'll feel better."

Better than what?

He wanted his dinner. She knew it. The fire was a trick like his concern. She wished him away, closed her eyes, wrapped her arms around the chill. Beside her, his voice buzzed like a fly trapped in a bottle.

"No!" She turned her face to the pillow. "No!"

"Yes!"

He'd never stop, never leave her. His will was stronger than she. Buzz. Buzz. Assassin fly, stinging wasp, following her down the stairs and into the kitchen.

Her hands moved. She could see them from far away and wanted to laugh, but what came out of her was a whimper, quickly stifled. Slowly she shuffled to the table carrying soup, concentrating on not spilling it. One step, then another.

Jake was crouched by the fire lighting a match, and she wanted to push him in, to see him turn to smoke. At least the flowers had vanished. Now what she saw was flame, hot streaks of orange flickering over the walls. Hell, that was it! She had descended into the pit and would spend eternity here in this room with this man who wanted his dinner. Every day. Every night. That was her punishment for being a fool and a coward. For believing in fairy tales. She was the Snow Queen with an icicle in her heart, a cold blade pinning her to her chair forever.

"No," she said again, feebly, the small protest drifting away like her strength.

"I'm going back to bed."

Jake pushed back his chair. She saw his mouth move. Buzz. Buzz. She had to concentrate, lean forward to hear what he was saying.

"Before you go. . . . before you go . . . do you think you could make me a decent cup of coffee for a change?"

He wanted. She heard. Felt the fire, blue flame, bitter as salt. It burned, cleansed, wiped out her pain and replaced it with another.

She could be bleeding to death, and he would ask for one last service. She was nothing and would never be. She was a bundle of sticks, a pair of hands, the hole into which he thrust himself for release.

She held to the back of the chair and saw him, the fire reflected in his glasses, his face a blur. "Go fuck yourself," she said.

His mouth opened, his tongue flickered. Snake. He was a snake not a fly. He was enemy. "What?"

"You heard me." She turned and walked to the stairs that seemed to move like an escalator. Dizzy, she crawled up them, wounded, sicker at heart than she had ever been, lost in a forest of evil where red flowers reached for her and Ben was a wraith from a dream.

* * * * *

She recovered slowly. Dragging herself from chore to chore, it seemed she'd never be Nan again, filled with energy, bursting with ideas. And Jake's words were burned into her soul, a wound that refused to heal. She had spent the best years of her life with a man to whom she was nothing, who had said so quite clearly. The memory sickened her, haunted her, stripped her of what had been a growing ability to make decisions and act on them.

Physically weak, her mind followed suit. She drooped, unable to do more than the minimum required to keep Jake calm, although Jake, himself, had reverted into a sullen silence, refusing to talk about what had happened, burying himself in his work.

Jamie was studying for his SATs and preparing to apply to colleges, thinking, she supposed, of the day when he'd leave home and be free of his father forever.

"A time bomb waiting to happen," Ben had said, a phrase that frightened her whenever it came to mind. She stopped at the door to Jamie's room, saw him at his desk bent over a book, one hand ruffling his hair, and she went to stand beside him.

"How's it going?"

"Okay." He looked up and smiled, that sweet, blue-eyed smile she loved.

"Are they all over with tomorrow?"

"Yeah. I'll be ready to party."

"That concert is at eight?" she asked.

He nodded. "I'll probably stay over at somebody's house afterward."

With good reason, she thought. Jake had raised the roof over the fact that his son was spending an evening at a rock concert. Even worse, Nan had given Jamie the money for the ticket out of the jar of quarters she hoarded for such occasions.

"I don't want my son out in that mob with God knows who! Dopers! Drunks! You should have consulted me before you handed him the money. You really should have."

"Half his class is going," she had reminded him. "You can't keep him home while his friends go off and have fun."

"I can. I could have if you hadn't given in. Next time ask me first. I've tried and tried to give him some good taste, and what do you do? Let him waste money on trash."

"Oh, why can't he just be a teenager?" she cried. "Why do you always have to impose your own taste on him?"

"It's for his own good."

But it wasn't. It was to conform to Jake's ideas of life and work. "You'll ruin him," she said bitterly, the scene at the ranch uppermost in her mind. "And I refuse to be a party to it."

She squeezed Jamie's shoulder and noticed once again the strength in his adolescent body. He was growing into a man, yet she could still see him as an infant, a cherubic pink and gold child smiling up at her from his bassinet, a trusting and empty slate waiting to receive the world. And what had been written there since?

Oh, God, she thought, *what have I permitted to be done?*

"Listen," she said then, "why don't you bring the guys home after the tests? I'll make early supper, and you can all leave from here."

Usually he kept his friends as far away as possible. "That'd be great, but what about Dad?"

"He's got a faculty meeting. He won't be home till late."

Jamie smiled harder. "Thanks, Mom. You're super. How about Nick and Steve, and can you make chili?"

"You bet," she said and felt pleased with the fact that she

was able to give him some semblance of normalcy, a small act of kindness in a life filled with misunderstandings. She said nothing to Jake of her plans. The less he knew, the better.

She went about her preparations happily, delaying the actual cooking until Jake left. By the time the boys got home at five thirty, she had the table set, the chili was bubbling, and chips and salsa sat in the middle of the kitchen table.

"Gee, Mrs. Fletcher, this looks great. Thanks for asking us." Nick reached for a chip, and the others followed suit.

"Yes. Thanks, Mrs. Fletcher," Steve echoed. "Jamie's been telling us all about the ranch and your chili."

"Straight out of a lady named Lupe's recipe book," she said. "Why don't you guys wash up and then come eat?"

They didn't need urging. Leaving their back packs in a pile by the door, they went upstairs. "Like a herd of elephants," Nan thought. How could three pairs of feet in tennis shoes make so much noise? Nevertheless, the sound and the laughter pleased her. Happiness in the house was so rare. She savored it as she put out bowls and got cokes from the refrigerator.

The boys were eating when the doorbell rang.

"Now who?" she said, stepping out into the hall where she could see the front door.

Jake was peering through the glass. God! What was he doing home? "Dad's here," she warned, then went to answer.

"Whose car is that?" he wanted to know. "It's blocking the garage."

"Nick's, I guess." Her heart was pounding. She felt as guilty as a criminal caught in the act. Worse, Jake was going to start. She knew it, and knew she wouldn't be able to stop him.

"Ask him to move it, and send Jamie out here."

"They're eating. Can't it wait a few minutes?"

"He can eat when he's finished. I don't see why I can't get into my own garage. And when do *we* eat?"

"I thought you wouldn't be home 'til late. What about the meeting?"

"Called off. Now send Jamie out here. And Nick."

She went back to the kitchen and carried out his orders with a growing sense of dread.

"Dad wants you," she said to Jamie, who was looking at her warily. "Nicky, your car's in the way. Give me your keys, and I'll move it. You go on and eat."

Nicky smiled, and his eyes turned to merry slits. "This is sure good," he said. "Can you give my mom the recipe?"

She nodded and went out the back door at a run. Jamie met her in the driveway, his eyes pleading. "He says I have to bring in some wood for the fireplace and split kindling. I don't have time, Mom. We'll never even find a place to park if we don't leave soon."

"I'll do it," she said. "Go back in and eat and try to get out before he thinks up something else."

She moved the car and assembled a pile of kindling, carried the logs into the house before Jake discovered her.

"I told Jamie to do that!"

"I know, but they're in a hurry, so I said I'd do it." She dumped the logs in the brass bucket and winced as a splinter pierced her thumb. She squeezed the wound and wiped the bright blood on her apron. It reminded her of the flowers of her delirium, red and pulsing. Jake didn't notice, merely turned and went upstairs, his feet heavy on the treads.

Nan went back to the kitchen feeling that she'd averted disaster. "Here's your keys, Nick." She tossed them, and he caught them one-handed.

Jake's footsteps thundered overhead, and his voice, when it came, shocked them all with its vehemence. "Jamie! You come up here right now!"

Mother and son looked at each other in dismay. "Go see what he wants," she advised, "and try not to get him too mad."

"He's always mad," came the response.

It fell to Nan to make light of the situation. She smiled at Nick and Steve. "How were they? The tests?"

"Not too bad, but we're glad they're over." Steve's smile was bright.

She put down a plate of cookies. "Well," she said, "you won't have to take them again, anyhow."

"We bet Jamie aced the math."

"You think? That's neat. He studied hard enough."

Steve reached for a cookie. "He's smart. He doesn't have to study that stuff like the rest of us."

Even her pride in her son and the rattle of dishes she was clearing couldn't cover up the sound of Jake's voice. "Concert or no concert, friends or not, you aren't going anywhere until this room is cleaned up! You tell those friends of yours that."

"Don't worry," Nan told the two boys who were looking at her. "I'll go see what I can do, and I'll get you out of here in plenty of time."

She left the room at a run. Upstairs Jake was hurling books and papers on the floor. "A mess! And you think you're going to run off and leave your room like this! You know how hard your mother works to keep this house clean, and what do you do?"

"All right!" she snapped, furious that he always used her when it suited his purpose. "All right! He'll clean it up. But for heaven's sake, his friends can hear you. What'll they think?"

"I don't care what they think! I don't care if they live in a pig sty. My son isn't going to." He turned and left the room.

"Go now," she hissed at Jamie who had tears in his eyes. "Go on! I'll do it."

"But Mom, he . . ."

"Never mind. All he'll do is yell some more. You have a good time and call when you know where you're staying. Whose house did you say?"

Jamie shrugged. "I don't know for sure."

"Call me," she said. "Now go!"

He bounded down the stairs, and a few seconds later she heard the back door slam. Hastily she picked up the books and papers and arranged them in piles on the desk. Then she smoothed out the rumpled bed, kicked a pair of tennis shoes underneath, and scooped up a pile of laundry she had forgotten to take to the basement. Then she looked around. Not so bad. She took a deep breath and went into the bedroom.

"Well? Is he doing it?" Jake came out of the bathroom wiping his hands on a towel.

"It's done, and he's gone. You didn't help, throwing his stuff all over."

"And you could have checked him out before I got here. Then it wouldn't have happened."

She faced him, her eyes burning. "You did it again, didn't you? You just can't help yourself. Like at the ranch. God knows what he'll do this time."

Jake threw down the towel. "He has to grow up! Be responsible. And all you do is baby him, let him get away with murder. Now if you don't mind, I'd like to eat. Ken's coming over to work on this paper with me."

"Your stomach above all else," she said, turning toward the door. "And don't bother to accuse me of anything because I don't want to listen. Not now, not anymore."

"What does that mean?" He followed her, his eyes bulging.

"You figure it out," she said and went swiftly down the stairs.

CHAPTER THIRTY

The phone rang shortly before one. Nan, who was reading at the kitchen table, picked it up.

"Hi, Mrs. Fletcher!" Nicky sounded cheerful.

"Hi. How was it?"

"Great. Really great. Listen, Jamie asked me to call. He's staying over at Ed's and wanted you to know, okay? And thanks for the neat dinner."

"You're welcome. Any time."

She hung up and glanced at the clock. Maybe she could get to bed early if Jake and Ken didn't want a late night snack.

But as she was walking toward the library, she remembered. Edward had gone away with his family for the weekend. In the core of her body she knew something was wrong, something terrible, and she ran into the library.

"Listen!" she said breathlessly. "Something's wrong. Nicky just called and said Jamie was at Ed's, but they're gone for the weekend. I know there's something the matter. I'm going over there."

Both men jumped to their feet. "Hold on. We're coming with you," Jake said.

They ran to the garage. Jake and Ken slid back the doors while Nan started the car. Ed's house was three blocks away, and she went through every stop sign before screeching to a stop in front of the darkened house.

"Where is he?" she cried, more to herself than to the two men.

"There's a light in the garage," Jake said. "Let's check back there. If he's not there, we'll go to Nicky's and get the truth out of the kid."

She had been here in daylight many times, but at night, in the dim light from the street, the buildings seemed menacing, filled with secrets. The door to the garage was locked, and so was the smaller one to its left. The window was ivy-covered, giving only a telescopic view of the interior—paint cans, a rake and shovel, the bumper of Ed's '59 Chevy that all the boys hoped would someday run.

Impatiently, she yanked at the vines, loosening their grip on the mortar and cutting her hands on the thick stems, but she was too intent on seeing inside to feel the pain.

"Jamie!" she called. "Jamie, are you in there?"

She heard nothing but the sound of her own blood roaring in her ears.

"Jamie!" she called again, and then saw him, a huge, shadowy figure made grotesque in the dim light.

"Jamie, let me in!" She pounded on the glass, shattering a pane.

"Mom!" When he answered, his voice was thick, glutinous, as if he had been gagged and was choking.

"What is it? Is he in there?" Jake and Ken came up behind her.

"Yes, and he's hurt. And the doors are locked. I can't get in."

"Mom!" The dreadful noise came again, and she watched, helplessly, as Jamie staggered toward her.

"Open the door," she called. "Let me in."

He stopped and stood weaving, shaking his head. "Can't."

"Why not?" She had to keep him talking.

"No key." He crashed into a stack of paint cans and sent them tumbling, nearly falling over himself. When he stood upright once again, he threw back his head and screamed. The sound sliced her flesh. She watched as he sank to the floor and began to pound it with his fists.

Without thinking, she attempted to climb through the broken window, but Jake held her back. "Don't go in," he said. "Go home and call the police and an ambulance. We'll try to get inside."

Without answering she turned and ran back toward the car, tripping once and falling, skinning her knees. Once in the house, she made the calls, her hands trembling, then ran out again like a madwoman, calling out loud, "Jamie, Jamie!" as if she could hold him by the thin thread of her voice spinning through the night.

She heard sirens as she jumped out of the car, and the next few minutes passed in a blur—police breaking in the door, paramedics dragging a struggling Jamie to the ambulance.

He was fighting them, flailing out with arms and legs, and making those sounds that weren't human, that corresponded to what Nan was feeling—animal anguish, terror, the inability of her mind to understand what she was seeing.

"Where are you taking him?" she cried at last, pushing her way to the door of the ambulance.

One of the paramedics gave her a swift glance and then his complete attention. He took her arms in a firm grasp. "To Saint Anne's. We'll meet you at the Emergency Room."

The touch of his hands broke her in two, and she began to weep. "Please," she said. "Please help him."

"We're doing our best." He released her and turned back to the ambulance where Jamie, subdued for the moment, was moaning.

At the hospital he fought again with that desperate strength like a cornered beast's. It took three attendants to get him onto the gurney and strap him down before they could wheel him away.

"What did he take?" the nurse at the desk asked. "We need to know."

"Take?" Nan's mind was blank. "I . . . I don't think anything except alcohol. He wasn't home. He'd been at the rock concert, but I don't think there's dope involved. Really. All I know is that his friend called and said he was all right."

"Friend!" Jake interrupted. "Do you realize he could have died because of that friend?"

She realized. And for all she knew, he might still die, and she was helpless to save him. She fought down hysteria, trying to remember what she had seen in the garage.

"I think all he had was liquor," she said finally. "There were bottles. I saw them. Beer. Vodka and gin."

Jake corroborated her statement. "At least two empty beer cases and a couple gallons of vodka. No telling how much really."

"No gasoline? Paint thinner?" The nurse was writing.

Paint thinner! Nan shuddered. "I don't think so. He . . . he smells like liquor, and I think I'd have noticed the smell of gasoline. Why would he drink that, anyway?"

The nurse shook her head. "No telling why he did any of it. But we need to know before we pump him out. And we need your permission. Sign here."

Numbly, Nan signed. Nan A. Fletcher. Her name. What did a name have to do with the life of a child? It was her body that had given him life, not her name.

She and Jake sat in the waiting room with its green linoleum, its harsh blue-white light, side by side but making no move to touch one another. She did not want his comfort.

She had only herself, a shell, a cage of flesh and bone, and her growing certainty that what had happened had been no accident.

After a long while Jake said, "You'd better know. There could be brain damage."

She stared at him. "How do you know that?"

"The doctor told me. It's only a possibility, but all that alcohol might have done something. They won't know until he's conscious and sober."

Now it's the sins of the fathers, she thought, but did not speak. There seemed no point in accusations or bitterness now. And besides, she was equally to blame, not by her actions, but by her passivity.

Please, God, she prayed. *Please. Not Jamie. Not my baby. Not my only one.*

How long they sat, motionless and silent, she never did know. It might have been days or all the years of her life that she spent staring at scuff marks on the floor, at her old loafers that she hadn't had time to change. They were turned up at the toes, and the right one was split at the side so her foot showed through. Her shoes looked like her life—cracked and breaking apart.

She didn't notice the doctor until Jake jumped up.

"Yes?" he said. "Yes?"

The doctor wasn't a young man. He had greying hair and his eyes were bloodshot. He looked like he'd gone without sleep for a week. "He's out of the woods. Asleep but stable. He should be ready to go home in the morning."

"Any signs of problems?" Jake was more subdued than Nan had ever seen him, more like a bad child face to face with fate than the grown man he was supposed to be.

"We think not. How did it happen? Any idea?"

Jake shook his head. "He was fine when he left home last night."

Nan didn't have the energy to speak, to explain the scene that had taken place and go on from there, the accuser. She shook her head and turned toward the door, then stopped.

"Can I see him?" she whispered. "Just for a minute?"

The doctor seemed about to refuse, then, seeing her stricken face, changed his mind. "Just for a minute. He's asleep and he's on an IV. Come with me."

She followed him down the corridor, aware of the swish of rubber soles, the breathing of machines inside darkened rooms.

At the door of one of them the doctor stopped. "Still asleep," he said. "That's good. He'll feel awful tomorrow, and for the next couple of days, but he'll recover."

She peeked in. Jamie lay in the middle of the bed, one arm exposed and linked to the IV. His breathing was deep but steady, and his face was as white as the sheet except for a dark purple bruise on one cheek.

"He was the most beautiful baby," she whispered, as much to herself as to the doctor. "And he's a nice boy."

"Ask him what happened," the doctor said, his bloodshot eyes searching and compassionate. "And don't stop asking until you know. Could it have been a suicide attempt? Ask yourself. Ask him. And if it was, get help, whatever you do."

She didn't have to ask. The answer lay in her life. She blinked back tears.

"Go home and get some sleep," the doctor advised. "He'll be fine, and you'll need your own strength tomorrow."

"Thank you." She put out her hand and he took it.

"It's the ones I can't help," he muttered. "The DOA's, the botched abortions."

Bone-wrenching sorrow swept her, there in the narrow corridor with the smell of antiseptic, the whir of machines, the breathing of her son. She peered up at the doctor wanting to give him something in return for Jamie's life.

"You mustn't agonize about them," she said. "Think of the saved lives, and that saving even one is important. People like you are important."

Hearing herself, she was embarrassed. What must he think of her, this dignified physician, this saver of lives? Who was she to stand lecturing when her own son had almost died because of her? She withdrew her hand and ran down the hall to Jake and bitter reality.

Outside the glow of the street lights paled as the horizon caught fire. "It's morning," she said, surprised.

Jake didn't answer. His chin was tucked deep into his coat collar, and he seemed dazed by the events of the night. No use explaining to him, she thought. He'd never understand, never see how his actions affected others, almost to the ruination of their lives. What happened now was up to her, as it had been all along, and she too lost to summon courage. *But no more,* she said to herself. *Not anymore.*

At home she stood a moment in the garden listening to sparrows arguing in the trees, and watching as the sun turned the leaves to gold. Finally she went inside and climbed the stairs to bed.

It seemed she had been asleep for only a few minutes when the telephone rang.

Jamie! she thought. *Something's gone wrong!* and she grabbed for the receiver nearly knocking over the lamp on the table beside it.

"Hello?" Her voice was trembling. "Hello? Hello?"

"Nan."

"Lottie!" She sat up, taking a deep breath. "What's the

matter? What time is it?" She blinked, trying to clear her head and see the clock.

"I don't know what time it is. But I thought you'd want to know."

"What?" She peered at the clock. It was a quarter to seven.

"I spilled a glass of water and called 911." Lottie sounded smug.

The anger, fear, anguish that she had successfully kept under control erupted. She thought she was going to start to scream and that when she did she would never stop. Roughly she shoved the phone at Jake who was awake and, mercifully, silent.

"Your mother," she hissed. "Your damn mother. You talk to her."

Then she went into the bathroom, sat on the edge of the tub and put her face in her hands. Her hot tears felt like a baptism of fire.

CHAPTER THIRTY-ONE

Jamie lay in his own bed, young and vulnerable, his long lashes dark against his pale cheeks, the bruise on his face garish. Watching him from her chair by the window, Nan kept replaying scenes from the past. Jamie on the beach at age two discovering the sea and trying to eat the sand; marching bravely off to nursery school, his companion blanket tucked firmly under one arm; staring up at her and Jake with tear-filled eyes and saying, in response to a brutal scolding, "Don't you know I'm just a little boy?"

It was this last that wrung her heart. Of course she had known. She had known everything about him, had tried to love and protect, but, involved with her own problems, she had been unable to protect him from pain.

He moved then and opened his eyes. "Mom?" he whispered.

"I'm here."

"My throat hurts."

She went over to him and sat on the edge of the bed. "I guess it does. You had a tube down it you know."

"I'm sorry," he said.

"It's okay. You want to talk about it?"

"Maybe." His eyes seemed very blue in the dim light, and very direct except for the shadows in them. "Will you listen?"

"Sure. I always listen. You know that."

"Yeah." He smiled, but it was a cynical smile that made her aware of her own uselessness. He pushed himself up on his elbows. "I did it on purpose," he said.

She heard him, and she heard other things—the ticking of the hall clock, the tap of a branch against the window, a crying inside her head as mournful as the wind.

"Why?" she whispered, although she knew the answer.

"I couldn't stand it anymore. Him. You. I kept waiting for you to do something, to help me. Since I was little I was waiting, but nothing ever happened, and he just got worse. I wanted to get rid of it all. To have it over with."

This was her punishment, and it would be with her always no matter where she went or what she did. In her innocence, in the depths of her personal anguish, she had nearly caused the death of her only child.

To ask his forgiveness seemed monstrous. How could he possibly forgive her? It was asking too much of anyone, particularly of a child. Nonetheless, she asked.

"Can you forgive me?"

"Forget it," he said and looked away.

That was more than she had a right to expect. She reached out and laid her hand over his. "I want you to listen to me," she said. "And I want you to know something."

He nodded, but she could see exhaustion overtaking him. She spoke quickly, with determination, knowing what she had to do.

"I'm going to get us out of here. You and me. I promise. I've been selfish and dumb and wrapped up in myself, and I kept hoping everything would work out, but it hasn't. I promise to help you, but you have to promise me something. Never to try . . . to try that again. You're a very special person, and I love you very much. Losing you would be the end for me as well as for you. Do you promise?"

His eyelids drooped, then fluttered open. "Promise," he mumbled.

"I want you to hold on a little bit longer. There are things I have to do. But we're leaving here. Together. I won't go without you, you hear me?"

He was awake again and interested. "You really are? You're leaving Dad?"

"I have no choice."

"I always thought you were such a wimp," he said, and then his eyes closed and he was asleep.

A wimp! she thought as she tiptoed out. *A wimp, a coward,* waiting to be rescued by the prince in the fairy tale, looking for an easy solution so that she only needed to go with the flow as she had always done. She had divided herself to have peace, but now even that had been taken from her because of her own blindness. Well, no more!

She set her chin, then frightened but filled with determination, she went to the study where Jake was packing his briefcase before leaving for work.

"We have to talk," she said without preamble.

He didn't look up. "Now?"

She sat on the edge of one of the chairs. "Yes, now."

"Not about anything painful I hope."

She clenched her hands into fists. Wasn't that the trouble? Neither of them had ever spoken about realities, had never pared the problems between them down to the bone. They'd been too busy, he finding fault and she retreating into herself.

"Don't you think it's time we did?" she asked. "Our son nearly died last night. He tried to kill himself."

Jake looked up then, his face white. "Who said that?"

She met his gaze steadily. "He did. Just now. I believe him, and the doctor was pretty sure of it. We've failed him, you and I. You with your obsessions about everything, and me with my acceptance of it all."

He closed his briefcase with a snap. "I don't have to listen to this," he said. "And you don't have to come in here and repeat his excuse for getting drunk out of his mind like it's holy writ. Use your head. He's shifting the blame on us, and you're accepting it. And as a matter of record, if he'd not been allowed to go to that . . . that circus, none of this would have happened. Nicky's a liar and a sneak, and I don't want to see him in this house again. Understand?"

"Oh, yes," she said bitterly, noting that, once again, he'd turned the blame on everyone but himself. "I do. And I understand something else. You've torn this family apart, and refuse to even try to put us together again, to even admit what you've done. To me, to Jamie, to yourself. All these years I've sat here like a dummy and never spoke up. Well, no more. I'm willing to accept my mistakes, to take the blame, but only for a part. You've nearly ruined your son. You've embarrassed him, withheld your praise, your love, your time. And so it's come to this."

"Feminist crap!" He put his hands on the table and leaned across it. "You've been reading too many of those women's magazines. Christ, you sound just like them! Next you'll be wanting a divorce like that friend of yours who thinks she's a painter."

She swallowed, frightened now that her chance had come. "I think I do," she whispered.

She'd stunned him. He was shocked but recovered quickly. "You think!" he snarled. "You don't think, and that's your trouble. You wouldn't last a month on your own. You'll never get a job, and believe me, I'll see you don't get anything that's mine."

"Ours," she corrected. "What we have belongs to both of us."

"Try and prove it! Try and get it! It's my money that bought you all of this. Do you think I like what I have to do to get it? Teaching a bunch of morons? Defending my ideas to a bunch of half-assed faculty? If you do, guess again. But I'm the head of this house in case you haven't noticed, and any court will see it my way." He stopped, breathless, then went on before she could respond.

"This whole conversation could have been avoided. Now I have to go to work when I'd just as soon go back to bed. And in case you forgot, my mother's in the hospital through no fault of mine. That's just great, isn't it? My son, my mother, and now you sitting there talking about divorce."

He stepped back, staggering a little. "She needs her things from her house. I told her you'd bring them this afternoon. I'm going to work even though my stomach is sick, and I hope when I come home you don't bring this up again. Divorce!" He laughed, a sound without humor. "And do you think anybody else would have you? I doubt it. I'll be home early, so make something light for dinner."

Across the widening fault line that separated them, Nan looked at him and smiled. Had he been more aware he would have seen it for what it was—a gesture of cold and utter contempt that signified his downfall.

CHAPTER THIRTY-TWO

Lottie was sitting up in the hospital bed watching the door. "What took you so long?" she said when Nan walked in carrying a bag containing her cosmetics, eyeglasses, the novel she'd been reading.

Nan halted just inside the room. Looking at Lottie, listening to her was like seeing Jake, having to cope with him all over again. She put down the bag with a thump and walked to the bed. For years she'd been a servant, to this old lady with her whims and ingratitude, to her son. It was past time for the truth.

"What took me so long," she began, "was that I had things to do. Important things involving your grandson. I didn't have to do this for you at all, but I did just like always. And what thanks have I ever gotten, from you *or* your son? None. You shouldn't even be in here. There's nothing wrong with you, and you know it. I should be home taking care of Jamie. He's the one with the problem."

Unexpectedly Lottie said, "Tell me what happened. I couldn't get anything out of Jake that made sense, but I want to know."

The new Nan spared nothing in the telling and watched as Lottie's face crumpled and she reached for a tissue.

She wiped her eyes, then said, "I wondered if it wasn't something like that. I've always admired you for staying with

Jake and wondered why you did. You're a good girl. A good mother. But Jake . . . he never lets go. He just goes on and on and never stops, and I don't know how you stand it. I couldn't, and he's mine." She blew her nose again. "Lately I've wondered . . . how did he get like that? Is it my fault? Did I do something wrong when he was growing up that made him what he is?"

As badly as she wanted to speak, Nan bit back the truth. Lottie was too old and looked too vulnerable lying there, somehow like Jamie, incapable of surviving another blow. And what, after all, was the use of casting blame now with the damage done and irreparable?

She shook her head. "Jake's an adult. He's supposed to be responsible for his actions, not you, not me. Although I've tried to make him see, I've failed. Obviously."

Lottie nodded. "If you want to divorce him, I won't hold it against you. You're young yet. You deserve better, much as it hurts to say it about my own son. But I've never held with that ' 'til death us do part' nonsense. There's enough trouble in the world without that."

Nan couldn't believe her ears. She looked at Lottie and for one moment caught a glimpse of another woman behind the wrinkled mask, a tough, realistic woman who had made a life and survived in spite of what had been severe emotional damage.

Abruptly she said, "I am going to leave him," and marveled at how easily the words came to her lips.

"You save yourself," Lottie ordered. "You save my grandson. He's a good boy. A smart boy." She pushed herself up higher in the bed. "At home, in the brown chair in the living room, inside the slipcover is an envelope. There's money in it, and I want you to take it. Use it for whatever you need. You'll need money, believe me."

"You mean this?" Nan was incredulous.

"Of course I mean it!"

"And you won't tell Jake?"

Lottie's expression was grim. "Don't be foolish. He'll find out soon enough anyhow. I'm trusting you to do the right thing. Don't let me down."

"I'll try not to." Nan spoke with difficulty, remembering the times she'd maligned Lottie, lost her temper over small happenings. "And . . . I'm sorry for not being more of a daughter to you."

Lottie's face softened and she reached out a not-quite-steady hand. "You were too busy taking care of my son and grandson. I know that. I just wanted some attention for myself."

"So does everybody."

"Get smart," Lottie said. "Be a little selfish and do what I told you. Life's too short to waste. I know. There were things I wanted to do and never did, and now it's too late. For me. But not for you."

Nan let go of Lottie's hand and bent down and kissed her gently, a small kindness, hardly enough to repay her. "Bless you," she whispered.

"You, too. Now go and do what I said. And put that money someplace safe. If you lose it, there's no more coming."

Lottie's apartment was dim, the curtains drawn, and it smelled like a house where no one had lived for a long time—musty, dry, and with the faint scent of lavender in the bowl of potpourri on the coffee table.

Nan stood in the tiny foyer feeling like a thief. When she finally crossed to the chair and found the envelope, she was afraid to open it. Suppose this were a joke, one of Lottie's notions? Suppose all she found were a few dollars crumpled with age?

She sat down on the couch and opened the flap, and her eyes widened in amazement. Inside was a stack of bills, all denominations, saved over the years by one who had lived through hard times and had never quite trusted banks.

Once, twice, three times she counted. Almost five thousand dollars. And it had been there all this time, hidden in the chair where she'd often sat. Five thousand dollars. With this plus her own savings she had enough to care for herself and Jamie regardless of what Jake did; enough so that she could begin again anywhere.

In the little house. The thought was an image of stone walls, blue-painted windows, jays fluttering in the oak trees.

It's yours if you want it.

She jumped up and went to the phone on Lottie's desk. *Let him be there. Let him answer.*

"Murphy's Mule Barn."

"Who? What?" She stammered then laughed as she hadn't in a long time. "Did you know it was me?"

"Mental telepathy. I was coming in to call you. It's been awhile. Are you alright?"

Was she? "I guess. Everything's gone wrong that could, but I'm okay. I . . . I asked Jake for a divorce. It was pretty awful, but I need to know if you meant it about being able to live in the old house."

All Ben's senses went on alert. She was in trouble. He knew it from the not quite controlled quaver in her voice. "Tell me," he said.

It was too soon. She hadn't the strength to describe the details, to have to remember how Jamie had looked in the blue light of the garage, the menacing sterility of the hospital room. "Not now," she said. "The important thing is that I'm leaving. Jamie and I are both leaving. If . . . if we could use the house it would be wonderful."

He wrestled down his joy. "It's yours. I told you. How else can I help? You want me to come for you? You want me to kill the son of a bitch?"

She laughed again. He'd never backed down from anything in his life, would take Jake on in a minute and be glad of the chance. "You're so good. So kind. I . . ." Her voice broke.

"Damn it!" He wanted to tear the phone out of the wall, to get to her, see her face, hold her. She was his and hurting, and he was two thousand miles away. "What happened? Don't cry. Are you there?"

"Yes," she said, and then her grief came out in a rush.

He drew a deep breath. "All right. Get hold of yourself. You'll do fine. Just tell me what to do."

"Be there for me. Please."

"I'll be wherever you want me. Always."

She sighed. He was so steady. So capable. Talking to him gave her a belief in herself she'd never thought possible. "I love you. Dearly," she said. "And I'll let you know what I'm doing as soon as I know. As long as you're there, I'm all right. I'm coming home, Ben. As soon as I can."

"About time." He chuckled to take the sting out and succeeded.

"Murphy's Mule Barn," she said. "Where'd you get that one?"

"I made it up. Fooled you, too, didn't I?"

"For a minute. You sounded good."

"Not as good as I will when you get here. Now be careful, do what you have to, and call when you can."

She wished she could touch him, put her hands on his face, feel the muscles in his broad shoulders, lay her head on his chest and know the warmth of his arms around her. She closed her eyes, but practicality pulled her back to the

216

present. There was five thousand dollars to be put into her bank account and the lawyer to call. She had plans to make, details to oversee. The time for dreaming was past.

CHAPTER THIRTY-THREE

"If there's anything in particular you want or like, take it with you when you leave," Leona said with one of the piercing glances Nan had come to expect. "After you're gone, you'll never get anything from him. Remember that."

With her mind made up, Nan was undaunted. "I know it sounds crazy to you, but this is the only way I can see to do it. I have to go someplace far away so Jake can't get at me. If I just move out and down the street, he'll camp on the doorstep, call me every ten minutes. And then there's Jamie. I have to do what I can for him. Take time for him. Tell him things he needs to hear. Ben has a house on the ranch we can live in. It's away from his and has its own address, so nobody can say I'm living with him."

Leona frowned at her. "Be careful," she said. "What you're doing isn't without precedent, but it's still unusual. One thing, though, and that is, even though the laws have changed, you have to make sure you don't move in with Ben or vice versa. You could destroy your chances in the final settlement if Jake can prove another man was supporting you."

Nan leaned back in her chair. "This is really happening, isn't it? Sometimes it's like a dream. I mean, it's like somebody else is doing all this, making all these plans."

"Somebody else is," Leona said with a smile. "The new you. And, incidentally, you look a hundred percent better than you did the first time you came to see me."

"I guess it's because I finally made up my mind. I wish now it hadn't taken me so long to figure it all out."

"But you did," Leona commented. "Some women never do."

Nan shuddered. "That's what scared me. Ben said something about looking back on my life and seeing it wasted—after it was too late. And Lottie said something similar. And I thought that not loving him, when he came into my life like a gift would be as big a sin as wasting whatever talent I have. It's all tied up together. Ben, me, Jamie, our lives, like a kind of intricate knot. Am I making any sense?"

"Absolutely," Leona reassured her. "I wish you could talk to some of my other clients. You're a brave woman."

"A desperate one."

"That, too. Now go and do what you have to and call if you need me. When you give me the go-ahead, I'll file. And I'll also file for monthly support so you won't have to use up your savings." She stood and held out her hand. "And good luck. I wish I could go with you."

Nan smiled. "When it's all over, maybe you can come out and we'll sit on the porch and I'll show you the mountains."

"Sounds good. Like heaven in fact. Now don't worry. Just keep going."

Outside in the waiting room, Nan stopped and looked at the little statue of Warrior Woman. She gave a sudden grin and flashed the victory sign. "I'm on my way, old girl," she said and went out singing.

What to take? Her notebooks, her published work, old photographs, clothes for her and Jamie—and he, of course, would want things, his computer and books, his tennis racket and baseball glove. And she would take her jewelry, all of it, and maybe the silver as Wendy suggested. Oh, God, so much to do in so short a time, and without help because no one but she knew!

It was the end of October. In early December, Jake was going to Mexico City, and she was headed West to a new beginning, like so many other hopefuls before her.

Nan was in the attic sorting through the stored mementos of nearly twenty years—Jamie's baby shoes that she'd never been able to throw away, his tattered blanket her mother had crocheted, the good copy of the Chanel suit she'd taken on her European honeymoon—things that still had value, if only to her, and that revived memories, happy and sad.

Half of her life was stored here and had to be left for someone else to sort. But not Jake, she decided. He, probably, would throw it all out into the trash out of bitterness or simply because his heart was not involved in piles of baby clothes. One man's trash was, indeed, another's treasure.

What to do? Nan sat back on her heels and frowned, chasing the elusive thread of a conversation she'd had with a neighbor about a shelter for battered women and children. What was it called? Refuge House, that was it, and surely they had need for these treasures, no longer used but useable.

She got up then, went downstairs, found the listing in the directory and dialed.

The voice that answered after several rings was cautious. "Yes?"

And Nan, who all her life had been attuned to nuance and patterns of speech, immediately understood. Fear and the necessity for anonymity were the rule at Refuge House. She identified herself and explained the reason for her call. "Can you use clothes, toys, old blankets and things?"

"We certainly can." The voice was more natural. "When were you planning to come?"

"Well . . ." Nan considered. "On Thursday, around three thirty?" That way Jessie could help her with the boxes and she could give more than clothes. There were pots, pans, skillets, towels she'd never use. In fact the house was filled with things that were now and always had been useless to her.

"Fine," the voice said. "You know where we are? Pull up to the front gate and press the intercom. Ask for me. Regina."

Nan spent the next hour sorting and packing, finally, with a tug at her heart, shoving her honeymoon suit into a box, then sitting back and remembering the good times and the bad. Oddly, there had been good times in her marriage, times when she and Jake had talked and laughed and enjoyed one another's company.

Looking back she realized that it was those times of ordinariness that had held them together. Always she had thought that Jake, somehow, had changed, that he would never attack her again.

But what had Leona said? "That's what all women want to believe. Even the ones with broken bones. They think, 'Oh, he's changed.' And he has . . . until the next time. But, people don't change their habits or personalities. A husband who beats his wife once will usually do it again, and one who destroys his wife's self-esteem does it for a very subtle reason."

Nan nodded to herself. Early on she and Jake had gotten caught in a pattern, she out of innocence, Jake because . . . she sighed, because that's how he was. Somehow his obsessions, his aggressions had become his reality. Perhaps if she'd stood up to him in the beginning, her life would have been different. Now it was simply too late. She didn't care what happened to him. All that was important now was herself and Jamie.

Nan stopped at the gate and looked at the cluster of buildings. "I guess this is it," she said to Jessie.

"Looks more like a prison to me," Jessie said.

She was right. An eight-foot cyclone fence topped with concertina wire surrounded the house and a square of concrete that might have been a playground. The gate was securely locked.

"Well," Nan hesitated, "the woman I talked to said to use the intercom. I'll try and see what happens."

Jessie rolled her eyes. "Is the women locked in or the men locked out?"

"Beats me." Nan got out of the car and pressed the intercom button. The voice that answered was a ghostly echo of one she had heard before.

"Regina?"

"Who is it?"

"Nan Fletcher. We talked the other day? I'm here with clothes and things."

"Just a minute."

The intercom went dead, and Nan stood peering through the fence at the barred windows, the cement yard lacking even a blade of grass. It was worse than a prison, yet they called it a refuge!

A woman came out and stood a minute before coming down the walk. She was plainly dressed in jeans and an old sweater, her red hair pulled back in a bun. "Mrs. Fletcher?"

"Yes."

"Okay. Just making sure. I'll open the gate. You drive around to the side entrance."

Nan slid behind the wheel.

"I still got the creeps," Jessie informed her. "Let's go to some church and drop this stuff off."

"Oh, come on, Jess. We're here. We'll just unload and go."

"Not through no locked gate we ain't." Jessie was looking out the rear window at Regina who was, indeed, replacing the locks. "What the Doc gonna say when you ain't home for supper?"

Nan started to laugh. "Oh, come on," she said again. "They're just being careful."

"I been lots of places," came the reply. "But I never seen one this careful. Even when little Leon was in the detention home."

"Then you just sit here, and I'll unload."

"You ain't goin' in there by yourself," Jessie said. "Little thing like you."

"Yeah. All five foot eight of me. Don't you worry. I'll be fine."

"You will 'cause I'll be right beside you makin' sure." Jessie with her mind made up was formidable. She got out and stood beside Nan, her hands clenched into fists.

Regina came up and unlocked a door that led into a small, bare room. The door in the opposite wall was locked and barred. "You can put the things in here," she said. "We'll unpack later."

Nan's curiosity nagged at her. "Why all the locks? Where are the women?"

Regina shook her head. "For safety," she said, her eyes wary. "You have to understand. These women have been beaten. Some of them are maimed for life. Their kids have been hurt. We can't take chances here."

There were women worse off than she was. Women on the brink whose lives had been threatened, whose babies bore visible wounds! "You mean their husbands might . . . ?" she couldn't finish, just looked her question at Regina, who nodded.

"That's right. Their husbands want them back. They want

their kids back, and they'll try anything to get them. They need help, too, of course, but there's no way we can give them access. We're not dealing with normal people here. We're dealing with anger. With despair. With potential murderers, though not a one of them would admit that. We're dealing with the victims, and we do what we have to do to keep them safe."

"How many?"

"Too many. We're over full right now. Thirty women and about fourteen kids. And two on the way. But we don't turn anybody who comes away. We can't. Most have no place else to go."

"Of course not." Nan turned on her heel. "Come on, Jessie. Let's get the boxes." And to Regina, "I stripped the house, and I'm glad I did. You need help more than anybody."

"Anything and everything. Just bring it on in." She stood at the door watching, and Jessie scowled.

"She don't trust us, neither. Even if we *are* women. The world's a sorry place, ain't it?"

"It is." Nan's mind began to whirl as it had done so many times in the past months. Violence, cruelty, misery seemed everywhere, even in what was supposed to be the sanctity of the home. She leaned against the car. "I don't think I can stand this," she said.

As usual, when she faltered, Jessie took charge. "You go sit in the car. I'll take care of this stuff. They can't scare me."

"I'm not scared. It's just too much."

Jessie grinned suddenly. "I ever tell you about my first husband? Leon's daddy with the glass eye?"

"No."

"I was young then. And tough. I was right out of the fields and had me some muscle. And one time that man tried to whup me, and I punched him out. I said, 'You try that again, and I'll do for your other eye. You be sittin' on the curb with a tin cup, you lay a hand on me.' "

"Then what?"

"Then he up and left, that's what. And good riddance. That glass eye gave me bad dreams. Still does."

"You ought to write a book," Nan said, laughing.

"That's for you. Why you think I tell you these things? So you know. I could tell you stories you wouldn't believe."

Like Lupe, Nan thought. Like Lottie and Helen and the mothers they never knew. So many stories, so many women and the tragedies that went unnoticed, so many wives beaten, silenced forever by the old beliefs.

"I wish you would tell me," she said. "But we'd better finish up and get going or the Doc will be home."

"Huh!" Jessie said. "He go on just like his old lady, and you there like a mouse with its eyes screwed shut. You ought to get you a boy friend. Go to a motel. Have some fun."

"My God, Jessie!" Was she actually suggesting such an act, or was she teasing? Nan wasn't certain.

"I mean what I say. You just too stubborn to listen."

Could she tell her now? Nan wondered. Give away her plan before time? No, she decided, as much as she wanted to share with another, she had to wait, to do it all alone and without help or risk the danger that Jessie would tell somebody else. Taking responsibility was difficult she decided, as she put the car in gear and started toward the gate.

Jessie, unaware of the struggle going on in Nan's head turned and looked back at the little compound, deserted and shadowed in the autumn dusk.

"They all locked up," she said darkly. "Every last one. And the rest of us ain't so well off, neither."

CHAPTER THIRTY-FOUR

"Are you sure you don't want to come with me? You've never been to Mexico City."

For the last weeks Jake had reverted to the man who'd courted her, polite, easy to be with, and Nan could feel her confidence wavering. *Why* couldn't he be like this all the time? Why make what she was doing more difficult?

She was at the sink rinsing dishes before putting them in the dishwasher. "I don't want to leave Jamie," she said, the excuse coming easily because it was the truth.

"I don't think he'll try that again. Besides, you and I need some time alone."

She gave an inward shudder. The time for that was long gone. "He probably won't," she said, "but still, I think I'd better stay home."

He moved to stand beside her, and when he spoke again it was with a pleading undertone. "I only asked because I know you haven't been too happy lately, and I've been trying. I really have, only you haven't noticed. Tonight I carried my saucer off the table."

To Nan's horror, she thought she was going to laugh— or cry. Biting her lip, she risked a glance at him, saw him as proud as a three year old expecting praise for what adults did without thought. And she was to provide it, as she provided all else. She, the mother he had never had, the wife he had never known.

"No," she said carefully. "I didn't notice. But thanks."

"Just so you know," he said, gratified, and added, "I'll want coffee when you're through in here. With lots of milk."

"Okay." She turned on the water full blast, wishing him gone before she threw the dish cloth at him, before she lost her frail grip on her overflowing emotions and told him exactly what she thought of his generosity.

"A saucer!" She was at Wendy's. "He carried his saucer and expected me to kiss his feet!"

"That man is certifiable, as I'm sure you know."

"You think?"

"Oh, come on!" Wendy shot her a look. "He's a nut case. You said so yourself. When in hell are you going to leave him?"

"In two weeks," Nan said and watched Wendy's jaw drop.

"You're kidding."

"Nope," she said. "I'm not. He's going to Mexico, and Jamie and I are going West. I'm renting a house from Ben, and you're the only person I've told."

"On account of a saucer?"

Nan laughed, but it was a pained sound. "That was just the frosting on the cake. Too much is broken to fix, and if I ever felt like trying, even that's gone. Jake isn't important anymore. But I am. Jamie is."

"God bless you," Wendy said, then her face crumpled. "What'll I do without you? Who'll I talk to? You're my best friend since forever, and now you're leaving."

At the sight of Wendy's tears, the finality of what she was doing hit Nan full force. She was leaving all that was familiar, leaving her security, her friends, her roots, the people and places that had shaped her as child and as adult. She was stepping off a cliff into the unknown.

"Don't cry!" She got up and threw her arms around Wendy. "If you do, I will, and I'm supposed to be happy, not bawling my head off. And besides, you can come out and visit. And paint. Wait'll you see what there is to paint. And meet Ben. He's wonderful. Kind of like us. Honest."

"It all sounds wonderful." Wendy sniffed. "And I'm so proud of you. It's just . . . it'll be lonely with you not here, that's all."

Nan hugged her tighter. "Life is lonely," she said, voicing her feelings as she had always done with Wendy. "All we've got is ourselves . . . such as they are. And, if we're lucky, once in awhile a friend to talk to. We'll never not be friends. We've gone through too much. We have a past. And if you come visit, we'll have a future. Will you come? Please?"

Wendy stepped back and wiped her face. "Okay. I promise. Because I have to meet this guy. Check him out. You can't be trusted."

"Yes I can," Nan said firmly. "I've thought about it, written out every scenario I could think of. I have to trust myself. Like I said, I'm all I've got."

"You've got more guts than anybody I ever met. Taking off like this."

"Guts have nothing to do with it. It's simply a choice between life or death."

"I still call it guts." Wendy reached into the refrigerator. "More wine from Howard the Undaunted," she said. "We'll use it to drink a toast. To you. To life, luck, happiness and the pursuit of dignity, because that's what it's all about. Your own worth. Mine. Our kids'."

With a whoop, Nan raised her glass high. "Dignity forever!" she shouted, then tilted her head and drank.

CHAPTER THIRTY-FIVE

It was the last time she would ever take Jake to the airport, the last time she would kiss him goodbye and drive home with a sense of relief as if she'd been let out of jail.

For the past month, she'd been acting a role, as usual, responding when spoken to, but it was as if the part of her that mattered had already gone, and what remained was a clone.

Oddly, no one seemed to notice. Maybe, she thought, they were too wrapped up in themselves, or worse, perhaps this is how she had always appeared, a rag doll lacking heart or feelings, a shadow figure, easily ignored.

Traffic at the airport was heavy. She circled twice then, finding no convenient parking place said, "Maybe I should just drop you off."

Jake was searching for his ticket which he'd misplaced. "It's a madhouse," he agreed. "Just stop at the front."

Obediently, Nan pulled up, and willing herself into a semblance of normalcy, took a last look at the father of her child, the man she had lived with for almost twenty years yet didn't know.

We are the hollow men/ we are the stuffed men/ leaning together/ headpiece filled with straw. Unbidden, the lines of Eliot's poem came to her, and with them sorrow, for Jake, for herself, for all whose hopes dwindled and came to dust.

She put out a hand, touched his arm. "Take care," she

whispered, knowing she could do nothing to change him, only send him on his way with a final blessing.

"You, too." He was oblivious to her concern. "Try and behave yourself while I'm gone."

"I always do."

He leaned over, kissed her cheek, got out and closed the door, and she sat for a time watching until he blended in with the crowd. Unaccountably, her eyes filled with tears.

Not with a bang but a whimper. Eliot again, wise, precise, writing to her and to all who had come to an ending. Would she, in time, be able to capture this moment, write it on paper for others to read? She didn't know, knew only that in a small piece of time she had banished the middle part of her life.

"What you gonna do with yourself now he's gone?" Jessie asked as Nan let herself in the back door.

It was the perfect opening. Nan took off her coat and threw her purse on the table. "Sit down, Jessie. I have something to tell you."

Jessie, recognizing the seriousness in Nan's voice, dried her hands and sat.

Nan began slowly. "In three days I'm leaving here. I'm taking my clothes and books, some things I value, and Jamie, and we're leaving and never coming back. I've had it with that man."

"That bad?" Nothing about men had ever shocked Jessie.

"That bad. I can't stand it anymore."

"Huh!" Jessie looked down at her lap. Then she said, "I told you before, but you didn't listen, so I'm tellin' you again. You don't have to go off to nowhere all by yourself. You don't have to give up all this—big house, nice life. What you do is, you get yourself a boyfriend. You go to a motel. You have a good time, then you wipe you' ass and come on home. Lots does it. I know."

"Jessie!" Nan stifled laughter.

"You heard me."

"I'm afraid I did. But it won't work. I have to get out. Jamie tried to kill himself. I have to get both of us out of here before something worse happens."

Jessie's lip quivered. "What I'm gonna do without you? Without that child? I been here since you came. You like my family."

"You've been my family, too," Nan said, "and I'll miss you something terrible, but I have to do this."

"I'll go with you." Jessie straightened and for a moment looked to Nan like Warrior Woman, ready to defend and protect.

"Not this time," she said, knowing she loved the woman as much as she'd ever loved anyone. "Maybe . . . maybe you could come see me when I get settled. And I'll write. I promise."

Jessie got up looking regal and fierce and gathered Nan into her arms. "Honey, all these years I been wonderin' how you took it. How you could put up with that man. I have eyes. Ears, too. I heard, though I didn't say nothin'. Now I say, you go on. It's past time, and you ready to fly by yourself. Me, I'll stay here and pick up the pieces because there's goin' to be one big explosion when that man come back and find you gone."

"You really think I can do it?" Nan felt ten years old, comforted by the woman's strong arms.

"You sure can, honey. You're something else."

She could feel Jessie's heart beating loud and steady. It sounded like a drum.

"What's happening?" Jamie came in and dumped his

231

backpack on the table, then stood looking at the two women, his curiosity undisguised.

"He don't know?" Jessie murmured.

Nan shook her head. She had put off telling him until she was certain everything was in order. Now she said, "Come on in the library a minute."

"Oh, oh. Serious." He looked at Jessie for confirmation. "Who died?"

"Nobody. Not yet, anyhow. You go on with you' Mama."

Nan walked down the hall ahead of him, her heels clicking on the black and white marble. In the library she sat down on one of the wing chairs that flanked the fireplace. "I promised you I'd get you out," she began. "And I am. In three days you and I are leaving. I talked to your headmaster, and he says you can finish your last semester through the mail. Your grades are good, your college applications are all in. You and I are going to Ben's. We'll be living in the old house, and I'm filing for a divorce from your father."

"Geez." Jamie sat down on the chair opposite. "Geez, Mom." His voice cracked with what sounded like anxiety.

"What's the matter?"

"I . . ." He struggled, searching for words. "I thought . . . I mean, like, what about my friends? And graduation? The senior prom? Christmas is coming. You want to do this *now?*"

Her first reaction was anger. She'd flung him a life line, and he was refusing it. He'd called her a wimp for doing nothing, and now that she had, *he* was waffling.

Tight-lipped she said, "If you want to stay, that's okay, but I'm leaving here."

"It's not that. It's just . . ." His eyes pleaded. "It's scary, Mom. Leaving everything. Going away. And what'll Dad do?"

He was, she saw, a child again. Still. His securities were

hers—home, house, friends. While she had thought through her own doubts and misgivings, she could hardly expect him to do the same in a matter of minutes. She got up and went to him, regretting her anger.

"I've wrestled with this a long time," she said gently. "I never believed in divorce or in splitting up our family. But too many things have gone wrong. Maybe it's too late to make everything right, especially for you, but I'm going to try like I promised I would. And as for your friends, your graduation, you can come back and be with them when the time comes. Dr. Peterson told me you can graduate with your class, and that you'll probably graduate with honors. As for Christmas . . ." She hesitated, thinking ahead, imagining Ben, a huge tree, the scent of pinon logs burning. She adored Christmas, the choosing and wrapping of gifts, and had always been disappointed that Jake didn't share her excitement. He usually gave her a check for a hundred dollars in a business sized envelope, explaining that the money was both for Christmas *and* her birthday, and Lottie did the same. Every year, it seemed, she had swallowed her feelings and thanked them. But no more.

Discussing her love life was something she had never done, but honesty won out over her reservations. "We'll be at the ranch. And, I have to tell you that Ben and I love each other. Where this will lead, I don't know. But he's genuinely concerned for you, for what happens to you. I know this for a fact, and I think you do, too. He wants us both to have a chance, and I'm doing this for you as well as for myself. Now you go and think about it. What you do is up to you. But . . ." Her voice broke. "But I so wanted you to come with me. I love you very much."

He sat, his hands balled into fists, staring at the floor, while inwardly Nan wept. She couldn't go without him!

Wouldn't no matter what she'd said. She'd see him through if necessary, brave Ben's anger and possible rejection, somehow save herself by herself if that's what she had to do. But leave him behind with Jake? *Never!*

She touched Jamie's bent head, let her fingers sift through his fine hair. "Take your time. I'm here for you whatever you decide."

When he looked up, he was smiling, and his eyes sparkled. *With tears?* she wondered, guilt stricken. Were all her good intentions to be undone by her child's tears?

He said, still in that cracked voice, "I didn't think you'd do it. I thought you were just talking like always. But I hope it works out with Ben. He's nice."

The knot of tension between her shoulders relaxed a bit. "You mean it's all right?"

"Yeah." He heaved himself out of the chair. "Yeah. And . . ." he stopped, then said, shyly, "I'm proud of you, Mom."

"You are?" People, she thought, even those she knew, would always amaze her, Jamie perhaps most of all.

"Yeah," he said again. "Who else do we know who'd do this? Who'd even think about doing it even if they wanted to?"

She knew the answer. "Nobody."

"Right. But you're different. You've always been, I just had trouble seeing it because . . . because I felt so bad all the time. But I'm sorry I called you a wimp. You're not. No way."

She fought down her own tears—of relief, of pride in this manchild who, like her, had come through the fire and was ready to fly.

"Thanks," she said. "I never wanted to fail you, and I don't intend to start now. How about you and me go out to dinner? You choose."

"Great. Then can I tell Edward?"

She thought a minute. "Can you wait a few days? I don't want his mother calling me. And after dinner I think we ought to go tell your grandmothers."

Jamie's mouth twisted into a wry grin. "What do you think they'll say?"

"Who knows?"

"Aren't you scared?"

"No!" she said, too loudly, refusing to admit that she'd put off telling either woman until nearly the last.

"You are!"

"So what?"

He shrugged. "So don't be. They're old. They wouldn't approve no matter what you told them."

"I don't believe you said that."

"Well, I did. You know how they are. Anything different, any change in how things have always been, and it's your fault. It'll be your fault no matter what, so let's go tell them and then come home."

"I guess I'm still wimpy," she said with a laugh. "You're right. They do scare me. But I'll survive. Just don't mention Ben."

He gave her a severe look. "Ben's not any of my business. Or theirs."

"Thanks again," she said, hoping her courage would hold out until the last scene, the final bitter word. If ever she were to lose the child, the time was now.

"Why are you here?" Lottie stood in the door, her head tilted like a bird's.

Like a canary in a cage. The thought came to Nan unbidden. The old woman had been beating at the bars with futile wings for more than eighty years, had worn herself out until only rage remained, visible in the hot coals of her eyes.

Nan stepped inside, pulling Jamie with her. "Can we sit down a minute?"

In answer, Lottie turned and shuffled into the living room. Without her cane she was awkward, leaning on the back of chairs, her dressing gown flapping with each step.

"We've come to say goodbye," Nan said when they were seated in an uncomfortable circle. "Jamie and I are leaving at the end of the week."

"Where are you going?"

Nan had expected that and shook her head. "I'm not saying. Not yet, anyhow. I'll keep in touch, but where we're going is a secret for now."

Lottie smiled. It was a conspiratorial smile, and her eyes gleamed with grim humor. "So you're doing it. Better late than never I suppose."

When Nan didn't answer, she turned to Jamie, and her expression softened. "I expect great things from you. And I want you to look out for your mother."

"Mom can look out for herself," he said, rising to Nan's defense.

"That remains to be seen." Lottie turned back to Nan. "You have my money in a safe place?"

"In a checking account. Don't worry." Of course, she thought, Lottie's first concern would be for "her" money.

"Well I do," Lottie said. "And I will. And I warn you, there's no more when that's gone."

They sat in silence—three generations, each struggling for recognition, each bound by the strictures of family, propriety, and time.

Suddenly Lottie said, "I wish it was me. I wish I'd done what you're doing when I still had the chance. But I was always bound. Even after Jake's father died, I just kept on like I was. There's so much I never did. So much I wanted. So much? . . . so much . . ." Her voice trailed off into the musty corners of the apartment.

Like dry leaves. Like pressed flowers in a book with brittle pages. And there was nothing Nan could do or say to resurrect the years of lost dreams. Nothing except to go on and do what she had planned. She shivered, more from her insight into Lottie and her past than because the room was cold.

She got up slowly, reached out and helped Lottie to stand. "I'll phone," she said.

Lottie's head snapped up. "Write!" she commanded. "The phone's expensive, and you'll be on a budget. Now give me a kiss and don't worry. I'll take care of Jake."

Of course she would. He was hers, faults and all, and she loved him because she had no one else, because her blood and bone had formed him, carried him, nurtured him however unwisely or unwell. The love of mothers for sons was composed of passion and intellect and something else that eluded definition. Some hope of glory denied to the vessel, some intimation of the joyousness of flight.

"Leaving? You can't! You can't just walk out as if you have no responsibilities. And people will talk. You know they will." Helen was standing in her living room, her posture that of a general giving commands.

Nan cringed, even though she'd known what her mother's first words would be. To Helen, to Jake, to Lottie, she was still a child to be scolded, made to behave, stood in the corner. She squared her shoulders. "I know it's hard to understand," she began, choosing her words with care. "But I've thought it over. For a long time I've been thinking about it, and I've decided what I'm doing is right. I'm not here to ask permission, but to tell you what I'm doing. I hoped . . ." she hesitated a moment, "I hoped you would see my side of it, no matter what opinions you had. I guess I was wrong."

"I don't know *who* you are!" The cry was torn out of Helen's throat. "All your life I've tried to understand you, but you never let me. You turned away from me, shut me out. I always thought mothers and daughters were like friends, but not with you."

Nan sighed. Who was to blame? The three year old? The mother filled with hope and unacknowledged hunger? Wherever the blame, whatever was said now could never eradicate a past built on fear and distrust, and, as usual, they had strayed from her initial purpose into a battle of wills. *Love me! Give me! See me!* Perhaps all mothers and daughters were at cross-purposes, or perhaps she was as she had suspected, a hawk hatched in a duck's nest, misplaced from the beginning.

She said, "Mother . . ." and waited.

Helen didn't answer.

"I'm me," she said, desperation lending her impetus. "Me. Not you, and not whoever you dreamed up or imagined. I'm not Shirley Temple or any of those precious, make-believe little girls you admired. I want things. Not the things you want but other things because I'm not you. I'm a real person and I'm separate from you. Can't you see?"

Helen's eyes flashed, steel-blue, behind her glasses. "I can't, and that's the truth. You're a stranger, and it hurts. It hurts."

The loving arms, the maternal understanding Nan had craved all her life and had done without were still denied her—not by herself but by the woman who had borne her. She choked back tears.

"It hurts me, too. I wanted . . ." She stopped, realizing that any explanation would lead to more accusations and heartache. "It hurts me like it hurts to leave here, but I'm doing it. To save myself and Jamie."

Helen's response came unexpectedly. "And about time. I never could stand that man. Neither could your father. We hated coming to your house, having to watch while he humiliated the two of you."

"Why didn't you say something? Ask me?"

"You married him." Helen's answer was clipped.

And was punished for it, Nan thought. *Punished for being different, from straying from the fairy tale path, for disappearing as a child and never emerging again.* The vividness of that earliest memory made her nauseous, and she swallowed hard.

"You could have helped me," she cried out. "You're my mother, like you said."

"I didn't think it was any of my business. Besides, you never took advice from me, even when you were little."

They could stand here and argue all night, stand like mock soldiers whose wounds, nonetheless, were real and deep. Nan shook her head and held out her arms in a last attempt to break the barrier between them. "Let's forget all that. Can we? Please?"

Helen turned away toward Jamie. "How we loved you," she whispered. "How I'll miss you. Give me a kiss like a good boy."

And Nan, watching, knew the truth. She was only a daughter, and a prodigal one. She was alone with only her own fragile beliefs, as she had always been.

"I'll be in touch," she said coldly.

Helen's expression turned to concern. "Where are you going?"

"I'll let you know."

"I wish I could come with you. It would be an adventure." Longing shone in Helen's eyes, and for the first time Nan felt compassion for this woman with the mind and heart of a child and the inability to deviate from the narrow path she had chosen to pursue.

Once more she opened her arms, and this time Helen came into them. "You can come and visit when we've got settled," she said, noticing with another jolt of pity that Helen barely reached her shoulder, and that her hair was pure white like the dandelion clocks that she used to scatter with a breath.

Helen raised a hand and touched her cheek, and Nan felt the tremor in her fingers.

"God bless you both," Helen said, and then, with an effort, "I love you. In spite of everything. You do know that, don't you?"

Speechless, Nan nodded once, struggling with the knowledge that love was both weapon and treasure, that it could kill as well as conceive. Once she had lied to Lottie, but now the admission came straight from the hidden chambers of her heart.

"I know. I do know. And I love you, too." Then turning, she ran for the car, blinded by tears.

CHAPTER THIRTY-SIX

Jamie was silent on the way home, probably stunned by what he'd just witnessed. But as Nan pulled into the driveway he said, with an embarrassed laugh, "No wonder you were scared. She acted like she hated you. Then she said she loved you. I wasn't sure what to do."

"Me, neither. It was worse than I thought, but it's done. For now," Nan added, knowing that she and Helen, regardless of what had been said, were antagonists whose differences would always intrude.

Jamie squirmed in his seat. "Do you . . . do you think Dad will ever say that? That he loves me?"

His question took her by surprise, and yet how well she understood. *In all of us is the hunger to be loved. By our parents most of all,* she thought, frowning as she searched for an answer that would give him both comfort and hope.

"I've told you before that he loves you," she said. "Just like he loves me. But he can't show it. Can't let go of whatever it is inside that dictates his actions. But to answer your question," she took a breath, "yes, I think someday he will because it's true and he'll have to face his problems, face you or risk losing you as he's lost me. It might not happen next week or next year. You might be as old as I am and will have forgotten this conversation. But when it happens, you have to accept, tell him your own truth, otherwise his admission will have meant nothing. Do you understand?"

"I guess. I guess it was hard for you, too."

"Nothing good ever came easy," she said. "But I want you to remember that you're loved. By us, by your grandparents. And that you deserve to be loved. Got it?"

He sat a minute, head bowed. "Yeah," he said. "But isn't it funny how people are? Everybody's all screwed up, even grownups."

She laughed. "Oh, baby, you don't know the half of it." She got out and pulled her coat collar tightly around her throat. The moon had risen, and the frost that lay on the grass shone silver in its light.

At the front door, she hesitated. Home, she thought, but it wasn't. It was simply a place where she had labored for the better part of her life, where she had lived and left no signature of self except in the garden where Jake had never intruded. Most of the furniture, and even its placement, had been decided by him. All she had done was caretake, and those few things she loved were packed and waiting in the hall. The horse painting she had carried back from Scotland; the Dutch fruit and flower painting she had loved at first sight; the silverware, as Wendy had advised, and her jewelry, all of it, topazes, diamonds, garnets and rubies stowed away in her trunk; several small old rugs whose design and colors she never failed to notice; her clothes, books, papers, a box of photographs. Odd that, after twenty years she had so little to take with her.

Odder still that a little less than a year ago she had stood in the yard and asked herself who and what she was. And then, miserable, desperate, wanting to belong somewhere, with someone, she had found Ben.

Now she was embarking on a journey of discovery, a flight that would end in Ben's arms. And yet she knew she was not doing this only for him. She was saving herself because she needed to touch the world, to speak out in her own voice that had been dormant so long. And she knew that he, unlike Jake, would understand.

PART THREE

When he comes, Sister Anne, tell him I'm gone and that he won't find me. Tell him I'm not afraid anymore because I've lost the child.

Tell him to look for what I am in the garden, in the branches of the chestnut tree, in the books that I will write.

Better yet, tell him nothing. The empty house will speak for me, the echoes of anger, the tears that were shed.

I have waxed the floors, polished the furniture, put clean sheets on the bed. I have paid the bills and taken out the garbage.

I have done my best, even now, and so tell him goodbye and that the years left are mine.

The road stretches out in front of me as it did for so many thousands of others—a ribbon of hope. The sun sets like an explosion on the flat land of the mid-west, and no matter how fast I move toward it, it eludes, moves further away like a mirage.

Tell him I'll make it on my own, that other women have done this before me, and that I walk in their tracks, throwing my heart ahead, dreaming my own dreams, alive as I've never been alive.

Tell him I'm singing a love song to the earth that stretches out like a tapestry, red-gold, indigo, the dun of stubble fields, their ragged edges stitched by the darkness of raven's wings.

Tell him I feel for him in his loneness, for he is lost and I, inexplicably, have been found.

CHAPTER THIRTY-SEVEN

She was in Illinois. Ben opened the big atlas he'd carried to his desk and stared at the map. Still miles to go, the Plains to cross, and it was winter.

"Any sign of a storm, you hole up and stay put," he'd told Nan on the phone, and was dismayed when she laughed.

"I'll be fine," she said.

But damn! She had no idea what a blizzard on the Plains was like—the wind, the snow thick as a rug, the cold that knifed your bones until you took the easy way out and simply went to sleep.

"Listen to me!" he said, desperation lending an edge to his voice. "I know what I'm talking about."

She was still laughing. "And so do I. We'll be fine. This is wonderful, all this country. I feel like a pioneer."

"And a bunch of them never made it." He was worried, sick in his gut. Her out there alone without a fear in the world and laughing.

"But I will." She was firm.

"You call me tomorrow. And the day after. Head for Taos, and I'll meet you."

"Honest?" He heard it then, the smallest doubt as if she hadn't been sure of him.

"Yes," he said. "I've waited long enough."

"Me, too." She was laughing again. "Oh, Ben, me, too."

"Just be careful. And call. I'll sit right here every evening."

"Yes," she said. "Every night. Yes, yes, yes."

He flicked on the television and looked at the weather map. Except for a storm in the northwest, the country was clear. With luck she'd be where he was before any weather hit. With luck he'd be able to protect her in a few more days. If anything happened . . . he clenched his jaw. She was his, damn it! His to take care of, cherish, spoil. She needed to be spoiled. Taught how to play. She needed to love and be loved without punishment. A few more days. He wished he could hurry time, say the magic words and have her with him now.

Lupe came to the door, her eyes dancing. "How soon?" she asked.

"Four days. Maybe three if the weather holds."

"It will."

How was she so sure? How were these two women possessed of such a firm belief, while he, alone, suffered and worried? He scowled at her. "How do you know?"

"Because the hard part is done. The rest is easy."

"I wish I believed you."

"I tell you the truth. Like always. But you don't hear. She's made up her mind. Nothing ever stopped a woman who made up her mind, and for sure not this one."

Nan, bringing in cattle, spreading her arms to embrace the mountain. Nan with laughter welling up like a spring at the sight of a colt, a field of poppies. And she was coming . . . to him.

He said, "I'm meeting her in Taos."

Lupe nodded. "Then get started instead of sitting here thinking bad thoughts. Go there and wait."

"And quit bothering you?" He glanced at her, saw the smile cross her face.

"I'll tell her where you are," she said. "I'll tell her to hurry."

"No you won't! You'll tell her to be careful. I've waited this long."

"Yes," she said. "And it's meant to happen, so it will."

From where did such unshakable faith come? He'd never been like that, at least not since Margo. In his experience the world was a bitter place with scant room for hope. Maybe, he thought, there were things Nan could teach him. Things like optimism and the sweetness of being with someone you loved day after day. He'd been a prisoner of his own wariness for more years than he could count, his happiness locked away, his suspicions ruling his every act.

He looked up at Lupe and smiled, white teeth flashing in his tanned face. "I'll go pack," he said.

The valley below was snow-covered as far as Nan could see. The whiteness dazzled her, and the purple shadows under trees and along the crooked edges of streams. She wanted to get out, roll in the snow, touch it, taste it, put her hands around the shapes of shadows and drifts. It was for this that she had come, this piercing joy, this freedom to feel without fear of being jerked back into the reality of another.

"Oh, look," she said, more to herself than to Jamie. "Oh, just look at it." It sounded like a prayer.

He'd become used to her moments, more frequent in the last few days, and he smiled with understanding. "It's okay. You can stop here if you want."

She giggled like a girl and reached for her sunglasses. "No stopping. We'll be in Taos in a few hours, and Ben will be there."

"You want me to disappear?" he asked.

She shot him a look. "Why?"

"Well . . . I thought, you know. Maybe you guys want to be alone."

He was thinking about sex, as she had been for the last thousand miles. And probably feeling cut out of her life. She reached across and patted his knee. "This is me you're talking to. What did you think? That I was going to drag him off to bed and leave you?"

"Well. . . ."

"Well, nothing. We're going to play tourist. I always wanted to see the pueblo, and you should see it, too. We'll have dinner. The three of us. We are not shutting you out. Got it?"

She spoke around her own yearning, trying for lightness. She'd never slept with any man but Jake in her life, and that made her an innocent. Although her body was crying out for Ben, she was terrified. What to do? Say? How to act when the day was over and it was time to make a decision. His room or hers? Should she act coy or be honest? God! Adult love was more hazardous than the gropings of adolescence! Her love for Ben was real, but the dance of courtship was a dance she'd never learned.

"Don't worry, Mom," Jamie said. "Just do what comes naturally."

Had he read her mind? Was he giving her advice when it should have been the other way around? "How do you know so much?" she asked with a hint of indignation. "What've you been doing I don't know about?"

He looked away. "Not much."

"Thank goodness. And if you're doing what I think, use a condom. You hear me?"

Jamie's face was red. "Geez, Mom!"

"I mean it." This was a talk that was long overdue, one that he and Jake should have had. Except that they obviously

250

hadn't, and she was now a single parent having to explain the facts to a teenager who knew more than she did.

"Look," she began, then stopped, frustrated. "It's easy to make a mistake and forget. Doing it right is lots harder than just following your instinct. But it's also being a man and responsible for your actions. I don't expect you to be celibate, but I do expect you to be careful, in your choice of a partner in particular. Sex is different when you love someone. It's not a blind act but something beautiful between two people. That's all I'm saying, but it's important."

Here she was, talking as if she knew, when the truth was that she'd reverted to her fairy-tale belief, and if being with Ben wasn't as she'd imagined it, she'd be shattered. She loved him, wanted him, but would that prove to be enough?

Oh, get a life! she scolded herself. *You won't die. You can't. Not now.*

She took a long last look at the glittering mountains, the dark pines and their blue shadows. Here was her life—in the seeing, the connection with the world. Whatever happened, she had always possessed a passion and the need to make that passion tangible. Whatever happened, she still had herself.

She shifted gears and pulled out, headed downhill toward destiny.

CHAPTER THIRTY-EIGHT

A light snow was falling as Nan and Jamie drove into Taos. On either side of the single street, lights were on in adobe houses, yet Nan felt that somehow she was far from cities and the noise of civilization, that she had stumbled into an asylum, a place that had retreated from modernity, where the old ways ruled, and where, when darkness fell, silence would take over and the voices that spoke from the mountains.

Ben was sitting in the lobby of the inn watching the door. She saw him as she entered, shaking snowflakes from her hair, and stopped, hearing the beat of her heart like an Indian drum in her ears.

"I made it," she said.

"God bless you." He took her in his arms, and she felt his warmth, his strength, his hunger that matched her own, and her legs seemed to go out from under her, so that she clung to him a minute, gathering her own strength.

"Where's Jamie?" he asked.

"In the car. I parked illegally."

"You're already registered. I got three rooms. For the kid's sake. Okay?"

She nodded, glad that whatever they did, it would be in private. She tilted her face for a kiss. "I can't believe I'm here."

"And liable to be snowed in," he said.

"How long?"

He laughed. "Who knows? Could be a week. Do you mind?"

"No. It's wonderful. The mountains. And how it smells outside, just like your fires at the ranch. And you're here. That's best of all." She rested against him, eyes closed, and he saw the signs of fatigue in the delicate lines around them.

"Come on. Let's get you settled. Jamie, too. Then we'll eat. Hungry?"

"Always." There were things she wanted to say, but suddenly she was shy, as shy as she'd been as a girl. Here she was in a hotel lobby with the man she loved, not quite sure how it had happened, how she'd escaped into Paradise, or what she was supposed to do next.

"I'll get your bags and Jamie," he said. "Here's your room key, ma'am." His eyes twinkled. "You're a woman in a thousand, you know. Hell, in ten thousand. One for the books." He bent down and kissed her again, gently.

He was proud of her. No one had ever been proud of anything she had done. Not Jake, not Helen. Her smile was radiant. "I'm here," she repeated, and in the saying knew that whatever happened next would be right, that like a moth that flies a thousand miles to find its mate, she, too had flown and found her place.

There was a Christmas tree in the lobby and a huge fire of piñon logs, and she stopped beside it, sniffing the fragrance that was so much a part of the Southwest. On the walls old retablos and santos had been hung, and she gave thanks to the saints for bringing her through, to the God who had lent her courage.

Her room had a fireplace built into a corner, and wood stacked ready to be lit. On the walls were pictures of broad-shouldered women bearing bundles of corn or red peppers, or holding pottery made with their own strong hands. She looked a long while. In womanhood was strength and courage. In womanhood was battle and the sweetness of loving when the fight was won. In womanhood was herself, brought up in a culture far removed from triumph, but nevertheless triumphant.

The power that had been taken from her, the words, the purity were returning in a flood of seeing, and she thought that someday soon her voice would be loud enough to reach behind the mountains to the darkening sky.

And after all there was no need for coyness, for the putting off of the inevitable. They came together, woman and man, as lovers have always come together—in passion, in the tenderness of two spirits long denied.

He kissed her—lips, breasts, the secret place where no man had ever kissed her. She had kept herself for him, tongue and lips, and knew vindication. She had been born for this man, and he for her, and when she cried out, it was not from pain but from a pleasure that threatened to annihilate her. She was the fire that flickered, the shadows trembling on white walls. She was the man on his knees, and the woman beneath. She was all things, all lovers, and the taste of her own explosion was in her mouth and burning behind her eyes, and in the touching of the man she had chosen—mate, lover, friend, self—mirror of her own passion, twin to the singing of her heart.

Ben woke in the middle of the night. The fire had burned down, the room was cold. Outside snow fell steadily, felt rather than seen, a silent presence wrapping around them as they slept.

He bent over Nan, saw her hair tangled, her cheeks still faintly flushed. She lay curled into herself, for warmth, he thought, or perhaps to contain the hours they had spent.

Quietly he went to the cupboard for a blanket, placed it over her. He would keep her warm all the days of his life.

She moved then, opened her eyes, smiled the smile of a child that knows it is loved, and fell back to sleep where the dream came to her again, she, the man, the sense of unity. "I will take care of you the rest of your life."

"And I, too," she answered, finding words for the first time. "I will care for you. Always. Forever. No matter what."

The dream turned to the whiteness of snow, and she slept as she had not slept in years, deeply, soundly, undisturbed.

At breakfast Ben handed the keys to his truck to Jamie. "I need your help. On my way up here I found two dogs dropped off on the road and brought them along. How about taking them out for me?"

Jamie's eyes lit up. "I always wanted a dog. But Dad . . ." He shrugged and looked at Nan.

"Jake worried about his rugs," she explained.

"The hell with Jake. You've got two dogs, pal. They're waiting." Woman and boy were still under the bastard's thumb. But give them time. Give him time—and Nan in his arms at night.

Jamie shoved back his chair and eyed their plates. "Any leftovers?"

"Take mine. I fed them hamburger last night, but they're half starved. You're in charge."

He and Nan watched him go, then smiled at each other. "How'd you know he needed a dog?" Nan asked.

"All kids do. Especially kids like him."

"You're so good."

"At what?" He raised one black brow and grinned wickedly.

"At everything." She reached over and covered his hand

255

with hers, a spontaneous gesture that surprised her. "I've never done that before," she admitted. "Touched a man because I wanted to."

"Touch me anytime. Anywhere." He was still grinning, but he wished suddenly that he'd found her when she was eighteen, unscarred and unafraid, as filled with love as she was now. Well, at least he *had* found her. He still couldn't believe it and shook his head. "What do you want to do today since we're snowed in?"

"Be a tourist. See everything. Go back to bed." Her eyes glinted, then faded into distress. "And call home so my mother won't worry."

She still called it home, he noticed. "Call now," he said. "Get it over with. Then we'll go walk around town."

Helen's voice was cautious. "Yes?"

"It's me."

"Thank goodness! I thought it might be *him*. Again," she added darkly, and Nan's hands began to shake.

"He knows?" Even her words came out wobbly, and she hated herself for succumbing to fear.

"He certainly does. He called the other night and said he hadn't been able to reach you. He asked where you were."

"And?" Nan held her breath.

"And I told him you were gone. He wanted to know where, and I said I didn't know. He's at the house now and wants you to call, and I wish you would. I'm not up to this."

Nan was frozen in place. He knew! Now he'd come after her, force her back, lock her away. He'd find her no matter where she went. She'd be looking over her shoulder, cringing at the ring of the telephone for the rest of her life, and no one, not even Ben, could help her.

Sister Anne . . . Sister Anne . . .

"Are you there?" Helen asked.

"Yes. But I don't . . . I can't call him yet. It's too soon."

"Are you alone?" Suspicion crept into Helen's voice.

Nan managed a laugh. "I didn't run off with the milkman if that's what you're thinking."

"This isn't funny!"

"Just . . . oh, just give me a few more days. Please. Tell him you haven't heard from me. Can you do that?"

Helen sighed audibly. "Alright. But it isn't fair—to me or him. He's *your* husband."

"Not for long. I'm filing for divorce. He'll probably get the papers any day."

"I hope you know what you're doing."

Did she? "Oh yes," she said, remembering how Ben had covered her in the night, kept her warm, watched over her as no one had ever done. "Yes," she repeated. "I do know."

She walked slowly out to the old cemetery where Ben and Jamie were throwing snowballs for the dogs to chase. Father and son. How she wished it could have been like this, without anger, neuroses, punishment. She wiped away the tears that came and bent to make a snowball of her own.

Ben had been watching her. "Bad news?"

"He found out." She searched his face hoping for comfort.

"You look like he's going to pop up from behind a tombstone," he said, taking her arm. "Relax. He's got the Indian sign on you but forget it. He can't hurt you anymore."

"It's not that easy. I thought it would be, but now I'm scared." She touched her tongue to the snow and tasted the cold.

She still hadn't learned her own strength, hadn't figured out that she'd done what few abused wives had ever succeeded in doing. But she would. He'd see to it.

"Come on," he said. "Meet the pups. And forget him, like

I said. He's not here, and he won't be. You are. I am."

She wanted to believe him, but she could feel Jake's rage from two thousand miles away. Tomorrow or the next day she'd have to call, hear his voice, defend herself while being made to feel the child again—guilty and ashamed.

Somehow Jake would find a way to punish her—and Ben. She bit her lip to stop it from trembling. No way would she let him attack Ben! In her hands, the snow had hardened into ice. Without stopping to think, she threw it as hard as she could at a tree, saw it connect and splatter.

"Take that, Jake!" she muttered. "That's for starters!"

Ben chuckled. "Who taught you to throw like that?"

"My father. He wanted a boy, but all he got was me."

"Hell," he said. "I wouldn't trade you for any boy. Especially not after last night."

"I love you," she said. "You know that?"

His arm was steady around her waist. "If you don't, you gave a good imitation."

One of the dogs spotted them and came running, light as a leaf, and she stooped down to greet it. "It's an Irish wolfhound!" she exclaimed. "Who'd dump him?"

"People are rotten."

She put her arms around the pup's neck. "Hello, Clancy," she said. "Where have you been all my life?"

In answer, Clancy looked her straight in the eye and licked her nose.

"Your mother has the knack of naming animals," Ben said to Jamie as he came up with the other pup, a yellow labrador. "First Monarch, now Clancy."

"What about him?" Jamie pointed at the dog at his heels.

"MacDuff," Nan said without hesitation.

They all laughed, and Ben said, "MacDuff it is. Now let's get them back in the truck and go do the town. First though, you ought to know that Kit Carson is buried right here in this cemetery."

Jamie looked around. "You mean Taos was here then?"

"Sure was. The mountain men came here, the Spanish lived and traded here, the Indians revolted here and killed a lot of innocent people in the process. Carson's house is a museum. We can go see it if you want."

"And in this century D. H. Lawrence and Georgia O'Keeffe came," Nan added. "Lots of artists and writers have, and it's easy to see why."

"Someday they'll say, 'Oh, yes. Nan Fletcher stopped here on her way South,'" Ben said. "Mark my words."

She shivered suddenly, and he turned to her. "Cold?"

"No. It was just what you said. It sounded like gospel."

"It was. And when we get back to the ranch, someone's coming I want you to meet."

"Why?"

"You'll find out," he promised. "A man has to keep some secrets."

And he would, so there was no point pestering him. "Okay. Let's go see the pueblo," she said. "Before my feet freeze to the ground."

It was the color of the earth, and it had been here for centuries, stacked like children's blocks around the worn dirt plaza. The incense of piñon seemed unusually pungent, overpowering the scents of snow and bread baking in the outdoor ovens. From somewhere came the sound of a drum and a single voice chanting words that were unintelligible, yet that Nan understood in her blood.

"Let's go see who that is," she urged. "Come on," and headed across the plaza to the houses clustered near the river.

They found an old man in a small room, and Nan stood in the doorway watching and listening, feeling her spirit take flight. Oblivious, the singer kept on, his voice rising and falling, the beat of his drum keeping time.

Earth time, Nan thought. *The motions of stars, the journey of sun and moon and seasons.* She closed her eyes and swayed to the rhythm, and was startled when the drum stopped and the old man spoke.

"One dollar."

Her eyes flew open. "What?"

"One dollar," he repeated with an unreadable look.

He wanted money! Payment for her dreaming. Indignant, she shook her head, then saw Ben reach into his pocket.

"You're going to pay him?" she demanded.

"You pay to go to a concert, don't you?"

"But this is different."

"To you, maybe. Not to him. Come on." He put the bill into a basket on the floor then went out. She followed, dazed by the abrupt transition from spirit to commerce.

"I still say that was demeaning. For him *and* me," she said.

"He's an artist. He gets paid just like you do for writing."

That made sense, but she felt something had been ruined, the purity of her pleasure stolen. "Life is too much with me, I guess," she said. "Maybe I don't understand."

"And maybe you're a romantic. The old guy has to eat like the rest of us, and besides, he's figured out how to make the white man pay."

She stopped walking, the truth of his words becoming clear. Beneath the seeming peace and simplicity of the place lay the bitterness of the conquered for the conquerors and the desire for revenge, even a small one.

"Nothing is what it seems."

"Not much," he agreed.

And us? she wondered. *Are we what we seem, or something other?*

A gust of wind blew off the mountain, cold and tasting of snow, and she wrapped her arms around herself. "Let's go. Let's get warm, and have lunch, and forget this place." But she knew she would never forget. That in her mind she'd return again and again in search of answers she might never find.

The woman was wrapped in the blue swirl of a butterfly's wing, her face upturned, her arms raised as gracefully as any dancer.

"Butterfly Woman," the clerk said, noting Nan's interest. "Not your usual Kachina."

Cautiously Nan put out a hand, touched the carved wood as if the woman within, emerging from the winged embrace, would somehow speak.

"She's lovely," she murmured. And so was the price. Way above her budget. Reluctantly she moved to another counter, acknowledging the fact that she was a great deal poorer than she'd ever imagined, and that items bought on whimsy were, from here on in, beyond her.

Ben recognized the longing in her eyes. She was seeing herself, the woman freed, a radiant metamorphosis. When she moved off, he spoke quietly to the clerk who smiled, nodded, and wrapped the figure in tissue.

"Where is she?" Nan came back, a concha belt in her hand. "What happened to her?"

Ben handed her the package. "Merry almost Christmas," he said.

The warmth that shot through her was like lightning, swift, brilliant, stunning. "How . . . how did you know?" she choked around the lump in her throat.

"It was written all over you. She is you, and you're her. I couldn't let you leave without her."

261

"Oh, my God," she said. "Oh, Ben. Nobody ever . . ." Then she was silent, words rattling in her head that she couldn't get out.

All she could do was stare at the carving she held in her hands, learn the subtle design, the face and partially revealed torso of the woman who seemed to be her mirror image. And he knew. Ben knew!

She cast off all vestiges of her past and put her arms around him. "Thank you," she whispered. "So much. For everything."

Catching Jamie's eye, the clerk applauded. She was an older woman decked out in necklaces and bracelets that jingled like bells. "Merry Christmas," she said. "It's so good to see two nice people in love."

Once Nan would have been mortified. Now she turned and beamed at the woman. "And to you, too."

"And Happy New Year," Jamie added, coming to stand beside them. "Especially that." He was holding an ornate, sand cast belt buckle. "Mom, can I buy this?"

She did a quick addition in her head. Not only had she no presents for him, she had nothing for Ben. "Why don't you two go on back? I want to do some shopping."

Ben took the hint. "Come on," he said to Jamie. "Let's check the dogs and then repair to the bar. Women shopping are too much for me."

She watched them go down the street, two tall men in western boots. Father and son. How she wished it were so!

"Such a handsome man." The clerk fluttered jeweled fingers. "You want a present for him I'm thinking."

Nan nodded. "Something special. He's a rancher."

"I always thought I'd like ranching," the woman said. "But I never got the chance. I came out here when my husband died and got into the Indian jewelry business. It's been fun. And profitable, but still . . ." Her words dwindled and hung in the air like a mantra Nan had heard before.

"But you've had fun," she reminded her. "That's the important thing."

"At times," came the response. "I never remarried. Once was enough, believe me." She busied herself moving a collection of animal fetishes on the countertop. "It was so long ago it hardly seems worth talking about. But I still have nightmares. You know?" She looked questioningly at Nan.

"About what?"

"He broke my arm once. I should have left him then, but I didn't. I didn't have anyplace to go, you see."

She said it so simply, as if it were an obvious fact, and perhaps it was, Nan thought. Perhaps there were thousands of women like this one, like the women crammed into the prison of Refuge House; beaten women with no place to go.

"I left," she said abruptly. "That's why I'm here. He didn't beat me. He just owned my soul."

"A vampire." The woman looked at her through lashes beaded with mascara. "The silent killers. No marks to prove anything, right?"

"You know then."

She smiled crookedly. "Sweetie, I could name you at least five women right off the top of my head who're stuck in that situation. Too scared to make a move, sure nobody'll believe them. If you got out, more power to you."

Silent killers. An apt description. "I wish I could help somehow," Nan said.

"Get on one of those talk shows, why don't you? You know the kind."

Nan shook her head. "I don't think I could. I'm a writer, not a talker."

Gently she picked up one of the fetish animals, an alabaster horse with a turquoise mane. "This is lovely. Is it . . . is it very expensive?"

"For him?" the woman asked.

"Yes. He's a horseman. He might like this."

"Take it. And Merry Christmas, like I said. You deserve it."

"I can't!"

"Sure you can. Besides, your man did me a favor buying Butterfly Woman. She's been here as long as I have. Waiting for you probably. They do, you know. Fetishes, kachinas seem to know who they belong to, so take the horse. It's Zuni. The real thing, too. You can buy the kid's buckle. He seems like a nice kid."

"He is. He had it rough, too, but I think he'll be okay."

"I saw it in his eyes." The clerk was wrapping the fetish carefully. "Once you've seen that look, you don't forget it. You want the concha belt? It suits you if you don't mind my saying so."

Nan had forgotten the belt she'd wrapped around her waist. In the bright shop lights the conchas gleamed with the purity of fine silver. She had jewelry, but none that felt as right as this.

"Oh, the heck!" she exclaimed. "Yes, I want it. It's a present to myself. I'll wear it." She pulled out her credit card feeling slightly defiant as she remembered all the years of doing without, looking with longing into shop windows, envying her friends their fashionable clothes.

Snow was falling as she left the shop and made her way carefully down the street. At the town plaza she stopped short, staring at the *luminarias* that lit the way to the church, each candle a golden blossom in the fading light. And the magic of place overwhelmed her, held her spellbound, with the snow blowing past, and the piñon smoke sweet in the air.

For centuries these *farolitos* had been lit at Christmas. For years this plaza had echoed with the feet of those making their way to the church—Indian, Mexican, the conquerors, the armed and the unarmed had walked here, on this street at dusk in the light of a hundred candles. Time was nothing to this place, to the guardian mountains, to the desert below cut by the mighty river that flowed south.

People lived and died, yet the nature of humanity, the goodness and the evils, the petty crimes and the moments of passion remained and would remain, and perhaps the echo of her love for Ben would be here centuries from now—the music of a Navaho flute, the notes of a wind chime, the flowering of a candle in the snow.

"I keep thinking this is a dream," she said to Ben that night. "That I'll wake up and be back there, and Jake will be yelling at me. But I don't *want* it to be a dream. I don't want to wake up."

He reached out and pulled her close so her head lay on his shoulder. "I was feeling like that, too. But it's real. All of it. You. Me. We were made for each other. The worst is over, and you can forget Jake. He'll never hurt you again."

But he would, she knew. He'd try. She would have to call him in the morning and try to explain the unexplainable, then hear the bitterness of his wrath.

She threw her arms around Ben, felt the heat of his body, the thrust of his arousal. "Hold me," she begged. "Hold me close."

How could he not? She was woman, passionate, loving, yet needing the strength that he had in abundance, strength she had awakened in him. He felt that he'd been asleep for a hundred years, the masculine version of the myth, a man who had been brought to life by the touch of this woman's hand, by the hunger in her eyes.

CHAPTER THIRTY-NINE

She looked at the telephone as if it were her enemy. "Just do it," she scolded herself. "Get it over with."

But her hands were shaking so badly she misdialed the number, and whoever answered sounded annoyed and slightly out of breath as if she had been running or making love and resented the intrusion.

"Sorry," Nan apologized and hung up, then cast a desperate look at Butterfly Woman on the table beside the fireplace. The very sight of the carving gave her courage. She dialed again.

Jake answered on the second ring.

"It's me," she said, and thought the pounding of her heart could be heard at the other end.

"Where are you?" He sounded stern, like a preacher about to call fire and brimstone down upon her head.

She sat up straighter, her eyes fastened on the statue. He'd not terrorize her. Not this time. "New Mexico," she said, then waited for the explosion.

"What the hell's the matter with you? Driving all the way out there, taking my son away. It's kidnapping, you know. Breaking the law. I could have you arrested for stealing the money in my checking account."

"No," she said clearly, hoping to pierce his self-righteous anger. "No, it is *not* against the law. Jamie's past the age of consent, and the money is not *yours*. It's ours. I'm not the fool you tried to make me believe. I checked everything with my lawyer before I left."

"Lawyer? You went to a lawyer?" She had shocked him.

"Of course."

"You mean you planned this? That all along you've been lying to me? I knew you weren't happy, but this is beyond belief." He went on, his voice rising into hysteria. "How do you think I felt? I called and I called, and you didn't answer. Then your mother told me you'd left. That's what she said. 'She left,' like she didn't care how I felt either. When I came home, you know what I found. You even took the silverware."

Ah, yes. The silver. Equally as important as his son. She held the receiver away from her ear as his accusations continued.

. . . "some of my papers were in the garbage. I got sick. So sick. I went to the hospital . . ."

When she didn't respond, his tone sharpened. "Say something!" he commanded. "Didn't you hear me?"

She remained non-committal. "I heard you." *Always the hospital. Always a refuge.* But there was no refuge in the end.

"You really don't care. After all I did for you."

"What?" she asked. "What did you do?"

His laugh was bitter. "You'd have been an old maid. You know that. I married you, took you to Europe, bought you jewels. And all the time you were hating me."

The phrase rang in her head. *Old maid. Old maid,* the curse of the unwanted, the fear of every girl-child, instilled in them by mothers. But if she had been so undesirable, why had *he* wanted her?

She fought down the angry retorts that came to mind. "Don't try to make me into a nothing," she warned. "It won't work. Not anymore. I've had time to think. And, just so you know, I'd rather be an old maid as you so kindly put it, than your goddamn, worn-out whipping boy. That's why I'm here. It's why how you feel doesn't mean anything to me. 'Make me a decent cup of coffee for a change.' Remember that? I do. That made all the difference."

"That was a joke!"

"Some joke!" she shot back. "I could have been dying and all you thought about was your stomach."

His anger was almost tangible, and she steeled herself.

"How do you think you're going to live? Huh? Answer me. You can't do anything. You never could. And if you think that women's crap you write will support you, guess again."

It was the old, demeaning threat. She, woman and worthless, was supposed to grovel at his feet, beg for forgiveness, for food, water, her very life.

"Don't talk to me like that," she said coldly. "And don't insult my intelligence. I'll manage. I got here without you, and I'm not coming back. So go get your own lawyer before you threaten me or make fun of what I do again."

"You better hope I don't." He was snarling, losing control. "You're menopausal. It happens to women, and everybody knows it. A good lawyer will see the problem, and you won't get another cent."

She pounded her fist on the bed, wishing she could reach out and smash his face. "Don't you blame my body," she hissed at him. "I'm a long way from menopausal, and I'm as capable of logic as anybody. If you want to know who's the crazy one, go look in the mirror. Better yet, go see a psychiatrist like I told you to do years ago."

And that, she thought, had gotten to him. After a long silence he said, "I want you to come home."

"No, Jake," she said. "I've left you because we had no home. And I'm not coming back. I'm sorry it had to happen this way, but it was the only way you'd ever let me go. Understand?"

If he did, he wasn't admitting it. "Take all the time you need to think it over," he answered. "Because you'll be sorry if you don't."

He slammed down the receiver. It sounded like a gunshot, and she grimaced. "Sorry," she snorted then. "I'm sorry, alright. Sorry I ever met you. Menopausal! Menopausal, my left foot!" Then she went out to find Ben.

The snow lay behind them, and the mystery of the northern mountains. Ahead, the desert stretched out, dormant in winter, the branches of cottonwoods and mesquite bare against brown earth and blue sky. The mountains on either side seemed more distant, softer in the winter light, as if they had receded into themselves and were sleeping.

"Pluto's cave," Nan said.

"Who?" Jamie was puzzled.

"Didn't they teach you anything in that fancy school?" she demanded. "Pluto stole Persephone. Took her home with him to his cave. But her mother, Ceres, went looking for her, followed the trail of flowers her daughter had dropped. When she found her daughter, she had to strike a bargain with Pluto, because the gods had promised that Persephone could come home if she hadn't eaten anything while underground. As it turned out, she'd eaten half a pomegranate, so Ceres and Pluto made an agreement. He'd have Persephone half a year, and Ceres would have her the other half. That's how the Greeks explained the seasons."

"Kind of like custody in a divorce," he said.

His reasoning surprised her. "Not quite. And if you're thinking about yourself, there's a difference. You'll be in college in another few months, and it's up to you what you do with your time. I hope you'll choose to spend time with both of us, your father and me. He *is* still your father. And, by the way, he accused me of kidnapping you."

"Are you kidding?" Jamie's eyes were huge.

"No. He did. And when you talk to him I want you to make it clear that you made your own decision. Not that it matters." But it did, to her.

"I wanted to come! You know that."

"But he doesn't. He has no idea what it was like." She clenched her hands on the steering wheel. "I probably shouldn't be talking about him, but I have to be honest. He can't conceive that he hurt you or me. Am I making sense?"

"Sort of, but it's hard." Jamie fiddled with his seat belt. "I mean, it's like he's nuts or something."

There it was thrown in her lap, and was she supposed to admit to a child that his father had problems? "Jamie . . ." she began, then stopped, not knowing how to explain. "Look," she said finally, squinting through the windshield at Ben's truck up ahead, "look, he can't hear himself, okay? He can't put himself in anybody else's shoes. If that's nuts, so be it. But he's still your father, and you're still dependent on him for your education. What you do is your decision, and I wish it weren't. I wish we were a normal family, but we aren't and won't ever be. Oh, Christ!" She slammed the wheel with her fist. "I don't know what to tell you. I don't know how to make any of this easy for you."

He said, "Mom . . ."

And she saw him again in the hospital bed barely alive, hooked to machines, his face white and bruised. "I did what I thought was best for us both," she said. "I got us out. But from here on, I don't know any more than you."

Jamie's face twisted, but when he spoke it was lightly.

"Hey, Mom, take it easy."

"How can I? I feel responsible."

"Maybe that's your problem."

Yes. She was the adult, and wished she wasn't. "I guess so," she said.

She saw Ben's turn signal flash and followed him onto the exit ramp. "When we get settled, we'll talk some more," she promised. "And don't be afraid to say what you think. I'm here for you even if I don't have all the answers."

Ahead of them, the dogs were watching out of the window of the camper shell. Jamie grinned. "They'll be glad to get home, I bet."

He was like mercury—changeable, elusive, serious one minute, laughing the next. "No gladder than me," she said. "I'm planning to sleep for a week."

A sickle moon hung over the western mountains as if it had been painted on the evening sky. How perfect it was! How delicately curved! Nan opened the window a crack and breathed the sweetness of the desert air, then folded her hands in her lap and let the tension flow out of her.

They had switched vehicles. Ben was driving the car, and Jamie followed at the wheel of the truck, so she had nothing to do but sit beside Ben and look out.

"Nearly there." Ben turned off on the dirt road. "I bet you're worn out."

"Happily so."

"And this time you don't have to leave." He reached over and put a gentle hand on her thigh.

"Not ever?" He hadn't mentioned marriage in the three days they'd spent in Taos, and her conversation with Jamie had left her jumpy and unsettled.

"Not ever," he said. "Did you think I was going to let you

go? That I spend my time in bed making love with every woman I meet?"

He was irritated, and she couldn't blame him. Her doubts were her own. "No," she said. "I know better. I'm just feeling kind of fragile. Seeing problems where there aren't any."

"Don't go looking for trouble," he advised. "Life's hard enough. Get settled in and relax awhile. You've had a hell of a bad couple months, in case you don't know it. But nobody here will push you into anything, including me."

He wondered if she was trying to tell him something—that she'd changed her mind and wanted her freedom. That what they'd shared in Taos had been wonderful but was over now and finished. In his experience, that was what women did. They took, they counted heads, and when they'd gotten what they wanted, they said so long and walked away laughing.

He turned and looked at her. She was watching the fading light over the mountains with that intensity that had first attracted him. Cautiously he asked, "Are you trying to tell me something?" then held his breath waiting for her answer.

She understood with that uncanny knowledge about him that came from deep within. "Actually, I was trying to ask a question." She laughed once, nervously. "I got all wrapped around my own axle and thought you mightn't want me anymore. I thought maybe I disappointed you."

"Never!" He let out a sigh of relief. "At least not so far. If you ever do, you'll be the first to know."

"It's just been scary." She curled up on the seat. "I mean, doing what I did, and knowing I loved you, even when all my experience said not to trust my own feelings. I still have a lot to learn about trust and stuff."

"We'll learn together." He lifted his hand and caressed her cheek. "Isn't that part of what love and marriage are about?"

He'd said it! Marriage! He actually wanted her enough to

share his life! She felt like an orphan brought in from the storm, like a woman lost who had been found. She was free to love him as she had wanted to do almost from the first.

"Learning how to live with you will be a happy process," she said. "The reason I was born."

"Amen." He pointed. The lights of the ranch were bright in the valley below. "Amen," he repeated. "And welcome home."

CHAPTER FORTY

The house was as she remembered it, blue-painted window frames, tile floors, and outside the murmur of the creek.

"Now you are home," Lupe said, holding her close. "You have come, and we will have Christmas like it should be, with presents, happiness, love all around."

In Taos Nan had thrown caution to the winds. She bought *ristras* of bright peppers to hang on the porch, a Christmas wreath for the door. She'd fallen in love with a hand-painted Nativity set, purchased Navaho saddle blankets for Ben and Wish, bright western shirts for Jamie and Bay, a red velvet skirt for herself. And for Lupe a triple strand of coral and turquoise beads. For her, it was truly a time for rejoicing and giving, and the hell with her budget!

She fussed over the placement of chairs, the hanging of the paintings she had brought. She went to town and bought plates and bowls from a local potter, and more rugs for the floor. It was her house, and she was making it for Ben, never mind that he had a house of his own filled with treasures.

"Stop!" Lupe told her. "Keep your money. Go out and ride a horse if you have to do something. You are here, and we are all happy. Come and help me in the kitchen. I am making special dishes for Christmas, and we have guests coming. You and I will do it right."

Nan juggled her time. Nights with Ben, occasional rides into the mountains, hours at her desk in the sun room that overlooked the creek, searching for the right rhythms and words to tell the stories she had wanted to write for so long. And then there were the telephone calls—from Helen and from Jake who insisted on his right to phone, to speak to her and to Jamie, who always, after the conversations, looked like he'd been beaten.

She dreaded the sound of the telephone, the fear that came each time she lifted the receiver and heard Jake's voice, accusing, pleading, angry. She had escaped him, but he could still reach out and find her.

"Come back," he said. "You know, I had a heart attack and went to the hospital."

Guilt, she thought. *He's trying to make me guilty.* "How long were you there?" she asked, giving no sympathy.

"They kept me overnight."

"Then you didn't have a heart attack." Lord, he was becoming just like Lottie, using sickness to get his own way.

"You've done a terrible thing," he said. "You've broken up a family. If you come back, I'll forgive you. I'll never say a word about what you did."

How incredible! And how like him, to put the entire blame on her. *What she'd done indeed!*

And what had she done except strike out for life? What had she done but escape? She stifled her shock and laughter. She had flown—moth, butterfly, migrating crane—away, away to her place of belonging, and what he said, what he in his self-delusion believed, was nothing to her.

She called Leona McGivern to tell of her safe arrival.

"How are you?" the lawyer asked.

"Fine, except I keep thinking I'm dreaming."

Leona chuckled. "And Ben?"

"Wonderful. Like always. Being with him makes me see what an idiot I was to stay with Jake. I mean, I could have been living like this all along. Did you file the divorce papers?"

"Not yet."

Frustration got the better of her. Did she have to think for everybody? "Why not?"

"You didn't tell me to."

"I thought it was understood. Just do it," she ordered, then realized that in two days it would be Christmas. "After the holidays," she amended. "No sense rubbing it in on Christmas."

"All right." Leona hesitated, and warning bells went off in Nan's head.

"What now?"

"Well, there's a law in this state that gives Jake the right to wait three years before making it final. Just so you know."

Nan resisted the urge to throw the phone across the room. "Why didn't you tell me this before?"

When Leona answered, she was purposely calm. "You needed encouragement. It was important to get you out. Besides, would knowing have stopped you?"

Logic. Such a wonderful tool! "No," Nan admitted, "but where did this law come from? How come I never heard about it? Wendy didn't have to wait for three years."

"Her husband chose not to exercise the privilege. But to answer the rest of your questions—the churches got it through with the help of a few congressmen who talked a lot about the sanctity of marriage regardless of the cost to some. It's foolish, but unfortunately it's law."

"So a bunch of unmarried, self-righteous clerics are running my life," Nan said out of tight lips. "So I'm supposed to sit here and wait when all I want is out!"

"We'll do the best we can," Leona said. "And you might try talking to Jake."

Nan rolled her eyes. "I haven't been able to talk to him in eighteen years. I know him. He'll put it off to punish me. And I'll be stuck because of some damn fool law."

Leona's sigh was audible. "You're better off now than you were. Think about that. Meantime, I'll file, and file for support, and you go on and have a Merry Christmas. Look on the bright side."

She was making it sound simple, but nothing was ever simple. "Bright side!" she snorted. "All right. But let's have some action. I hate standing still."

"My how you've changed." Leona's voice was full of humor.

Nan took a breath. "Bet your ass," she said.

She heard Ben's pickup coming down the road and ran to meet him. "Three years!" she said after she'd kissed him. "She says I have to wait three damn years until it's final. What'll we do?"

"Calm down." His hands lingered on her shoulders. "And tell me."

When she finished, he said, "So we'll wait. You're here, and that's what counts. No more sneaked phone calls, no more missing each other like a toothache that won't quit. Count your blessings. I do."

Ah, he was wonderful. Still . . . "I want to be rid of him," she muttered. "I want to be clean. I feel like Lady Macbeth, and him out there trying to get at me."

"I know." And he did. Hadn't he lived with memories and reminders for more years than he cared to talk about? He gave her shoulders a squeeze.

"Remember how, when you were a kid, a year seemed to last forever?"

She nodded.

"And now a year goes by so fast you wonder how you missed it?"

"Yes," she said. "That's true. Sad but true."

"Well, three years will go like that. Except we're together. And that's what matters. For me, anyhow."

"For me, too. I just thought that once I left everything else would happen like dominoes."

"Optimist!" he said. "Anyhow, I came for a completely different reason. Tomorrow's Christmas Eve, and Milton Shuttleworth will be here for a week. I want your permission to give him your stories to read, and I want you to come and meet him."

"Who's he?"

"The editor-in-chief of St. James Press. He comes every Christmas. We've become good friends."

"Oh, my God!" The whole world knew about St. James Press, one of the last privately owned publishing houses left. "He's coming here? What'll I wear?"

Ben threw back his head and howled. "Who gives a damn? You always look beautiful. Anyway, he's not interested in your clothes, just you, those stories you write."

"Oh, my God!" she repeated. "I'm not good enough. He'll laugh. I know it. Why didn't you tell me sooner, so I'd have a chance to do something really good?"

"Let him be the judge of that. You just come up for drinks and dinner and be your charming self. And bring the rest of your work. I've already given him what you sent me."

"They're not good enough," she repeated, mentally sorting through the stories in folders, those clamoring in her head. "Shuttleworth's a legend, and I don't think I'm ready to show anything."

"Relax and trust me."

"Easy for you to say. It's not your stuff being axed. Milton

Shuttleworth! I can't believe this." She would, she knew, hold up her head and smile, and cry her eyes out in private when he gave his opinion. Still, she was going to try.

She wore her red velvet skirt and concha belt, black boots and a garnet necklace from her jewelry box. In her hand she carried a briefcase—an old one of Jake's that she'd taken from his closet when she left. At least she could look professional in spite of the Christmas clothes and the fear like an ice cube in her chest.

She was good—but not good enough. Shuttleworth would read her work then hem and haw and tell her, very politely of course, that they had no room on their list for her, and wish her luck at another house.

That was how editors did it. Politely, saying nothing and everything, they dismissed you—and your hopes and dreams, your precious time. "Women's crap," Jake had called her work. It wasn't. She knew it wasn't, but still . . .

She swallowed hard, pasted a smile on her lips, and opened the door to the main house. Behind her Jamie whispered, "Go it, Mom!"

"Shhhh!" she hissed.

"Here she is!" Ben left the man and woman by the fireplace and came to her.

It seemed like the first time when she'd stood in the hall feeling awkward and happy both at once, except she wasn't supposed to be like that now. She was supposed to be in charge. She squared her shoulders, touched Ben on his arm, and advanced into the living room. If her knees were knocking, no one could see beneath the velvet skirt.

Milton Shuttleworth was a small man, white haired with sparkling blue eyes magnified by wire-rimmed spectacles. *The Christmas elf,* Nan thought as she shook hands.

279

"This is a pleasure," he said, sounding as if he meant it, then turning to include the vivid woman beside him. "My wife, Rachel."

If he were an elf, his wife was a humming bird, small, dark, brightly cloaked in turquoise and rose silk with an exquisite squash blossom necklace that gleamed in the firelight. She took Nan in with one, penetrating glance. "I'm so happy to meet the writer who's stolen my husband away. He's been buried in the study reading your stories all afternoon."

She spoke without malice, tempering her words with a smile, and Nan suddenly felt at ease, drawn into a charmed circle. "Is that good or bad, do you think?" she asked.

Rachel patted her arm. "We'll let him speak for himself. For now, tell me about you. Ben says you're here to stay. And," she dropped her voice, "I hope that means what I think it does. It's about time some woman took him in hand. He's a very lonely man. We always wondered why he never remarried, but I think he was waiting for you."

The woman's warmth was undeniable. Nan accepted a glass of sherry and took a sip, then cocked her head. "I'm a runaway wife. I chucked it all and came back where I belong. And that's a story, too."

"Tell me."

There was no doubting Rachel's interest as she sat down on the couch and patted the cushion beside her.

"It's a long, strange journey," Nan prevaricated. Unfolding the ins and outs of her life to strangers seemed to be all she'd done for the past few weeks, and every time it brought Jake to mind—Jake whom she wanted to forget. But Rachel was watching her with piercing dark eyes. *Like a fortune teller,* she thought. She glanced over at Ben, but he was deep in conversation with Milton, and Jamie and Bay had disappeared. She was on her own and wondered how much influence Rachel had over her husband.

"Let's just say I've been a writer all my life. Since before I knew how to write," she began. "I worked for a newspaper, got married, and was convinced in no time that I was worthless. And believed it. My lawyer calls it abuse. I believe that, too. I left with my son, and we're both starting over. And I'm going to try my damnedest to publish and succeed where I failed before."

Rachel nodded. "I wish my patients could meet you."

Nan looked her question with raised eyebrows.

"I'm a psychologist," Rachel said. "Family counseling. You wouldn't believe the women who come to me thinking they're ciphers, who've been totally blotted out. And sometimes the reverse—men so cowed by their wives they're sexless. It's a sad situation always, and I'm seeing more and more of it. Why, I don't know. But you've already succeeded, and I congratulate you." She lifted her glass. "Here's to you. And to Ben." She flicked a glance across the room.

Milton saw her gesture and came to stand beside them. "I hope after dinner you and I can have a talk, Mrs. Fletcher."

"Nan," she corrected. "Please."

"And I'm Milt. Nobody calls me Milton except Rachel when she's annoyed with me." He smiled at his wife, and Nan sensed the love that existed between these two elegant people, one of whom possibly held her future in his hands.

"Milt." It sounded strange. Never in her life had she imagined that she'd be calling the editor of St. James Press by his first name.

"I've read the stories Ben gave me," he said. "They're jewels, you realize."

Her mind was as blank as her face. "Jewels," she repeated, in a whisper.

"Surely you know that."

"I hoped. But whoever can be sure?"

"I think you can. But we'll talk after dinner, and here's Lupe to tell us it's ready." He smiled again, that elfin shivering of his face that was so different from what she'd expected, and gave her his arm to escort her to the dining room.

She was supposed to eat and contribute to the conversation, but Lupe's Christmas *posole* stuck in her throat, and she found herself drinking water by the glassful, one minute wishing the meal was over, the next that it would last forever. *Jewels*. He *had* said it. She'd heard him. Not women's crap but treasures.

Ben watched her with amused understanding. She still had no idea how lovely she was or what talent she possessed. He remembered how trusting she had been with him in Taos, the way her body had moved in time with his own, how she had opened her arms and her heart and welcomed him. He hoped she knew she was safe with him, that he'd made a vow never to hurt her, and that he intended to do all in his power to foster the uncanny ability that she had and seemed unable to recognize. His gift of the old house was part of his vow, and this meeting with Milt, and he'd think of other ways as time went on, because if she denied that part of herself, she wouldn't be who she was meant to be, which was what he wanted with all of him.

"You two use my study," he said as they left the table. "Take as long as you need."

Four of her stories lay on the desk. Milt seated himself behind it, humming under his breath as he picked up a sheet of paper on which he'd scribbled notes.

"I'm always on the lookout for new writers, but I never expected to find one on my vacation," he said with a twinkle. "However, obviously I have. This is extraordinary work, and I see you've brought others."

"A few. Some unpublished stories that I guess may not be good enough."

"Let me be the judge of that." He sat back in his chair. "Have you thought about putting together a collection?"

"It's every writer's dream."

"And a novel? I feel there's a novel in you."

He was going too fast. She'd hardly allowed herself to think at all, and here he was talking about novels.

"Maybe," she said. "I really hadn't got that far. But there are so many things I'd like to write about, so many stories to tell."

There was, in her, a chorus of voices—Lupe's, Jessie's, Wendy's, Lottie's and her mother's—their hopes, sorrows, their search for self and dignity.

"Write it in a book," Jessie had said, her dark face filled with the hunger for expression.

"Chew off your foot!"

"Love me!"

One by one, these women had handed her their lives, the gift of their burdens, and her need to speak for them was strong.

"I've never seen myself as a novelist," she said after a minute. "But that doesn't mean I'm not. I've come to believe that we shouldn't impose limits on ourselves, at least not without trying. So yes, there may be a novel in me. And a collection. And poetry. I started out as a poet, so who knows?"

"Who, indeed?" Milt beamed at her. "If I may, I'll read these others tonight. That is, if my dear bride has no objections."

"Somehow," Nan said, "I don't think she will. She's wonderful."

"And she has a life of her own aside from me. She understands."

"You're very fortunate."

He cocked his head. "And so, I would imagine, are you. You have a gift. Use it well."

"I hope so."

"I have no doubt, Nan," he said. "None at all."

The phone rang at 7.30 the next morning. *Christmas morning,* Nan thought groggily, reaching for the receiver. She'd been unable to fall asleep the night before, unable to stop her mind from going off in all directions—stories, novels, Ben who'd arranged for this miracle.

"I hope I didn't wake you," Milt said.

She gathered her wits. "No, not at all. And Merry Christmas."

"To you, too. I read until after midnight, and I'd like to come down and have a serious discussion with you whenever it's convenient."

"Any time," she said, wondering if it was bad news, if after all, she'd failed.

"Fine. I'll be down about ten. And, Nan . . ."

"Yes?"

"Relax. Like I said, these are jewels. I want to talk business."

He meant it. She was sitting on her bed on Christmas morning receiving the most wonderful present ever. Her entire life was being vindicated. "I don't know what to say. I guess . . . I think I'm stunned."

"So was I," he said. "See you soon."

The phone clicked off, and she sat looking at it in a daze until she heard Jamie calling.

"Hey, Mom! You awake?"

"In here."

He stuck his head around the door. "There's a horse tied

up outside. With a ribbon around its neck."

"A horse!" She pulled on her red chenille bathrobe and searched for her slippers. "What kind of horse?"

"Come see. Bring some apples."

She opened the door and saw Monarch, his bay coat gleaming, wearing a new halter and sporting a glossy red ribbon."

"Hello, baby," she greeted him. "What're you doing down here all dressed up?"

He nickered in answer and stretched out his nose, scenting the apples in her pocket.

"Merry Christmas." Ben came around the side of the house. "I figured since you're his godmother, you ought to have him."

Abruptly she sat down on the step. "For me?"

"I don't see anybody else who's qualified as godmother."

She burst into tears and hid her face in her hands. First Butterfly Woman, then Milt and his praise, and now a horse of her own, the one thing she'd yearned for since childhood.

"Whoa, girl." Ben came to sit beside her. "Here I was expecting a kiss, and all I get is tears. Haven't you heard about looking a gift horse in the mouth?"

How could she explain? She wasn't used to presents, or kindness, or the kind of love that flowed so bountifully out of him. She had always been the giver, and if at times she'd yearned for conditions to be reversed, she'd never believed it would happen. She wasn't worth all this attention. She was only Nan, an ordinary woman who had, somehow, stumbled into paradise.

"It's too much!" she choked. "I don't deserve all this."

Her cry struck straight to his heart. What had been done to her was cruel. He wanted to wring the necks of every person who had ever contributed to her lack of faith. He cupped her face in his hands.

"Listen to me," he said. "And listen good. You deserve the sun and the moon. Just leave it to me, and don't worry about what else you deserve. Okay?"

"But . . . all I got you was a little statue and a s . . . saddle blanket. I wanted the sun and moon for you, too, but I couldn't afford them."

"You're here. That's gift enough for the rest of my life. I want to spoil you, and I want you to let me."

"But . . ."

"No buts. You have to learn to receive, and that's an art in itself. But it shouldn't be too hard, and I'll be a good teacher."

Once again she marveled over how all the lessons that had been pounded into her head were wrong. Where she came from, too much happiness was sinful and cause for alarm. Disaster was certain to follow. And selfishness, making demands, taking without giving, was equally wicked, alien to womanhood whose *raison d'etre* was to suffer and do for others without complaint.

Regardless of the fact that she had rebelled against such teachings, they'd left their mark. Once more she'd been guilty and afraid. She had too much. The worst was sure to come. And here was Ben, smiling, looking at her with love in his eyes, advising her to forget, to be in some way the child she'd never been allowed to be, the woman she wanted to become.

"I'm like a bag lady, I guess," she said. "Carrying my past on my back wherever I go. I probably should just dump it, but it's not easy."

"You'll manage. My money's on you. And I'm going to help you train Monarch. By the time he's ready to ride, he'll be part of you, and you of him."

286

"He's what I always wanted. But my mother said horses were dirty, and anyhow we couldn't afford one."

"I'll have to meet her someday," he said. "She's got lots to learn, too, evidently."

Nan laughed at that and wiped her face on her sleeve. "Please. Not now. It's Christmas." She glanced at her watch. "Oh, God, Milt's coming over, and I'm all cried out. I'd better go wash my face and put clothes on."

Ben helped her up, and she lifted her face to kiss him. "Thank you," she whispered. "For your faith in me, your presents, who you are. I don't quite know how to say it right, but I'm trying."

"Write it," he suggested. "I'm sure you'll find a way."

"How long will it take you to put a collection together?" Milt was sitting at the old oak kitchen table, a cup of coffee and thick ranch cream in his hands.

He was dead serious, and Nan responded in kind. "How many stories?"

"You have eight here. I'd like another five, maybe less, depending on length. Let's shoot for about three hundred pages."

She searched her thoughts for those elusive words and images that signified a project. "Six months."

"Alright. Here's what I'd like to do." Milt twinkled at her over the rim of his cup. "With your consent of course. I'll send a contract when I get back. We can pay a three thousand dollar advance. I know," he waved his hand, "it's not much, but stories by unknowns don't exactly make the top of the list. You'll get half on signing and half when you send the completed manuscript. And I won't cheat you on the contract. You don't have an agent, do you?"

She'd never even thought of the possibility. "Do I need one?"

"At some point perhaps. But, as I said, I won't cheat you. And when you have an idea for a novel, send it. A couple chapters and an outline, and I'll see about giving you a larger advance. Agreed?"

Nan looked down into her cup as if she could read the future in the swirls of cream. "It sounds too easy. Don't I have to be read by some editorial committee?"

"My dear Nan." He beamed at her again. "I *am* the editorial committee. My father founded the Press in 1918, and I still own sixty-one per cent of the stock. If I say 'publish,' it's done. And that's what I'm saying. I do know talent when I see it, which is rare these days. All this sex and violence and no depth, no hope, just the bleakness of despair. You, my dear, have depth, and a certain optimism that appeals, believe me."

She heard him, let it sink in, tasted the first flush of a joy so intense she thought she might die. Then she said, "I'll write my heart out for you. That's a promise."

He reached across the table and shook her hand. "I'll hold you to it. A gentleman's agreement. Or," he amended, "an agreement between a very rare lady and a bookish old codger who's delighted with his new found treasure."

He meant it. There was no mistake. "Milt," she said, abandoning her notions of propriety, "be careful or I'll fall in love with you."

"Career hazard," he flashed back. "Love away, but keep Ben happy."

"I'll do that. And I'll look forward to seeing you and Rachel here every Christmas. Is that a deal?"

"Naturally. We wouldn't miss it for the world."

The phone rang, and Nan got up to answer. "Finish your coffee," she said. "I'll only be a minute."

"It's me." Jake was glum.

"Hi."

"I thought you'd call."

"Why?"

"It's Christmas. You could at least have had Jamie call. You can imagine the kind of day I'm having."

"Oh," she said, unable to call up the guilt that was supposed to be her response.

"Is that all you can say?"

She was supposed to crawl, apologize. Instead she gave vengeance free rein. "I've been busy. I'm signing a book contract."

That stopped him. "A contract?" he repeated. "You mean somebody's going to pay you?"

"Yes," she said, and then, unable to restrain herself added, "They are. Looks like that 'women's crap' I write may support me after all."

He ignored the dig. "You'd better get a lawyer to look at it for you. You know you can't understand that kind of thing."

Of course not. She was Nan the Inept. She said, "I'll do fine. And I can't stay on. I'm in the middle of a business conference." It sounded good.

Jake said, "On Christmas? Just what in hell kind of business is going on? Where'd you meet this guy? Who is he?"

Be firm, she reminded herself. *Don't let him accuse you.*

"I met Milt and his wife at a party. Since his time here is limited, we're talking now, though I don't see that any of this is your business. And Milt happens to be editor-in-chief of St. James Press and a gentleman."

When Jake answered, she heard something almost like respect in his voice, and she smiled at her face reflected in the mirror on the wall. *You see,* she said to the image, *you see what you can do?*

"I'm taking my mother to dinner," he said. "If Jamie could

call soon, I'd like to talk with him."

"I'll make sure he does. And give Lottie my best."

She hung up, ran her hands through her hair, and went back to the kitchen.

CHAPTER FORTY-ONE

"Call your father," she told Jamie when he came in, the dogs at his heels.

"Do I have to?"

"Yes. I said you would, and it is Christmas."

"And he'll start on me like always."

Something in his response caught her attention. "How so?"

Jamie shrugged. "Like why did I leave? I'm ruining all my chances. Stuff like that."

She sighed. Naturally he'd work on Jamie, the weakest link, the kid without defenses. And naturally she wasn't to be allowed her time to savor her luck and future. "Look," she said, "just call and get it over with. Tell him you have to take out the dog or something. And try not to let him make you feel guilty."

"Sure." He stalked down the hall.

Nan rinsed the coffee cups and gave biscuits to the dogs who retreated beneath the table to work on them. Their contented chewing was a happy sound, but it appeared that reality would always intrude on euphoria, that she'd never be permitted to sit and gloat without having to deal with other problems.

When Jamie came back one look at his white face told her that Jake, indeed, had been at it again.

"What now?" She clenched her fists, prepared for the worst.

"He said he wants me to go back. If I don't, he's not going to pay my last semester's tuition. I won't be able to graduate. I won't get into college. God, Mom! Merry Christmas! My own father."

"He *said* that?"

"Yeah. Now what am I supposed to do? I'm stuck. It's okay for you, but I'm in the middle." Suddenly, viciously, he kicked at one of the chairs.

"Calm down!" she snapped, though she was far from calm herself. "I don't think he can do this. I think he's just making noise. But I'll call the lawyer. Failing all else, I'll pay your goddamn tuition, and tell him to go to hell."

"You can't afford it!"

"Don't tell me I can't! *He* can't, is what. He can't use you to get at me, and that's what he's doing. He has no right to talk to you like that. Threaten you." Nan laughed bitterly. "He hadn't ever the right, but got away with it. Don't worry," she added, seeing his stricken face. "You don't have to go back. No matter what."

"He's my father!" It was a cry of anguish.

"My mistake, not yours," she said. "If he died, I'd dance on his grave. Now, let's forget it, or try to 'til tomorrow when I can make some phone calls. I've got some presents for you."

He looked at her, his expression oddly mature. "Are presents supposed to make it all go away?"

She felt like he'd punched her and wanted to hit back, but reason won out. "He's *not* going to ruin Christmas. He is *not* going to intrude, and it's up to us to keep him out. This day began with a miracle, and I refuse to let him take it or our happiness away. Now, you want your presents or not?"

He flinched, then grinned. "You're really wild when you

get mad," he said. "Okay. I guess I'd like my presents. And I've got one for you. Ben helped me pick it."

Ben again. The man was too good to be believed. "I could really get used to all this giving," she said, coming around the table and linking her arm through his. "Come on. I hid yours under the bed."

"I hid yours under mine," he said. "Meet you back here."

By mutual consent, she and Jamie did not mention Jake's ultimatum. "No sense ruining everybody's day," she said, "and besides, Ben will just get upset."

Jamie agreed. He was wearing his new shirt and belt buckle, and was delighted that Nan had pounced on the hand-embroidered shawl he'd given her.

"It's gorgeous! It's incredible! How do I look?" She threw it around her shoulders and pirouetted like a Spanish dancer.

"Your friends wouldn't recognize you. Probably even Dad wouldn't know you."

A look in the mirror showed a far different woman than the one who had left home three weeks before. Her face was fuller, her eyes brighter, and the shawl, the red skirt added the flair that had been missing in her person and her life.

Was this what love did? she wondered. And success? Took a black and white photograph and painted over the shadows, adding color and contrast that had never been visible? If so, she approved as Jamie so obviously did and, regardless of Jake she was going to enjoy the day, have fun, pass out the gifts she had brought and give thanks for the blessings that had been heaped on her.

"You're as rosy as a poinsettia." Ben greeted her with a hug and a kiss, and as usual she wanted to stay in his arms.

"Later," he whispered in her ear, making her laugh deep in her throat. "Jamie can spend the night, and I'll make sure you get home safely. Check under the bed and on it. If that's all right with you?"

Nan giggled again. She'd probably never get used to being loved, teased, cared for. Who would she have been if she'd not hidden away for most of her life, if she'd never met Jake?

"You're thinking again." Ben interrupted her questioning.

"How can you tell?"

"I'm a Nan watcher. That's like a bird watcher, but much more interesting." And that, he reflected, was the truth. Her face, her moods, the intensity of her thoughts fascinated him. "What's bothering you?" he asked. "Something is."

Was she so transparent? She shook her head. "Nothing. Let's give out these presents, and remind me to call my mother. I was so excited over Monarch and Milt's news I forgot, and it is Christmas."

"Use my phone if you want."

"Later. Right now, it's time to celebrate."

She almost succeeded in banishing Jake in the hours that followed. Almost. But as she knew he would, he'd managed to insinuate himself into her pleasure even from thousands of miles away. At some point she'd have to talk sense into him, accuse, argue. The idea wasn't pleasant.

After dinner she excused herself and went into Ben's study to call Helen. *Like a kid crying to its mother,* she thought as she dialed, annoyed with herself but needing to share her burden with someone who felt about Jake as she did.

"This is unconscionable!" Helen's outrage was almost tangible.

"It is," Nan agreed. "And I'm not sure what to do."

"Taking it out on a child." Helen went on. "He's a monster." She paused and Nan heard the click of a cigarette lighter. In times of tension Helen always reached for a cigarette.

"*I'll* pay his tuition." She exhaled loudly. "That child is not coming back to live with that man. Not after what happened before. Do you hear me?"

"Loud and clear," Nan said. "But don't do anything until I get in touch with my lawyer."

"I'm calling Lottie. She should know what kind of a son she raised, and her always boasting about him."

Nan chuckled to herself. Helen and Lottie, bitter enemies banding together to take on one man. "Go ahead," she said. "And let me know what she says."

"I certainly will. Where is Jamie? I want to wish him Merry Christmas."

"Out with Bay. We got invited to the ranch for dinner."

It was a graceful white lie, but not graceful enough. Helen's radar clicked on. "You're with that man."

"He owns the place." Nan tried to sound casual. "And, he has a guest who's a publisher. Who read my stories and wants me to do a book. He's sending a contract."

"Are you good enough?" Helen was doubtful.

She should have expected that one. In her mother's world no one wrote books, they only read them. Writers were alien beings whom no one knew or even wanted to know.

"Yes," she said shortly. "Yes I am."

"Well, we'll see won't we?" Helen's answer was clipped, as if she didn't want to admit to being the mother of a woman who actually wrote the books she saw in stores.

What had happened to the woman who had stolen her child's words? Who had wept with pride and shivered with delight over the visions of a three year old?

"You thought I was good enough once." The accusation escaped before she could stop it. "You took my poems and read them to everybody."

"You remember that!" Helen was pleased. "I still have those poems you know. Would you like them to keep?"

Nan shivered, the day, the faces, the quaver in Helen's voice still vivid. "You keep them," she said. "I've got to go. I'm using Ben's phone."

"Behave yourself." Helen was back on track. "Remember who you are."

There was that chasm again, a space so deep it would never be crossed, and she was on one side and her mother was on the other. She was a mirage, a shadow figure shouting into the abyss, but those who heard were few. So it had always been, for herself and for everyone. Who you were was a matter of self-definition, and the truth of it came from within.

"Merry Christmas," she said and hung up, pressing her hands to her temples where a dull throb warned of a beginning headache. Too much sherry, too many emotional highs, and all she wanted was Ben.

As if he heard her calling, he appeared at the door. "Problems?" he asked, his dark eyebrows raised.

"Just tired. It's been quite a day." She managed a smile.

"Come on. I'll take you home. Jamie and Bay are fooling with the new computer. A good night's sleep will help."

She didn't want sleep. Not yet. She wanted Ben with a desire so strong her chest ached. "Stay," she said. "Don't leave me."

Her blatant need tugged at him, her vulnerability so at odds with her independence.

"All you have to do is ask." He picked up the shawl that had slipped from her shoulders and put it around her. "I wasn't going to force my wicked passions on you."

She managed a snort of laughter. "My mother just warned me to remember who I am. As it turns out, I'm a shameless hussy. I want you. Let's get out of here."

She stopped in the kitchen to say goodnight to Lupe who was flaunting her new necklace on top of her apron, and in the living room where Milt and Rachel were sitting beside the fire in the silence of true companions.

"It's been the most wonderful day," she said, smiling at them, visualizing herself and Ben seated here reliving their own memories in years ahead.

"I wish you both many more." Rachel took her hand. "And if Milt gives you a hard time, I hope you'll call me so I can straighten him out. I read a few of your stories, and they speak, most eloquently if I may say so, for all of us. It's a pleasure to have been here and met you."

"Thank you. For everything." On impulse, Nan bent and kissed Rachel's cheek, then turned and kissed Milt who beamed at her.

"My dear, thank *you*. You've made my day. Now go on, both of you, and do what young people do best."

Together they stepped out onto the terrace. Lupe had lit *luminarias* whose lights were poignant and small in the midst of the immense darkness. The mountains that rimmed the valley stood out, black against a black sky.

Nan stood, head cocked, listening to the silence that, as always, startled her. "It might be the first night of creation," she whispered, "with only the world and nothing and no one to disturb it."

"Sometimes I believe the theory that we, all of us, are evolving into chaos." Ben was behind her, his hands on her shoulders. "Especially when you remember that not so long ago, half the world was as quiet as this. No cars, no sirens, no radios or TV, just a few people. And the land."

He bent and rubbed his cheek against her hair. "You sure you feel up to having me stay tonight?"

His touch, his concern moved her more deeply than she'd ever been. She turned and faced him, saw the glow of the tiny candles reflected in his eyes.

"I'm sure," she said.

CHAPTER FORTY-TWO

The ringing of the phone woke her. She reached for Ben, but he had gone at first light, taking care not to be seen leaving the house. Would it ever end? Would three years of sneaking, lying, deceiving ever pass?

She rubbed sleep from her eyes. "Hello?"

"You're there." Helen was accusing.

"Where did you think I'd be?" she shot back, knowing her mother's mind.

Helen chose not to answer. She said, "I talked to Lottie. We're having lunch. Then we're going to talk to Jake. She agrees with me that he can't do this. I really think he is crazy."

"I told you," Nan said, suppressing a grin at the thought of the two enemies united in a common cause. "I told you how he was. You didn't listen."

"This is different."

It wasn't, but Nan wasn't about to stop the combined forces. "Good luck."

"Jamie's our grandchild. That creature isn't going to victimize him."

"Go it, Ma!" Nan shouted, wishing she could eavesdrop on the confrontation.

"You sound different."

Nan sat up in the bed where she and Ben had made passionate love only hours before. "I *am* different. I'm who I should have been."

"Nonsense!" Helen snapped. "You always talk some kind of code that makes no sense."

It had to come to an end. She had to be rid of her burden, the memory of violation. Nan took a breath and blurted out what she had held in abeyance for most of her life. "I was a little girl with pictures in my head. They were beautiful. They were mine, my poems, and you stole them. Like they didn't count for anything except giving you some kind of a kick. I was making your life. I was the reason for your existence, like you told me once, but even then you didn't think about me. I didn't count. It was what you wanted that was important. That day you stole my poems I wanted to die. I did die, right there at the table with those people I didn't know. They were strangers, and so were you." She stopped, reliving it again, the actual, physical pain.

"Oh, I'm not blaming you. It's past time for that, but it happened, and I was too little to understand. All I knew was that I couldn't trust you anymore, and I was scared. But there wasn't any way to tell you. Little kids don't have words for when their world goes haywire. They just hide, like I did. Or they try to kill themselves like Jamie. I became nobody. But I'm not that anymore. I'm me. Nan. The mother of your grandchild and proud of it. I'm the owner of my own mind and life, and you can take me as I am or leave it. Just stop telling me I'm different from some ideal you made up when I was three. Or five. Okay?"

She stopped, leaning back against the headboard of the bed, her breath quick and shallow. It was said. She closed her eyes and waited.

"But I loved you!" Helen choked with what sounded like tears. "You were so dear. So quick. So gifted, and I was so proud. I wanted to share you with everybody, share my excitement. Can't you see?"

But everybody could have cared less. And Helen, in her delight, her innocence had closed off the fountain of spontaneity.

Innocence, Nan thought, *is the greatest evil. From Eve to the present.* But she couldn't say it, couldn't destroy Helen's beliefs regardless of her question of the day before. "Are you good enough?" which, in its naïvete seemed to contradict everything Helen had just claimed.

It was the old game—dreams versus reality—and Nan had neither the ability nor the desire to demolish the imaginings of an old lady. "I can see now. But then all I knew was that I was afraid. My whole world fell apart. But you couldn't know, and I couldn't tell you."

"It wasn't meant!" Helen cried. "I'd never have hurt you. You were a child. You were all I had!"

"I know," Nan said softly, fearing an outburst of tears. "I do know. Sometimes I worry about what I've done to Jamie without realizing it. Being a parent is scary. We start out knowing nothing with a blank slate to write on. And what we write ends up engraved like in stone. And all the advice in the world can't keep us from making mistakes. I . . . I didn't mean to accuse you." Her apology came hard, but it was necessary. "It happened, and I outgrew it, so don't worry. I'll be fine. I am fine. It's the next generation we have to worry about."

"About Jamie," Helen began.

Nan cut her off. "You and Lottie do your damnedest. If you don't have any luck, I can manage to pay the tuition."

"The little shit," Helen said quite clearly.

Nan's jaw dropped. "What did you say?"

"You heard me. And I meant it."

Nan chuckled. "Call a spade a spade. Well, go to it, and

give the little shit my regards."

Helen's response was stiff and in character. "Don't use me as an excuse. Once said is enough."

And coming from her that was fact. "Okay," Nan said. "Call me after the explosion."

She lay back on the pillows and imagined the two women setting forth on their errand of justice. Jake didn't stand a chance against them—Lottie of the acid tongue and Helen the guilt-bearer. Still, it was best to make sure of Jamie's rights.

She picked up the phone and dialed Leona and was informed that the lawyer was on a two week vacation. No help there, but it was probably just as well. The scene would play itself out.

She stretched lazily, wishing Ben hadn't left, intuiting that it would always be this way between them, her need hot and urgent, surfacing at a touch, a word. She'd never felt like this about any man, had never trusted a man enough to let herself go, shed her inhibitions like so many layers of protective clothing, and then glory in it.

Around her the house was quiet. She slipped on her robe and went to the kitchen to make coffee feeling a lightness, a release from the bonds that for so long had rendered her voiceless. Early morning had always been her writing time. And now she had silence and all the time in the world.

The coffee made, she carried her mug to the sun porch. Five more stories! Which ones would she choose out of the multitude that waited?

She stared out the window, saw the mountains taking shape in the early light—peaks, hollows, canyons seeming to lift out of shadow into brilliance, and in the valley, yellow winter grass leaning in the wind, undulant as waves in an endless sea.

Still she sat, waiting for the words to come, the voices to speak, for pictures to form as the mountains formed, solid, indelible. And at last she picked up a pen and began to write.

A dam had burst. Words poured out like music; faces took shape; people moved through all the rooms of her life, rooms she knew intimately and that echoed with emotions, real and imagined.

Faster she wrote, her pen skimming across the pages, an extension of self. Had she been writing with her own blood, she would not have been surprised. What surprised was the flowing, the precision of thoughts she hadn't known she possessed. What surprised was the almost physical pleasure she felt there, at her desk, with the mountains looking on, and the restless valley alive to every nuance of wind, every shadow of cloud, given definition by the motion of hawks, the pulsing of raven's wings through unseen air.

Time held its breath, became nothing. She wrote until the sun crested and began its descent, until the ringing of the phone brought her back from her journey. She looked up dazed, uncertain, irritated.

"Yes?" She tried to keep annoyance out of her voice. Whoever it was could not understand her distance traveled.

"It's me."

Always Jake, intruding, seeking, demanding.

"What now?" This time she permitted her irritation to show.

"Your mother and mine were just here. A pair of harpies. You sicced them on me, didn't you?"

"I didn't, as a matter of fact. They were disgusted when they heard what you did to Jamie."

"And what about what you did? Taking him out of school was foolish, you know. You didn't think, just like you didn't think about me, what you've done. I want him to come back and finish properly, and none of this nonsense you and he cooked up without my permission."

She doodled on the page before her, slashing black lines that ripped holes in the paper. "You threatened your own son. You terrified him, used him without a thought about how he'd feel. As usual," she added, and drew a heart pierced with a dozen arrows.

Oh, she was angry! Her body writhed with the fury of an animal mother protecting its child. "This is a child's life," she said. "And a fragile child at that. Like you made him. And I helped. I sat by and let you demolish him. I let you pick on him, embarrass him, drive him to suicide, and I hate myself for it. I hate you even worse. You hear me? I think you suck."

Jake was silent, probably stunned by her use of the vernacular. She hoped so, hoped she'd penetrated his aura of self-importance.

She pressed on, taking advantage of his wordlessness. "Lottie and Helen see it that way, too. I don't know what they said to you, and I don't care, but I'm with them. We all know what you are. You've proved it this time, so don't try to get out of it or blame me for your neuroses. It won't work. Not anymore."

"I don't want to talk about anything painful." Jake was on the defensive, using his old excuse.

She hissed through her teeth. "You never did. You've never faced yourself. Well, the time to start is now. And," she swallowed, her throat gone dry with rage, "and I'd appreciate it if you'd stop calling every hour on the hour. I have a book to write and these interruptions are disturbing. I'd also appreciate getting the divorce finalized as soon as possible."

He didn't answer. Her doodles became fierce and abstract—jagged, erratic—like the track on a heart monitor. "Well?"

"I . . . I'll think about it."

"You better. Putting it off will only make it more painful, as you put it. And I'd advise you to cough up Jamie's tuition unless you want to ruin him more than you already have."

"I did. Lottie and Helen took my check with them. You can't imagine how they spoke to me." He was baffled. Indignant.

She smiled. The scene pleased her. "What goes around, comes around. Now you know how the rest of us felt while you were degrading and yelling all the time. You abused me, Jake. That's what it's called, how you acted. You hurt your only child, and God knows who else. You turned me into a slave without caring at all, except for yourself, and I don't think I'll ever forgive you. I'm getting off now so I can tell Jamie. Maybe *he* will forgive you at some point, but don't hold your breath."

"Nan . . ." He was pleading.

"What?" she snapped, wanting only to be rid of him.

"This isn't right, you know. It isn't. Nobody's acting the way they should. You're all against me, all pointing a finger, making me out to be some monster. It isn't fair." He was whining like a baby caught in wrong-doing. She could almost see him, lower lip jutting out, a frown between his eyes as he asked her, the mother, to make it right, put his world back the way he wanted it.

She felt a twinge of pity. He was a child—and a bully, taking advantage of every weakness, of her whose impulse, always, was to give. But no more; not to him.

"I can't help you, Jake," she said. "You'll have to fight this by yourself, and hopefully you'll grow up someday."

She put down the receiver amazed at herself. From somewhere she'd found the courage to talk back without shrinking away or succumbing to belief in her own unworthiness. She'd fought—for Jamie and her own person—and won, at least for the moment.

She glanced outside, saw the shadows of afternoon moving up the slopes of the mountain. She hadn't eaten, hadn't dressed. On her desk lay a pile of pages, another miracle, proof of a day's work, a lifetime of experience.

A jay rose squawking from the branches of an oak, his wings a vivid, iridescent blue, and Jamie came down the banks of the creek, stopping to watch, his face the face of the child she remembered, sweet, trusting, filled with expectation.

They were connected, mother and son, as she was connected to the world. It was here, in the room, in the sunlit valley, the pulsing of earth, in joy and tragedy, the small battles and the large.

Swiftly, so swiftly she was taken by surprise, she sensed the presence of the muse, questioning, challenging, speaking in myriad tongues, shouting in a thousand voices, beguiling, demanding her devotion.

As if in prayer Nan clasped her hands. Everything was all of a piece, joined by the smooth red muscle of the heart.

"Yes," she whispered, to the silence, to the unseen presence that waited, as it had always waited, for her response. "Yes."

Once again the phone rang, shattering the moment. So it had always been. Day or night she was on call, an emergency service for those in need, her own needs put aside, lost, forgotten.

The ringing insisted, but this time she declined to answer. Instead she walked through the door into the mystery of sunlight and ran down the path toward the creek, her red robe flying, her arms outstretched embracing the world.